Praise for the Ne
Don

"A daring double life . . . reveals the full extent of his dangerous voyage into the underworld."
—*Time*

"Thoroughly absorbing true-life adventure."
—*Newsday*

"The tension builds with the machine-gun rapidity . . . the suspense of a fictional mystery yarn but the chilling ring of reality."
—*Virginian Pilot*

"Excellent . . . for a view of how the Mafia operates, none can match Joe Pistone."
—*Seattle Post-Intelligencer*

"Unprecedented. . . . A chilling chronicle of Pistone's undercover work in the Mafia." —UPI

Continued . . .

"Truly exciting . . . so skillfully written it's worth your time." —*Palm Springs Desert Sun*

"Oozes with names . . . and plenty of behind-the-social-club-door gossip."
—*New York Daily News*

"A penetrating look into the Mafia inner circle . . . frightening . . . daring."
—*Fort Worth Evening Telegraph*

"Compelling, gripping, revealing . . . raw, hard-hitting nonfiction at its best."
—*Toronto Star*

"Immensely satisfying." —*Oakland Press*

"New ground is broken! . . . There are few ways, short of participating in it, that you'll get a better look at the business of crime than by reading Pistone's recollections of his life in it." —*Canton Repository*

"Fascinating!" —*Dayton News/Journal Herald*

"So entertaining, you have to remind yourself it's deadly serious." —*Boston Globe*

Also by Joseph D. Pistone

Donnie Brasco: My Undercover Life in the Mafia
Donnie Brasco: Deep Cover

MOBBED UP

A Donnie Brasco Novel

Joseph D. Pistone

ONYX
Published by New American Library, a division of
Penguin Putnam Inc., 375 Hudson Street,
New York, New York 10014, U.S.A.
Penguin Books Ltd, 27 Wrights Lane,
London W8 5TZ, England
Penguin Books Australia Ltd, Ringwood,
Victoria, Australia
Penguin Books Canada Ltd, 10 Alcorn Avenue,
Toronto, Ontario, Canada M4V 3B2
Penguin Books (N.Z.) Ltd, 182–190 Wairau Road,
Auckland 10, New Zealand

Penguin Books Ltd, Registered Offices:
Harmondsworth, Middlesex, England

First published by Onyx, an imprint of New American Library,
a division of Penguin Putnam Inc.

First Printing, April 2000
10 9 8 7 6 5 4 3 2 1

Printed in the United States of America

To the men and women of the
Federal Bureau of Investigation, who put
their lives on the line each and
every day in defense of the country

ACKNOWLEDGMENTS

I wish to thank Louise Burke and Joe Pittman of NAL Books for helping to make this new career a reality. Also, my eternal gratitude to my agent, Carmen La Via, of the Fifi Oscard Agency, for his total support and understanding. Thanks, too, to John Lutz, for his valued contribution.

1

It was the kind of gray, cool morning that made people hunker down within their souls and simply go through the motions of life so time would pass. The tendency was to look beyond the morning, at least to some cheap food and conversation at lunch, then maybe a beer or two in the evening. A get-by kind of day where nothing much either good or bad figured to happen, and people were lulled into thinking of small comforts while life was on hold.

Of course, life is never on hold.

This time he was Donnie Barns. Most FBI agents used their real first names when working undercover, because without that instant recognition and response at the name's mention, the bad guys would know you for what you were.

But Special Agent Joe Pistone had lived for six years as Donnie Brasco while gathering evidence against the East Coast Mafia, and though there was a half-million-dollar open contract on his life that forced him to use various other names since then while assuming false identities in order to survive, he was still by now more Donnie Brasco than he was anyone else. It was "Donnie" that made his head turn and changed the light in his eyes and gave him his best chance to stay alive.

A tall, muscular man with dark hair, he squinted his keen blue eyes against the light mist and jockeyed his propane-powered Clark forklift out of the hangar and across the wet concrete apron toward the gaping cargo doors of the Logan Air Express plane that had landed that morning at La Guardia Airport after a flight from Canada. The plane was a former military C-130 Hercules transport that had once hauled jeeps, tanks, artillery, and troops. Now it hauled heavy equipment and whatever other civilian freight needed moving.

Donnie tromped down on the accelerator pedal and ran the forklift up to top speed, which was about fifteen miles per hour but felt like thirty. It had no suspension to speak of, and a thinly padded seat. The shock of the smallest object or irregularity in the concrete ran through the heavy little vehicle and Donnie's entire body. He had to grip the steering wheel hard to hold on to it.

He made a sharp turn beneath the plane's towering tail assembly, causing the rear wheels to skid slightly, then gunned the engine and went jouncing and clattering up the wide ramp into the fuselage.

Four days ago the same plane had flown a load of Hobson backhoes and a disassembled road grader north. On the return trip it had brought in crates of frozen produce. With cargo capacities the size of major caves, the big planes hauled just about anything that took up at least some space and paid minimally.

Donnie maneuvered the forklift so its steel twin

prongs slid between the upper and lower horizontal boards of the wooden pallet, then used the levers on his right to tilt back slightly and raise the heavy stack of tied-in crates. Slinging his arm over the back of the seat and contorting his body so he could see to drive backward, he reversed the forklift and ran it toward the ramp and carefully down onto the concrete. He placed the pallet of produce near the base of the ramp, then gunned the forklift engine and went back into the plane for a second load. This pallet he placed on top of the first, then backed up the forklift, lowered the heavy steel prongs, and neatly slid them back into the bottom pallet so he could haul the two-tiered combined load. He worked the hydraulic levers and lifted the load only about six inches off the ground, keeping the center of gravity low.

Continuing to drive in reverse so the load wouldn't block his view, he returned to the dry hangar, breathing propane exhaust all the way.

As he made his way to the loading dock to place the pallets on a waiting truck trailer, he noticed the blond head of Karl Barkov, one of the many Russian immigrants or sons of immigrants working in Cargo. As Barkov pushed a steel-handled, flat wooden cart in the direction of the dock, he glanced over and smiled in a way that made Donnie curious.

Barkov was one of the reasons why Donnie was working undercover at La Guardia. Horizon Movers, the company that was contracted to load and unload cargo in this area, had been a largely Italian company with Mafia connections until recently, when the Russian Mafia had moved people into it. Smart, ruthless people like Barkov.

Donnie's job was to find out why.

Some of the powers-that-be at La Guardia didn't like what they heard about Horizon Movers, so they provided the FBI with the opportunity to move Donnie in as a new employee, complete with phony work record and mandatory membership in mob-controlled Dock Workers Local 672.

Careful not to upset his load, Donnie eased the forklift forward slowly over the steel plate that bridged the gap between the dock and truck trailer he was loading with produce crates. The forklift speeded up slightly as its wheels skidded down the shallow dip of the plate into the trailer. He felt the floor give slightly as the trailer settled lower beneath the weight of the vehicle and its heavy load. The engine was suddenly louder and the fumes heavier and smellier inside the trailer.

This was only the third trip Donnie had made to and from the plane, so there was plenty of room in the trailer. He drove ahead slowly and blindly about twenty feet, then used the right side of the trailer as a guide as he inched the load forward, the long steel prongs tilted back slightly to shift the weight so the forklift had more traction and control. Something had been left to rot when the trailer's cooling unit had been turned off, and he tried not to breathe too deeply as he worked a hydraulic lever to shift the load horizontally to the left so he could see better.

That's when he realized he wasn't alone in the trailer.

A man was standing off to the left in the dim light. Donnie glanced behind him and against the bright rectangle of the trailer mouth he saw the dark silhouettes of three other men approaching.

He recognized the larger of the three—Mako Fazio, a hulking Mafia soldier who specialized in strong-arm tactics. That Mako worked here at La Guardia was in itself evidence that something illegal was going on. Guys like him usually held regular jobs for reasons other than paychecks.

Guys like *us*, Donnie corrected himself, knowing there were similarities between him and Mako. He clung to their differences to preserve his self-respect.

"Hey, Donnie, my man!" Mako yelled with mock cheer and camaraderie. "So what's the good word?"

Donnie eased the load to the floor to anchor the forklift. He let the engine idle. Maybe the combined smells of rotted meat, leaking propane gas, and exhaust fumes in such a confined space would help to keep this conversation brief and to the point. "You tell me, Mako."

"Word's fuckin' 'Ouch!' " Mako said through a nasty grin.

His huge right fist slammed into the side of Donnie's face like a meteor, toppling him from the forklift.

That was sure brief and to the point, Donnie thought, as the back of his head bounced off the trailer floor.

2

Donnie knew what was coming next and rolled away fast to his right. Mako's size 13 steel-toed work boot only grazed his ribs as he scrambled to his feet. His face and the back of his head throbbing with pain, he blinked and tried to clear his mind.

Mako was closing in with a predator's smug confidence, walking around the lead-weighted back end of the forklift, light on his feet for someone the size of a city block. Donnie knew he had to remove his martial arts training temporarily from the arsenal at his command. He was simply Donnie Barns from the West Side. Average guy trying to scratch out a living. A brawler rather than a weight-trained, skilled practitioner in the deadly arts.

He took the play away from Mako immediately, kicking him in the shins to divert him, then slapping him hard on the ear and side of the face, bringing involuntary tears that would obscure vision. Nothing exotic in that attack, simply aggressive, old-fashioned alley fighting.

Mako knuckled moisture from the corner of an eye and shrugged lazily. It was all the same to him if the rabbit wasn't going to go limp in the jaws of the lion. Might even be more fun that way. When Mako threw a hard right, Donnie slipped the punch and countered with a left hook to the ribs, a right to the gut. Mako was powerful but raw, and going soft in the middle. Another hard right to the stomach brought a *Whoosh!* of foul-smelling breath from him. He backed away, a little surprised at the fight and strength in Donnie.

The other men—half a dozen of them now—drew closer in a semicircle, intensely interested but silent. They didn't want to draw attention to the trailer and have the fight interrupted. Donnie noticed a blond head among them, a curious smile. Barkov.

Mako's big fist rammed into Donnie's sternum, knocking him against the trailer wall. He danced to the side and another punch, this time aimed at his head, whizzed past him and hit the wall with a wood-and-metallic thunder that sounded like an armor-piercing shell striking the trailer. Donnie moved in a tight circle while Mako was shaking his sore hand and punched him in the kidneys. Mako responded by nailing Donnie with a left to the heart, almost causing him to black out as he stumbled backward. Heart in my throat, Donnie found himself thinking, trying to swallow the lump of throbbing pain just beneath his Adam's apple.

When Mako growled and lunged at him Donnie had just enough presence of mind to fall back against the forklift, elbowing Mako as he charged past. He saw that Mako's momentum had carried him between the double stack of crates tied in on the pallets. Donnie reached out for a black-knobbed lever beside the forklift's seat and pulled it toward him, sliding the prongs to the right. The load shifted and pinned Mako against the truck wall with hydraulic force.

Mako was some bull. He freed one arm and began tugging and shoving at the crates, making room for himself. The exhaust and propane fumes in the trailer were nauseating Donnie, adding to his weakness, but he summoned what strength he had left and stepped forward, slamming his fist again and again into Mako's face, twisting his punches at the end to tear flesh. The trapped giant flailed his free arm but Donnie easily fended it off and kept landing punches, getting his body into them now, feeling the shock of them running up his arm into his right shoulder.

When Mako was limp, Donnie stepped back and worked the forklift lever, moving the load to the left. Mako stumbled out from between crates and wall, knocking two of the crates to the trailer floor, and slumped down to sit cross-legged. Blood was streaming down his face and trickling onto the front of his blue work shirt.

Donnie sat down hard on one of the crates and rested his elbows on his knees, his head bowed. He needed to catch his breath for real, but he made a show of it.

"You fucker!" Mako said, wiping blood from beneath his nose and flicking it away. "You done some boxin' somewheres."

"When I was a kid," Donnie said.

"You was a pro?"

"Naw. Didn't take a pro to whip your sorry ass."

"Hmph! You still got fight in you."

"More fight than you've got sense."

Mako leaned his back against the trailer wall and worked his way to his feet, keeping his distance from Donnie. "You only won round one," he said.

Donnie looked up at him. He knew he could move from where he sat in a hurry if the big man wanted to start round two immediately. "See what I mean about you having no sense?" he said.

"Bastard busted one of my teeth." Mako let his mouth hang open and probed around with his tongue to see if there was more damage. There was a lot of blood in there. "Next time I'll use an iron bar on you."

Donnie smiled. "I'll feed it to you sideways."

Mako grunted and returned the smile, then swaggered unsteadily from the trailer. The other men followed. But at the last moment Barkov turned back and approached Donnie.

"Know why he got tough with you?" he asked.

"His nature," Donnie said.

Barkov laughed. He was a handsome man except for a vertical scar that crossed his undamaged right eye and curved down the side of his face. Someone had slashed him with a knife and hadn't cut deep enough, and probably paid the price. "He tried to give you pain, Donnie, because the Italians here think you're too friendly with us."

"Who's us?" Donnie asked, dumbing down. He noticed Mako had loosened one of his molars as well.

"The Russians. Mako wanted to beat you up, make a girl of you in front of us so we wouldn't have anything to do with you. All he proved was you had—what do you Italians say—balls . . . *cojones*, hey?"

"I don't know," Donnie said. "Sounds Spanish."

Barkov cocked his head to the side. "You are not Italian?"

Donnie shook his head no, bringing on a burst of agony. "Nope. I'm an all-American mutt."

Barkov extended a sweaty hand and helped Donnie to his feet. "Well, nothing was said to you, but it was let known to some of us that we were to have little to do with you. They said you weren't to be trusted."

"Nobody has to trust me about anything," Donnie said.

Barkov laughed. "There's no reason for us not to be friends."

"Is there a reason we should be?"

"Yes. Anyone who beats up the goon Mako is a friend of ours—of mine. The enemy of my enemy is my friend, as we Russians say. And I admire the way you fight."

"So you're going to ignore the Italians' warning to stay away from me?" But Donnie already knew the answer to that one: telling a man like Barkov what not to do would almost guarantee his disobedience. The forbidden would be to him nothing more than a challenge.

Barkov stared at him, the scar making his grin slightly crooked. "It is like apples."

"Apples?"

"Yes. There is another Russian saying: The way to be sure your apples will be stolen is to lock them up." Barkov leisurely lifted the two crates from the floor and replaced them on the pallet, then walked from the trailer.

"I'll try to figure out what that means," Donnie said after him, climbing back up onto the forklift.

But he knew what it meant.

He reached up and gingerly used his fingertips to explore the lump on the back of his head.

It felt the size of an apple.

3

I thought you said you were making progress," Donnie's Bureau supervisor Jules Donavon said to him that evening over coffee at the Crispy Queen doughnut shop on West 72nd Street. "Your head looks like ripe fruit."

"The bruises will go away," Donnie said, "and they bought me the respect I need from the Russians."

Donavon bit into a messy cream-filled doughnut, then took a sip of coffee. As Donnie's supervisor, he was given wide latitude by Special Agent in Charge Victor Whitten. This freedom from binding Bureau rules was passed on to Donnie. Whitten and Donavon understood Donnie's special status in the Bureau. He was the only FBI agent with a half-million-dollar price on his head payable by the Mafia, the only agent who carried the curse of having to live under assumed identities for the rest of his days.

The Bureau owed Donnie.

Donnie's six years of undercover work had cost the Mafia dearly, having virtually destroyed its east coast operations. What was left of the Mafia figured they owed him something, too. The something was death.

As part of a marriage—or agreement—between the Russian and Italian mobs, a Russian hit man had been assigned to find and kill Donnie. Former KGB assassin Yesa Marishov was never completely out of his life, always out there somewhere on the map of Donnie's existence, like a heat-seeking missile prowling for the slightest warmth and direction. That meant Donnie seldom saw his former wife Elana, or his daughters Maureen and Daisy. He lived perpetually in a shadow world of peril and fractured identity. Danger clung to him like a disease, and because it was a contagious disease, it meant loneliness. His life had become a fearful exercise in survival, and his work had become his life. There was nothing else. There could be nothing else.

Right now his assignment was to infiltrate part of the cargo handler workforce at La Guardia to find out why the Russian Mafia was moving in on the traditional Italian Mafia's territory. During the past few years the east coast Russians had become a meaner and more potent power than the Italians, establishing a strong and ominous presence from New York to Miami. So pervasive were they in southeast Florida that the Bureau's Miami office had created a special Russia-Eurasia squad to cope with the inundation of this new breed of mobster. Redfellas, some of the FBI agents called them. Whatever was going on at La Guardia, it meant something important. The first step in figuring out what it was required becoming part of it.

That was Donnie's rare talent and specialty; transforming himself, blending and learning, observing, gathering not only knowledge but incriminating information. For this assignment he must become an honorary Redfella.

Donnie sipped his coffee from time to time but left his glazed doughnut untouched as he briefed Jules Donavon on the events of the last few days.

"Barkov bears more looking into," Jules said, when Donnie was finished talking. "We'll learn more about him and get the information to you."

"I can tell you he's smart, tough, and a leader."

"What about Mako Fazio?"

"He's dumb, tough, and a follower. He bragged to me once he was called Mako after the shark. Hammerhead is more like it."

"So what's kept the Russians from completely taking over whatever the racket is out at La Guardia?"

"I'm not sure yet. And maybe they *have* taken over."

"I'm thinking about that fight you had," Jules said. "The Russians at or near the top are more hands-on. They don't mind getting blood under their fingernails. But because Mako did the strong-arming, he's obviously no more than a soldier at best. Any idea who might be in charge?"

"Could be the Local 672 business agent, Sam Vargo."

"I doubt it," Donavon said. "More like the union to be passive and take a cut of whatever crooked money goes through the operation."

"Whatever Vargo knows, so does Lefty Ordaz, the cargo boss. They're thick with each other. But I agree with you that if Vargo's involved he isn't in charge. He's smarmy, backslapping, more a sergeant than a general. But he spends more time than he has to at La Guardia."

"You think he or Ordaz suspect you?"

Donnie considered the question, watching the doughnut-making machinery behind a glass wall knead dough, separate it, and drop it on metal trays to be deep fried. "There's no way to know for sure with either of them. Ordaz is carefully neutral where I'm concerned, and Vargo doesn't seem hostile or suspicious of me. In fact, he seems to like me. When he's around me he sometimes absently sings 'Danny Boy,' only he substitutes 'Donnie.' "

Jules wiped a dab of cream filling from his chin and shook his head. "The people we have to deal with . . ."

"He is pretty much off-key."

"How come you're not eating your doughnut? That Mako guy make it impossible for you to chew?"

"No. Somehow he missed knocking out my teeth."

"Think we should place a member of the EO Squad at La Guardia?"

Jules was referring to the Extraordinary Operations Squad, a group of agents with special skills sometimes called on and commanded by Donnie.

"Not yet," Donnie said. "At this point, it'd only double the chances of me being found out."

Jules shrugged. "Your call, Donnie." He glanced down at the table. "You gonna eat that doughnut, or just look at it?"

"Haven't made up my mind. Want it?"

Jules patted his flat stomach. "Yes and no. The diet. You know how it goes."

Donnie knew. He watched the play of contradictory

forces move behind Jules's eyes. It had always been difficult for willpower and whipped topping to coexist in Jules's mind.

Finally Jules pushed his chair back and stood up, a middle-aged man with salt-and-pepper hair, not as tall as Donnie but barrel-chested and lean-waisted, still in good enough condition to take the obstacle course at Quantico in stride, and wanting to stay that way. He and Donnie had both grown up in New Jersey, though Jules had lost all of his accent while Donnie retained some of his. They'd gone through Bureau training together, worked together, liked and respected each other. That translated into trust, and trust was the coin of their realm.

"Stay in touch and watch your back," Jules said. It was his frequent parting remark to Donnie.

Donnie watched him leave the doughnut shop without looking back and turn right when he was outside. He paused for a moment to smile at a young woman carrying an infant in one of those sling arrangements that rested the child against the mother's breasts. Secure baby, Donnie thought. Safe. What would it be like to feel that way again? He watched as his old friend fastened a button on his sport coat, hunched his shoulders against the evening chill, and trudged on toward Columbus Circle.

Donnie finished his coffee but left the glazed doughnut. He was seldom hungry after a conversation with Donavon.

For this assignment his flash pad—Bureau terminology for an undercover agent's apartment used during an operation—was a West Side walk-up, and his flash ride was a junk car with a finely tuned engine under the hood. The idea was for him to live in neutral territory in teeming and anonymous Manhattan. He could drive to La Guardia, bitch about the traffic, talk about moving closer if the job worked out. The Bureau hadn't furnished help in finding parking spaces, so Donnie walked or took the subway to most places around town.

After leaving the doughnut shop, he strolled several blocks to his apartment, which was in an old eight-story brick building with bowed out, rusty iron bars on the lower-floor windows to keep burglars and junkies out and the air conditioners from being stolen. When he was halfway home a fine mist softened the night and made the streetlights and headlights star. It was beautiful but the moisture worked down inside his collar and chilled the back of his neck.

He fished in his pocket for his keys as he climbed the three steps to the building's concrete stoop. Months or years ago a swastika had been painted in black on the wall near the front door. There was no way to scrub it away entirely from the porous bricks, so someone had long ago connected the swastika's cross strokes to turn it into a four-spoked wheel and painted flowers inside each of the circle's quarter compartments. Donnie liked that.

The mist had become a cool, steady drizzle and he was now in a hurry to get out of it.

Nobody's perfect; he didn't notice the venetian blind slat in his third-floor unit's front window drop half an inch back into place as he unlocked and opened the street door.

Working undercover was like doing a trapeze act in the dark.

Not being perfect could be fatal.

4

Some of the old tricks are the best. Or variations of those tricks, anyway.

Before unlocking his apartment door and entering, Donnie stooped in the dim hallway and deftly felt the hinged side of the door. Just beneath the lower hinge, where it was out of sight, the rounded end of a metal paper clip protruded a quarter of an inch. Which meant the door hadn't opened and closed in his absence, allowing the paper clip to drop.

Then why did he immediately sense he wasn't alone as soon as he stepped inside the apartment?

He was about to move back outside in a hurry when a lamp winked on.

Karl Barkov was sitting in the armchair that normally faced the TV. He'd scooted it at an angle to face the door.

He looked more like an executive than a dock worker. His blond hair was combed back slickly and he was wearing a camel hair sport jacket and dark brown wool slacks that had a nice drape to them as he crossed his legs. His shoes were oxblood wingtips. The facial scar that gave him a rough look at work now seemed to possess all the nobility of an honorable memento from a duel. A tan topcoat was folded neatly on his lap.

Barkov smiled at Donnie. "I noticed the paper clip and put it back where I found it."

"That's hard to do from the inside."

"I refastened it to the doorframe from the outside with some adhesive tape from your medicine cabinet, then came back inside and shut the door. Magic's always a disappointment when you learn how simply it's done, hey, my friend?"

"Not always," Donnie said. He felt a slight chill as he realized Barkov had probably been over every inch of the apartment. Then he realized he was safe. There was nothing in the place suggesting he might be an undercover FBI agent. All Barkov would have found was confirmation that the apartment's occupant was Donnie Barns. The Bureau had even seen to it that past-due credit card and utility bills were planted in the small desk in a corner of the living room. A few of his dress shirts had the letters "DB" written on their labels with laundry ink, as if to keep them from being lost at the cleaners. Some returned Donnie Barns checks marked INSUFFICIENT FUNDS were another authentic touch. Donnie Barns was who he claimed to be, all right, and he needed the job. The apartment would do what it was designed to do, which was lend credibility to his cover.

Unless something had been forgotten.

He did know the windows were locked and protected by steel grates, the one near the fire escape blocked by a gate that could only be opened from inside the apartment. Barkov had to have entered through the apartment's only door, just as he'd said.

"Where did you get a key?" Donnie asked.

"Would you believe the door was unlocked?"

"No."

Barkov shrugged. "I have many old skills. One of them is opening doors with a lock pick."

"That I believe. But I don't much like the sensation, coming home and finding someone who doesn't belong there. It's like discovering something with feelers in your salad."

Barkov chose not to be insulted. He uncrossed his legs and slung an arm over the back of his chair. "I surprised you that way to show how deep the water is where you're swimming. I thought, this Donnie Barns is a nice guy, straight and strong and simple. I want to be his friend, help him in his struggles. Then I thought some more about it and changed my mind."

"You don't wanna help me in whatever struggles you're talking about, fine," Donnie said in an irritated voice. "So leave."

"I meant I changed my mind about you being a simple man. We Russians say action should not be mistaken for simplicity. A man like you, there are thoughts swimming around in your skull, always. That means you need help all the more, because you'll figure out the deal. Oh, yes, you will."

"What deal?"

"The one where something unusual is happening at work."

Donnie put on a puzzled look. "I don't know what you're talking about."

"But you will, because you're smart. Then the Italians won't just send around a goon like Mako to beat all sense and reason out of you, my friend. They'll kill you."

Donnie stared at him. "Somebody wants my forklift job that bad?"

Barkov laughed, then shifted his folded coat from his lap to his left arm and stood up. He seemed larger in the tiny apartment than at work. Part of it was his surroundings, and part of it was because he was the kind of man who filled his space. "I like you even more because you're complicated. The time will come when you need help. I want you to know you can get it from me. Have you ever heard of the Westward Ho Social Club?"

"No."

"It's a sort of Russian gathering place in Brooklyn. I spend much of my time there. You should see it. Come there tonight as my guest."

"It's kind of late," Donnie said. He didn't like the thought of going with Barkov into enemy territory until he was better prepared. Donnie Barns wouldn't be keen on it, either.

"You seem a little bit uneasy. Some vodka will put you at ease."

"Maybe I am a little uneasy," Donnie admitted. "You said somebody might want to kill me just because he's Italian and I'm smart."

"Not just because he's Italian, Donnie. Mafioso. Mafia."

"What? You putting me on?" Donnie swallowed. Shifted his weight.

"You stepped on Family toes when you beat up Mako. You can't be too surprised. After all, labor unions, Mafia money and influence. Isn't it American tradition that these things are all of a piece?"

"This has to be a joke."

"Is Mako Fazio a joke?"

"The worst kind," Donnie said.

"And a dangerous kind."

Donnie gave it a few long seconds, as if weighing what he'd been told. "You hear about that kinda thing, sure. The Mafia, the unions. But I always figured they keep that stuff to themselves. Which is fine with me. All I wanna do is load and unload planes."

"And so you can. We'll help you to do that, convince people you can keep a secret."

"The secret I'm sure to learn?"

Barkov smiled. "That's the one." He slipped into his tan topcoat. It looked expensive, like the rest of his clothes. "Come on, Donnie. I want you to meet some of my friends. We'll take two cars so you can leave and drive back here whenever you want."

Donnie stood still as if trying to make up his mind. Then he lifted and dropped his shoulders in an elaborate shrug—Donnie Barns, still afraid and making a show of being cool. "Okay. Why not?"

But he could think of countless reasons why not.

He followed Barkov out into the hall and carefully locked the door behind them.

Not that it mattered.

A sleek black Mercedes was parked at the curb in front of Donnie's beat up, twelve-year-old Honda Accord. There was nothing to suggest that the Honda had a new and souped up Acura V-Tech engine and a modified transmission that allowed it to accelerate and hit top speed faster than almost anything else on the street. The first time Donnie had driven it he'd been startled by the way he'd been pressed back into the seat, then glanced at the speedometer and seen the needle zoom past the 100-miles-per-hour mark.

He started the Honda, waited for Barkov to pull away from the curb, then followed the Mercedes.

Barkov cut over to Broadway and drove south to lower Manhattan and the Brooklyn Bridge. Soon Donnie found himself following the Mercedes's bright red taillights through a maze of Brooklyn side streets lined with small shops and narrow brick apartment buildings. He was careful to make mental notes of landmarks so he could find his way back if he left the Westward Ho Social Club before Barkov. If he left the Westward Ho Social Club.

Finally he parked behind the Mercedes across the street from a flat-roofed brick building with a green canvas awning across its front. The windows of deserted shops on the ground floor had been boarded over, the plywood painted a dark green to match the awning. There were blinds or curtains over some of the upper floor windows, with light seeping through them or showing around the edges. Two men were standing near the entrance, beneath the awning to stay out of the light drizzle, smoking cigars and talking. They were both overweight, wearing suits without ties. Every few seconds the taller of the two would wave his cigar as he spoke, the ember tracing a red pattern in the night.

"This is it," Barkov said, standing in the street as Donnie climbed out of the Honda.

Donnie squinted at the building. "I don't see a sign."

Barkov grinned. "Must be an exclusive club, hey?"

"Hey," Donnie said, and followed him across the dark, wet street.

The two large men in suits suspended their conversation and stood silently, looking at Donnie but ignoring Barkov as they walked past. They were fat men, but they carried a lot of their weight in the chest, arms and shoulders, like professional wrestlers. The cigars they smoked gave off a stench like burning rubber.

Barkov pulled open what looked like a new steel-core door in the old drab building. He held the heavy door and stood out of the way for Donnie to enter first.

Donnie eased past Barkov and stepped inside out of the cool night air.

He tried to ignore the lump of fear in his stomach. Getting into the Westward Ho Social Club had been a snap.

Getting out might not be as easy.

5

A slight pause inside the door, and Donnie's trained eye took it all in. The inside of the Westward Ho looked like somebody's home rathskeller times ten. A long bar with red vinyl stools ran along one wall. Behind it was a large mirror backing shelves of multicolored bottles of liquor that reflected concealed lighting. The floor was gray-and-white-checked tile, patterned with dark scuff marks from rubber heels and extinguished cigarettes. Half a dozen men sat or stood at the bar. Another half dozen sat at small wooden tables. The place was ten degrees above normal room temperature, and the haze of tobacco smoke clinging to the ceiling would have made Joe Camel proud. To the left was the doorway to another room, this one with a couple of pool tables under stark fluorescent lights. The tables' felt was bright red rather than the traditional green. Donnie wondered if it was some kind of political statement.

Another door opened at the far end of the room in which Donnie and Barkov stood, and music from what sounded like a live band burst out. Against a dim backdrop Donnie caught a glimpse of lots of people milling around, beyond them more people dancing. A woman laughed loudly in a high, tinkling voice like breaking glass.

Then the door swung shut and the music and voices were abruptly cut off. That kind of soundproofing made Donnie nervous.

Barkov was grinning hugely. "Come, Donnie, we'll have some good Russian vodka."

"I'm more of a beer man." Donnie wanted his mind to remain as clear as possible.

"Okay, beer." Barkov nudged Donnie as they moved toward the bar. "Don't call them brewskies here, hey? Could get you hurt."

Donnie glanced over at him. He seemed serious.

Two men saw their approach in the mirror and moved out of the way to provide two stools next to each other. Donnie and Barkov stood near the stools but didn't sit. One of the men who'd moved, about fifty, tall and stooped but with wide shoulders and long arms, grinned at Donnie and Barkov. There was a wide gap between his front teeth.

"Gregory," Barkov said to him, "this is my friend from La Guardia, Donnie Barns. I told you about him."

"I remember," the grinning Gregory said in a deep, phlegmy rumble. He shook hands with Donnie. "You're a tough guy, huh?"

"When there isn't any choice, I guess I am."

"Barkov here says you got balls."

"Two of them." Donnie noticed a tattoo on Gregory's left index finger, crossed daggers with a numeral 4 between the blades. He knew it was a Russian criminal tattoo that signified a racketeer from the Caucasus, or sometimes Chechnya. Russian mobsters were big on tattoos; it was often possible to trace the background of an apprehended or dead criminal by the tattoos he'd obtained in various provinces or prisons.

A slender young bartender with a bushy mustache, sad blue eyes, and wearing a red ascot beneath a half-buttoned white shirt approached along the backside of the bar and asked who wanted what.

"We got Siberian Yellow here on tap," Barkov told Donnie. "Our own special label."

Gregory nodded his agreement with the recommendation.

"I'm up for it," Donnie said.

Barkov held up two fingers and the bartender drifted away toward the decorous, porcelain-handled taps. A short, stocky man appeared on Donnie's left. He was wearing corduroy pants and a tight-fitting black T-shirt that showed off a weight-lifter's torso. The only tattoo visible on him was a faded red heart above the name "Terri" on his bulging right bicep.

"Boris," Barkov said, "this is my friend Donnie Barns."

Donnie noticed he seemed to be the only one in the place with a last name but decided not to bring it up.

"Guy who ties knots in those Italian pricks," Boris said. He had hooded, serious eyes; a long, long chin. Shifting the glass he was holding to his left hand, he shook with Donnie. "Buy you a drink?"

"Thanks, but they're already on the way."

"Barkov says you're smart. He's smart enough to know."

Donnie looked over at Barkov. "I'm also curious."

The bartender arrived with their beers in tall glass mugs coated with frost. Barkov clinked his mug against Donnie's, then threw back his head and downed half his beer. Donnie took a long swig. Siberian Yellow was thick, with a rich malty taste. Probably half a million calories per mug. Donnie liked it.

"No need to be curious, Donnie," Barkov said. "I just wanted to bring you here so you could meet some people, they could meet you. They like the idea you did a job on Mako."

"And that you're *oomnyj*," Gregory growled. "Smart."

Boris nodded approvingly, then said, "We're not so sure about liking the curious part."

The doors at the far end of the room opened wide, and the music and voices were louder than before. There was a lot of laughter, too.

"Come," Barkov said, and tugged at Donnie's sleeve. He held tight to the material as they walked across the room to the open doors. "A wedding," Barkov pronounced, as they stood in the doorway.

Donnie, being *oomnyj*, had guessed it from seeing the bride. She was wearing an elaborate white gown and a tiara with a white veil folded back atop her braided yellow hair. She was pretty, and she was dancing like crazy. A tall, skinny guy in his twenties, grinning at her in a way that made him the groom, was facing her with both hands around her waist and whirling her and himself in tight circles. He had nimble feet and she was struggling to keep up. The long black tails of his tux stood out horizontally as he picked up speed. Something, an earring or barrette, flew from the bride's yellow hair and skidded glittering across the tile floor to disappear beneath a white-clothed table. Her smile never faltered. The six-piece band was wearing identical powder blue suits. They grinned in unison and launched into what sounded like a very loud polka. The groom swung the bride around faster, so that her feet actually left the floor. People fairly leaped from their chairs and were on the dance floor, whirling like the bride and groom. Donnie thought somebody was going to get hurt.

"In Russia there's an old saying," Barkov told Donnie. " 'All women should marry, but no men.' "

Donnie didn't think that, right then, the groom would agree.

On one wall was a large fireplace with blue and red flames flickering above gas jets in obviously artificial logs. Donnie saw that people were scraping their chairs across the floor, switching tables, moving away from the fire as if the phony gas logs might explode.

The music stopped, and a man sweating from dancing swaggered to a table, picked up a glass of wine, and gave a brief toast in Russian. He was drunk enough to slur his words, but not so drunk that he didn't deliver his message with gusto. People toasted, laughed, then hurled their wine and champagne glasses toward the fireplace. Glass shattered and glinted in the flames. That pleased everyone to the point where they raised their arms and cheered loudly.

The music became softer, slower. More wedding guests stood up from their tables and joined the bride and groom on the dance floor. The bride was leaning against the groom now, her head resting on his shoulder as he led her in a lazy two-step. Probably she was still dizzy from the last dance, Donnie thought. Or maybe she was simply in love. Either way, an affliction of her heart or her inner ear, she looked as if she couldn't stand up by herself.

Barkov punched his shoulder. "Just like in the movies, hey?"

Donnie felt a pang of fear. Barkov didn't say much by accident. Was he making reference to the movie *Donnie Brasco* that had helped to make a hero of Donnie by dramatizing his exploits undercover in the Mafia? The movie's success, and a subsequent book, had also made it more difficult for him to move incognito through the world.

But Barkov was staring contentedly at the dancers, an amiable man made more so by Siberian Yellow, enjoying seeing people having fun.

Barkov stood up straighter, and Donnie looked to his right and saw why. A man in his fifties, medium-height, broad but only slightly overweight, was approaching. He had on an ankle-length black coat with a gray fur collar. Beneath a sharp widow's peak and bulbous forehead, his face was broad and intense, his dark eyebrows almost meeting in a V above wide-set brown eyes. Though his features were a cruel mask, his eyes were merely inquisitive. A white shirt and tightly knotted gold silk tie were visible above his buttoned coat. His short, neatly trimmed gray beard was a shade darker than the coat's fur collar.

"Mr. Zelensky," Barkov said. "This is the friend I told you about."

Finally somebody besides me with a last name, Donnie thought, but apparently no given name.

"It's good to meet you," Zelensky said, but he didn't offer his hand to shake. "Karl says you're a man of courage and ability."

"Some of each on some days," Donnie said, wondering if Barkov had forgotten to mention smart.

Zelensky gave him a surprisingly warm smile, the gargoyle-like frown turning into the beatific gaze of a saint. "Let's hope you're also as smart as Karl says." His gaze flicked casually up and down, surveying Donnie. "You are Russian?"

"No," Donnie told him, figuring Zelensky had probably known the answer before asking.

"It doesn't matter. You're welcome here if you're a friend. I get to this country only infrequently but I know how it works; a big melting pot."

"Sometimes it's a stew."

Zelensky grunted agreement. "Soup sometimes, too. Or just water. Hot water." He'd been casting a long, last look around the room as he spoke. Now he fastened the top button on his coat. "A pleasure to meet you," he said almost absently.

"My pleasure," Donnie said, knowing he'd been sized up by an expert despite Zelensky's seeming lack of interest.

Zelensky plucked a black, fur-trimmed hat from his pocket and fitted it carefully on his head so he wouldn't muss his sleek gray hair, then walked toward the street door.

Remember that one, Donnie thought, watching him.

As Donnie and Barkov moved back toward the bar, Donnie let his gaze slide around the room. He didn't recognize any of the faces from the distant and dangerous past he'd lived in the New York area. He prayed no one recognized his face. His usual prayer. He knew he'd be discussed after he left.

"Another beer?" Barkov asked, sensing Donnie was preparing to leave, maybe wanting to make sure he'd stay long enough that he couldn't follow Zelensky.

"No, thanks," Donnie said. But he decided to put Barkov's mind at ease and not rush off. "So who's Zelensky?"

"Mr. Zelensky's . . . well, he's Mr. Zelensky."

Donnie knew that would have to be good enough.

Barkov was looking at him. "No good can come of you wondering about him. The important thing is that he doesn't wonder about you."

"I think I'll have another beer at that," Donnie said. "A short one. It won't affect my driving. I've sweated away the effects of the first one."

"Yes, it's warm. People have been known to perspire a great deal in here." Barkov strapped an arm over Donnie's shoulders and held up his two-fingered sign for the bartender.

During their time in the Westward Ho, Barkov hadn't again mentioned whatever it was that Donnie was supposed to figure out was happening at La Guardia. Donnie knew better than to ask about it. If and when Barkov felt the time had come, he would inform Donnie. Then Donnie would inform Jules Donavon.

Half an hour later Donnie emerged from the warmth of the Westward Ho into the cool night. Siberian Yellow was a strong brew, but he knew he'd been slowed down only marginally after nursing half of his last drink and leaving the rest to sit warming on the bar.

He climbed into the old Honda, aware that he was being watched. There was no reason at this point to suspect a bomb in the car, but he still clenched his teeth as he twisted the ignition key to start the engine.

He was breathing easier as he pulled away from the curb.

Caught off-guard for a moment in his relief, he didn't notice the black Ford Bronco fall in behind him at the intersection.

6

Donnie did notice the Bronco when its headlights, much higher than the trunk of the low-slung Honda, drew dangerously close as he carefully wound his way through side streets back to the bridge that would return him to Manhattan. The big headlights stayed glued to him through every turn he made; there could be no doubt the driver was following him and didn't care if he knew. When finally he turned onto the expressway and picked up speed, he half expected the vehicle behind him to pull up alongside.

But the looming, squarish, dark form behind the headlights remained about ten feet away from the Honda's rear bumper. Though Donnie slowed on the bridge so other cars honked at him and passed, their drivers sometimes glaring sideways at him, whoever was tailing him adjusted speed so that the two vehicles might have been connected by a taut piece of string.

Back in Manhattan, Donnie headed north and across town toward the Upper West Side. Now he used the Honda's performance engine to cut in and out of traffic, shot ahead with bursts of speed, managed to get a glimpse of his pursuer—an ominous black vehicle with tinted windows. It was moving adroitly through traffic, keeping pace with the smaller, more maneuverable Honda. It must have a special engine and suspension, and the driver had to be good to match Donnie's high jinks at the wheel.

Donnie was outwardly calm but his heart was hammering as he played brake and accelerator in a game of high-speed mental chess with the Bronco's skillful driver. He kept waiting for a cop to pick up the action and pursue both vehicles, but it didn't happen. This was Manhattan, and late as it was, traffic was still heavy. Donnie and the other driver were pushing limits, moving ever faster, sometimes with two wheels up on the curb when there wasn't room to pass.

Donnie kept a tight grip on the steering wheel as he barely missed a knot of pedestrians poised to step off the curb. He noticed a small girl among them, about the age of one of his daughters. This had to be ended. Somebody not involved was going to be killed.

It would be a mistake to return to his apartment if he couldn't lose the Bronco. Maybe a mistake to return even if he did shake his persistent shadow. Waiting until the last possible second, he cut right onto Central Park West, rocketed north, then barely avoided a wooden sawhorse as he veered into the barricaded 72nd Street entrance to Central Park, where there was no late-night traffic and pedestrians were less likely to be killed.

People seated on the benches just inside the park gaped as the Honda sped past. Donnie turned right, jumped the curb, and steered the Honda along a walkers' and roller-bladers' blacktop path that led away from the street. The smooth path was virtually deserted this time of night, as he knew it would be.

He killed the Honda's headlights and reduced speed by gearing down so he wouldn't flare the brake lights. Then he pulled off the path, onto the grass and dark shadows beneath the trees.

Behind some trees and tall bushes, he stopped the Honda, turned off the engine, cranked down the window—and listened.

He heard nothing but the muffled thrumming of the city outside the park. A horn honked several times far away beyond Central Park West. The distant, plaintive notes made Donnie feel secure and isolated. Apparently he hadn't been seen turning onto the trail, or later off of it to disappear in the foliage and shadows. Not for the first time, night had become his shelter.

To be safe, he waited at least five minutes before twisting the ignition key and restarting the engine.

Headlights flared brightly, blinding him, and with a roar the huge form of the Bronco appeared from behind a rise, bore down on him, and skidded sideways, blocking the Honda.

Donnie hit reverse, then tromped the accelerator.

The Honda crashed into a tree, jolting him so he bounced back then forward off the seat and into the steering wheel. His right elbow slammed into the dashboard.

The Bronco straightened out and moved much closer, against the front bumper of the Honda. The bright headlights were extinguished.

His eyes not yet adjusted from the blinding light, then darkness again, Donnie could only faintly see several men piling out of the Bronco. They advanced in the night toward his blocked car, nightmare shadows with substance.

He thought about getting out of the Honda and running, knew it was probably hopeless, but fumbled for the door handle and made his body obey.

By the time he was out of the car and straightening up they were on him. As the first blows began to hit home, he glanced around before ducking low and covering his head with his arms and hands. This was happening well off the street and the trail, in dim moonlight. No one was likely to come to his rescue.

A fist got through and bounced hard off the side of Donnie's head, stunning him.

The pain disappeared in a hurry, so he might have passed out for a moment.

But only a moment.

The pain was back, and he was being yanked to his feet by two huge arms at the end of which were fists that clutched his shirt front. A pale, oval face grinned down at him in the moonlight. Donnie wasn't surprised to see it was Mako's.

"Asshole," Mako said, "don't you know you ain't s'posed to drive on the grass?"

Donnie figured the question was rhetorical.

Mako adjusted his grip for comfort. His own, not

Donnie's. "Didn't nobody ever tell you Central Park's dangerous after dark?"

"Been told," Donnie managed to gasp. Talking wasn't easy, what with the knuckles digging into his throat. He saw two men standing behind Mako, and maybe there was another off to the side. Some odds.

"Know what's gonna happen now?" Mako asked. He was full of questions, one of those inquiring minds.

"You're gonna ask what I was doing at the Westward Ho Club."

"Naw. All we need to know is you was there, and you ain't never goin' back."

"How do you know I don't have a membership card?" Donnie asked. There was nothing to lose now. The Italian faction thought just buddying up to the Redfellas was reason enough to kill him.

"You and your membership card's gonna be part of the environment," Mako said. He turned his head as he spoke. "Freddy."

One of the men behind Mako moved forward. He was slender and looked like a nasty young Frank Sinatra, and he held a hook-pointed carpet knife in his right hand.

"Freddy a recycler?" Donnie asked. He was moving from terror to resignation. A part of him didn't like that even though it was a comfort. Too many men had died unnecessarily while making peace with their God.

Mako made an odd shape with his lips and looked off to the side, as if giving the question some thought. "Freddy's more the kinda guy that ends cycles. Know what happens when you slit a body from gut to gullet?"

"I never can remember."

"The gasses don't build up in the belly, so when you sink one it stays sunk and don't float up like a balloon. We're gonna drive you over to the reservoir an' gut an' sink you. We'll be a little touchy about drinkin' tap water for a while, then we'll forget all about you."

Donnie heard one of the Bronco's doors open and shut, then a voice in the darkness: "What's taking you guys so fucking long?"

He was sure he recognized the voice. It didn't give him much hope.

"Enjoyin' myself, is all," Mako said. "A man oughta try an' find some pleasure in his life."

"We're spending too much time here," the voice said. "This isn't anything personal, it's business. Just kill the fucker, take him to the—"

The man who moved into the moonlight stopped talking as he saw Donnie's face. He stepped closer, then grabbed Donnie's hair and yanked his head up, staring hard at him. "Holy shit! Look who it is! I don't fucking believe it!"

The two men studied Donnie, then each other in the faint light.

"It's him, all right," the man said with certainty. "You just never know who you might run into in the park."

"It's a small underworld," Donnie said.

He was looking into the mad, moonlit eyes of Vincent (Vinnie) Roma, who'd been a high-ranking Mafia soldier who had the good fortune to be vacationing in the Bahamas at the time Donnie broke cover years ago and destroyed the East Coast Mafia. Roma had barely escaped prosecution, mainly because he hadn't been caught in the initial net of arrests and had time to arrange for some of his friends to eliminate potentially damaging witnesses. He'd stayed in the Bahamas where he followed the trials and convictions of his fellow mobsters in the newspapers and on CNN. Donnie had heard a rumor he was back, and that he'd risen to the rank of capo.

"You've been upwardly mobile, Vinnie," Donnie told him.

Roma smiled. He was a short, swarthy man with thick black hair and glittering dark eyes in a round face. Al Capone without the scar. Or the balls. Had the meanness, though. "You know me, Donnie, a good organization man."

"I always figured you for more of a rogue."

Roma chuckled. "Just like you, eh?"

"Gee, I'd like not to think so."

"You know this asshole?" Mako asked. "You know Donnie Barns?"

"He's Donnie Barns, my ass!" Roma said. "This is the famous Donnie Brasco. Me and him go back. We know each other real well."

Mako stared at Donnie in surprise, and not without some awe. "Jesus! I seen that movie. Pacino an' Johnny Depp. Or was it Christian Slater?"

"It was Depp," Roma said. "I saw the movie six times. I didn't like it."

Mako tore his gaze from Donnie and looked back at

Roma. "So what's a hotshot movie hero like this doin' handlin' cargo out at La Guardia?"

"He's still working with the FBI," Roma said. "I'd say he's trying to infiltrate the Russian mob. That's probably why he beat the holy crap out of you, Mako, to get in good with the Ruskies. And it looks like it worked."

Mako tightened his grip on Donnie's shirt, but he backed away almost to arm's length. "So whaddya wanna do, Vinnie? Kill him some other way so it takes longer?"

Roma looked appraisingly at Donnie. "Yeah, that's what I want to do, but maybe I won't. Or maybe I will."

"Ain't there a half-million-dollar open contract out on this prick?" Mako asked.

"Sure is."

"That should be mine, then. Ours."

"Shut up, Mako."

Mako did.

Distracted and interested in the conversation, Freddy with the carpet knife had edged closer.

Close enough, in fact.

Donnie used a free hand to hack the man's bony wrist. The curved knife flashed in the moonlight as it slipped from numbed fingers. At the same time, Donnie let his body go limp and drop straight down, his hand extended now, ready to grab the knife as it fell, poised to gouge it into Mako's testicles or midsection with a tight upward sweep.

At a time like that, tenths of seconds are like minutes.

Donnie was short one. Mako merely raised his right knee and caught him smartly in the forehead, snapping his head back.

"Fucker never gives up . . . " Donnie heard Roma say.

The park got darker, then disappeared entirely.

When Donnie opened his eyes he was home in his apartment.

He squinted in the yellow lamplight, reentering the world in stages, and realized he was slouched in what had become his favorite chair. There was a residue of dread in his mind and an awful taste in his mouth. He probed with his tongue and felt teeth the size and texture of mossy tombstones. He attempted to move but his body would barely respond, making it not worth the effort. Maybe he'd been asleep a long time. Should he feel relieved? Had the Westward Ho Club, the car chase, and the Central Park encounter all been a dream?

Nope.

He swallowed, and his throat felt as if Mako's knuckles were digging in again. When his Adam's apple bobbed, it was painful and noisy. And there was Mako himself staring down at him. Flanked by Vinnie Roma and young Frank Sinatra. The Rat Pack gone from bad to worse.

"Surprised to be alive?" Roma asked.

"Shocked," Donnie said truthfully. What would

make Roma pass up the opportunity to kill him and collect the half-million-dollar bounty? A half-formed thought that scared Donnie was swimming like a shadowy shark in the recesses of his mind.

"Wake up Donnie all the way," Roma said.

Donnie's head was jolted to the side as Mako slapped him, then grazed his nose with knuckles on the back swing. The charge of pain did make Donnie somehow more alert.

"You got your senses about you?" Roma asked.

"That's a laugh," Mako said. But nobody even snickered.

Roma nudged Mako aside as if he were on casters and moved around so he was standing squarely in front of Donnie, staring down at him with the light at his back. Donnie looked unflinchingly at the doomful dark form silhouetted in the sickly yellow light. Roma slipped his hands in the pockets of his unbuttoned overcoat. So now the bullet or knife blade was going to come. They'd simply wanted him awake enough to realize what was happening. Sadistic bastards! Donnie considered kicking Roma in the crotch, scoring some points on the way out. But that didn't seem so important right now.

"You called La Guardia and told them you weren't coming in to work today," Roma said. "A touch of stomach flu, but you should be okay tomorrow."

Donnie didn't understand at first. He sat up slightly straighter in the soft chair. His head ached and felt heavy as concrete on his neck and shoulders. It took a few seconds for him to realize the call had been made by someone pretending to be him.

Roma smiled. "This isn't the night we had the little dance in the park," he said. "This is the next night. You been asleep almost twice around the clock, with a little help from a sedative we gave you."

"Why?" Donnie asked, trying to clear his brain without moving his head. He didn't seem able to focus for more than a few seconds at a time. The room was pitching gently, with a slow rhythm, like a ship anchored in calm waters.

"Why's he still alive, I think he's askin'," Mako said.

"No, our hero's smart," Roma said. "He's asking why did we buy us some time by keeping him under. Answer's because we're gonna talk business, and we wanted to make sure we were dealing from strength."

"Your idea of dealing from strength means a marked deck," Donnie said.

"Marked, stacked, whatever. You're in a game where we make all the rules. This isn't negotiations. This is you playing whether you like it or not, and us winning every hand."

Donnie was surprised to hear himself laugh. He could stall a while, regain some strength, fight them so they might have to kill him. Or maybe he could get to the window and through the glass, die on the pavement below so they couldn't torture him in their own good time. A fall from a window; it might look like an accident. Would Roma be able to collect his contract blood money then? When it came to murder, the Mafia demanded proof beyond a reasonable doubt, just like the law.

Roma sneered. "You can laugh, dickhead. But your little girl's not laughing with you."

Donnie shook his head, letting the pain make him more alert. "What?"

"That eleven-year-old daughter of yours, Daisy. She played some softball in St. Louis this afternoon after school, smooth little fielder but without much range to her right. And her head's not in the game. She went to get a soda at the refreshment stand between innings and missed her turn at bat. Never did show up, but they found her glove in the parking lot. Mom was all excited, but the teams played the last inning before everybody got excited along with her."

Donnie realized what had happened. They'd drugged him to buy time until they could contact someone in St. Louis who would abduct one of his daughters. He'd do what they wanted now, or they would kill Daisy and then him.

"Pretty little blond girl," Mako said with his shark-like underslung smile. "She was wearin' her ball-player's uniform when they took her. Wonder if she still is."

"Old enough to bleed, old enough to breed," Freddy with the Sinatra grin observed tauntingly.

Donnie made it through pain and grogginess all the way to his feet then threw a slow motion punch at Roma, who was closer than Freddy. Roma didn't bother trying to get out of the way. Before Donnie's fist had traveled ten inches, Mako reached over and casually shoved him back into the chair.

"The deal is," Roma told him, "you're going to keep right on learning about the Russians, doing the sneak and snitch act you're so good at, only you'll be reporting to us so we can clear everything before you pass it on to the FBI. You might cross us, but if we find out, you'll start getting packages in the mail, and when you open them up you won't like what you find inside. Then you'll start playing straight with us, doing what we fucking say, or you'll get the next package, the next small piece of your daughter. Then the next."

"Slightly used pieces," Freddy said. Roma glared at him and he lowered his head and backed away a step into the shadows. There were times when you never interrupted the boss.

"Nothing'll be missing from her that'll kill her, so long as you don't stray too far," Roma said. "That oughta be reassuring to you."

"All you'll get are fingers, toes, nipples," Mako said, "not necessarily in that order."

Roma didn't seem to mind that interruption. Bile rose in Donnie's bruised throat.

"You'll be reporting to Mako or me personally," Roma told Donnie. "We want to know why the Russians want in at La Guardia, what they're up to, who's important in their organization and how things work. Same kinda stuff the FBI wants to know, only we get the information first and have you pass it on to them the way we want it to read."

"How do you know what the FBI wants to know?" Donnie asked.

Roma and Mako exchanged glances and smiles. "Certain kinds of sedatives lead to talking in your sleep," Roma said. " 'Specially if you're asked questions forcefully enough."

"Sleep walkers, sleep talkers," Mako said, "they get into plenty of trouble." He grabbed a handful of Donnie's hair and jerked his head around so the pain took over. "You got enough trouble now, asshole?"

"Enough," Donnie said.

"Ease up," Roma said with mock concern. "Fucker's one of us now. Don't hurt him. He might as well be a happy employee. Turn on the TV so our snitch can relax."

Freddy jumped over to the ancient Zenith and punched the power button. A *Law & Order* rerun flickered to light and life without sound. Weary Jerry Orbach, playing one of the cops, said something you just knew by his face was worldly and cynical to his young Latin partner with the slicked-back hair. The young guy smiled handsomely and looked dubious.

"You're lucky I found a way to make you useful," Roma said to Donnie. "Now you just take it easy and enjoy yourself here, but make sure you get to bed pretty soon 'cause you gotta get up early tomorrow and be at work on time." He motioned with his head toward the TV, where Orbach and his partner were exchanging gunfire with some bad guys in a deserted warehouse. "That's one of my favorite programs. Very authentic. Pay attention to those guys, see how it's done."

"Some great actin' in that show," Mako agreed seriously. "I think I even recognized one of the judges."

"We're gonna leave you alone in this roach trap now," Roma said to Donnie. "You and your TV and your problems."

He turned his back on Donnie and swaggered to the door. Mako followed, then Freddy, Freddy shuffling backward and never taking his eyes off Donnie, never blinking, never letting up with the sick smile.

Freddy was the last out, but just before they all left, Roma paused and stuck his head back in the room to take a long look at Donnie.

"Thing to remember," he said, "is we're only borrowing your daughter, but now you belong to us."

8

It took Donnie a full five minutes to force himself up from his chair. The harder he tried, the deeper the soft cushions became. They were warm, enveloping. He could have stayed sitting there the rest of his life.

The inside of his head was still a mess and he knew it. When he did gain his feet, he staggered to the phone and picked it up, dropped it, picked it up again. He started to punch out Elana's number to confirm what he'd been told about Daisy.

Then he put down the phone, went back to the chair, and sat slumped over with his face buried in his hands. What he'd dreaded for so long had happened. He'd thought his family would be safe. He was divorced from them. Anyone would assume that even if located, Elana wouldn't know his whereabouts or how to get in touch with him. So she'd elected not to go into hiding for the rest her life and their children's. It shouldn't have been necessary. She and the girls should have been secure, out of the game and off the board, in no more danger than the families of people who'd gone into the Witness Protection program. The

Mafia lived by its own rigid and chivalrous code; wives were left alone.

But Roma was a wild card, acting on his own and playing off the board himself. And now Donnie's family had been made part of his work, his world, his predicament, the double life he was trapped in until death. He should be dead by now. He knew Daisy's chances. Men like Roma killed as naturally as they breathed in and out. Donnie looked down and saw his fists clenched so tightly his knuckles were pale. He tried to think clearly through his confusion and rage.

Roma had been telling him the truth, he was sure. They had Daisy. And Roma hadn't been bluffing about mutilating her in order to persuade her father to cooperate. He *had* been lying about not harming Daisy if Donnie obeyed his orders. When Daisy's usefulness was ended they would kill her, just as they would have killed Donnie if it hadn't been to their advantage to keep him alive a while longer. He and Daisy were both, in the minds of the Mafia, already dead. All that was left was for them to lie down and stop breathing at a time not of their choosing.

However hopeless it seemed, Donnie had to find a way to change that. To save Daisy even if he couldn't save himself.

He slammed his fist into the chair arm in frustration. His mind darted this way and that, trying furiously to escape the trap that had been sprung around it.

But he'd sensed the destination of his tortured thoughts from the beginning. There was only one thing he could do, even if it meant taking an initial risk.

He stood up and moved back to the phone with renewed strength and a determination to shake off the effects of the drug he'd been given.

Then he realized his line might be tapped, so he replaced the receiver, put on his jacket, and made his way toward the door.

The cool night air helped to clear his head some more as he walked to the deli at the end of the block and used its reasonably secluded public phone back by the cases of refrigerated milk and juice.

The phone on the other end of the line rang twice, then Jules Donavon answered.

Donnie identified himself and started bringing Jules up to date in a voice that sounded as if it came from inside a box. He swallowed painfully and noisily and his ears popped. That helped. His hearing improved immediately, and his voice sounded like his own except for a hoarseness that reminded him of a time at the Academy when he'd accidentally been struck in the throat during physical training.

"Christ!" Jules said, when Donnie was finished talking. "They snatched her to nail you to the spot, so we can't simply pull you off the assignment and get you outta there."

Donnie tried to clear his aching throat, making a noise like gravel tumbling in a cement mixer.

"If we'd suspected something like this, we could have gotten your ex-wife and your kids out in time, moved them someplace safe."

"There is no safe place for them," Donnie said. "There never can be."

"Not completely," Jules admitted. "But when something like this happens, we better protect Elana and your other daughter."

That was Donnie's instinct, too, but he knew better than to relocate them even if Elana would agree to it. And he had something else in mind. "Moving them won't work now, and it'd tip off Roma that something's wrong."

"You're probably right about that last part. Got any ideas?"

A customer came to the back of the deli and got a container of orange juice out of the case. Donnie waited until the woman had squinted at the expiration date on the carton then gone up front to check out. "Put the E.O. team in St. Louis to watch over them."

The Extraordinary Operations team specialized in exactly this kind of situation—one that was fluid, unpredictable, and dangerous. The pool of special-skill agents drawn on from time to time was always ready. As usual, Donnie would command them and report to Donavon. Special Agent in Charge Victor Whitten would authorize the operation. Knowledge of it might not get beyond him in the Bureau hierarchy. Bureaucracy imposed its limitations, and Whitten knew when and how to ignore them.

"It's done," Jules said. "I'll inform Whitten later and he'll back date an authorization."

"Rafe, Lily, C.J.," Donnie said, naming three of the team's best, "I want them." He'd worked with them often before and knew and trusted them in a way outsiders wouldn't understand. Now he was preparing to trust them with Daisy's life.

"I can send Lily to St. Louis soon as I hang up. Rafe

and C.J. will take a little longer, but Whitten can cut them loose from whatever they're working on and I can assign them to you. It'll just be Lily for a short while, drawing on St. Louis Field Office personnel."

Donnie felt slightly better. Smart, tough Lily Maloney would know how to watch over Elana and Maureen, and would do whatever it took to protect them. That included trading her life for theirs.

"Sounds as if Roma already has what he needs," Jules said. "Probably Elana and Maureen are safe for now. And with Lily on the job, nobody's gonna even steal the newspaper off your lawn."

My lawn, Donnie thought. Jules had always liked Elana and sometimes talked as if she and Donnie were still married, or might somehow get back together. But it was over and Donnie and Elana knew it, or so they told themselves, and his daughters had been drifting further and further from the center of his life. He longed to hold on to them, and he longed to distance himself from them to protect them. Being marked for death by the Mafia was contagious. People near you could die as instantly as you could in a bombing or unexpected blast of gunfire.

"Donnie?"

"I'm okay, Jules, just trying to think."

"Do what they say for now. Play it straight. Check in with me from public phones only. And we need to be careful if we set up a meet. If—when we find Daisy and get her back, things'll change."

"I know how careful we need to be," Donnie said, "and what the odds are." He stood leaning harder against the wall for a while. Damned place wouldn't stay quite motionless! Shelves of canned goods swayed. The paper products and cold remedies wavered like a mirage.

"Donnie, you sure you got it together?"

"Together, Jules."

"You want to call Elana, tell her what's happening? Or should I?"

"I'll do it," Donnie said. It was a phone call he'd hoped never to make. Its possibility had long haunted his dreams.

"Okay. I better hang up and contact Lily."

"Yeah . . . Thanks, Jules."

"It'll work out, Donnie. You're doing the right thing. This is rough, but you got good people behind you."

"I know, Jules."

"It'll work out," Jules said again. There was more hope than certainty in his voice.

The receiver clicked in Donnie's ear as the connection was broken.

He was alone.

A full five minutes passed before he found the will to lift the receiver again and call Elana's number in St. Louis.

She picked up on the first ring. Donnie could imagine her heart-shaped face florid with concern and streaked with tears. The vertical parallel worry lines above the bridge of her nose would be deeper than he'd ever seen them.

"It's Joe," he told her. By now his own name sounded unfamiliar to him. Donnie pretending to be Joe.

She waited a beat; she couldn't know if he knew, couldn't know what any of this was about. "Joe—"

"I know about Daisy disappearing," he said. The words felt like sandpaper brushing his throat.

"This has something to do with you?" Now she seemed angry.

"Someone recognized me. They took Daisy so they could get me to do what they say."

"Simple as that . . ." she said softly. "Simple as goddam that!"

"Elana—"

"Oh, you bastard!"

"I feel the same way you do about this."

"Do you *really?* So *what?* My daughter's still gone, and all because of your fucking—"

"Job," he finished for her. "Do you think I have any real choice in this, Elana?"

He waited through a long stretch of silence, listening to what might have been her sobbing.

But when she finally did speak, she didn't sound as if she'd been crying. Her voice was a low, resigned monotone. "We're wasting time and energy arguing about what caused it," she said. "We have to take it from where we are now. Who took her?"

"Someone in the Mafia." The words sounded brutal, hopeless.

"Good God! What do they want?"

"For me to be a double agent. To work for them without the Bureau's knowledge."

"You're going to do it, Joe."

"I'm going to pretend to."

"No, you're going to do it. Really do it. You're going to keep the Bureau in the dark."

"I can't. It isn't the best way."

"Then I'm going to the police."

"Don't do that, Elana. The Bureau already knows. They'll bring in the locals when the time is right."

"The time is right now!"

"Please! Going to the locals now might be fatal. The Bureau's trained for kidnapping situations. They're the best in the world and you know it. Let them call the shots."

"Let *us*, you mean. You're one of them."

"Of course I am. You've got to trust me in this, Elana."

"Damn you! If you endanger our daughter's life . . ."

What could he tell her? That he was taking the only and outside chance that Daisy might survive? That he might survive?

"All right," she sighed. "Maybe you do know best when it comes to something like this. It's your job, your life, your goddam world that we don't want any part of." Her fresh burst of anger was under control now. "Play your stupid grown-up cops-and-robbers game you're so good at. Try not to get our daughter killed."

"I suppose it is a game," Donnie said. "And I *am* good at it. Please let me make the moves."

"You really think what you suggest might work?"

"It can," he told her. "It's our best chance."

She said nothing. He could hear her breathing as if she'd run a great distance and was exhausted.

"Someone's already on the way to watch over you and Maureen," he told her. "You'll be safe because the Bureau will be shadowing you. And since the kidnappers have Daisy, they won't want to run any further risk or complicate matters. They've got the leverage they need."

Her deep breathing had become shallow and ragged. She was crying now, he was sure. But he knew her and knew her strength. She was still ninety percent composed, but her fear and frustration were forcing their way to the surface. It was the same vicious energy that was trying to tear him apart. He'd directed some of it to her. Contagious Donnie. Guilt closed in on him, tightening his throat, trying to bend him over from the inside.

"An agent named Lily Maloney will be in touch with you soon," Donnie said.

"The way you're talking, I mean your voice, is that part of this? Are you okay?"

He considered lying to her but he couldn't bring himself to do it. Lies, layer upon layer, was what had brought them here. "Okay enough," he said. "They got a bit rough with me, but that's over."

"You're sure you're going to be all right?"

"Yes." He said it too harshly with his new three-pack-a-day voice. "Ask Lily for identification. She'll understand. Do as she says. Make sure Maureen does, too."

"We will. Joe, where do you think they took her? How are they treating her?"

"Don't torture yourself speculating about it," he told her gently. "That's my job."

"Your job . . ." she said sadly, and hung up the phone.

Donnie bought a carton of milk, in case it was necessary to make his trip to the deli look legitimate. On the walk back to the apartment his legs seemed to get heavier with each step. Tears began tracking down his cheeks. It wasn't because of the cold.

When he dragged himself into the bedroom it took all his willpower to remain upright and not sink to the floor and curl up comfortably on the carpet before reaching the bed. Whatever drug he'd been given had left him mentally and physically drained.

Sleep wouldn't be a problem.

Dreams would.

9

"You're looking rough," Barkov told Donnie the next morning at work. It was one of those raw days that wasn't going to warm up much, with nasty gray clouds marbling a sky that seemed low enough to touch if you stood on your toes. Jet planes were dropping tentatively out of the mist like misguided angels, while others were disappearing into it with defiant roars that vibrated through the concrete staging area. "You still sick with the flu?"

"About over it," Donnie said above the roar of an ascending TWA jetliner. He hoisted a full propane tank onto the back of his parked forklift and hooked up the pressure hose, tightening the connection with his gloved hand. Because of the possibility of fire or explosion, the tanks were stored in a steel rack outside the hangar.

"Looks like your neck's all bruised. The Italians haven't been after you again, have they?"

Donnie made himself grin. "If they have, they've all got the flu and don't know it yet."

Barkov laughed, zipped his jacket tight around his own neck, and began walking toward the hangar, leaving Donnie to finish readying the forklift for the day's work.

Mako was stacking crates in the main hangar and pretty much ignored Donnie whenever they were within sight of each other. It was as if last night hadn't happened. As if Daisy were safe at home or in school today. Donnie had to fight down the rage that rose like bile in his throat whenever he laid eyes on Mako. The other Italians also didn't seem to view Donnie any differently, but that didn't surprise him. Here at work, probably only Mako knew about Donnie's dilemma and the pressure on him. The other Italian thugs would help to keep Donnie in line, following Mako's instructions, but they wouldn't need to know the reasons.

Donnie had the forklift stopped, waiting for another driver to bring a pallet to him to relay into the hangar, when the lift's engine suddenly went dead.

"How ya doin', Donnie boy?" a voice asked.

Donnie turned to see that Local 672 business agent Sam Vargo had turned off the engine.

"They treatin' you okay here, kid?" Vargo asked. He was a short, muscular man in his fifties, with handsome features spoiled by a low hairline and heavy brow that gave him a faintly simian look. But there was always a smile on his face, which at least made him resemble a happy ape. His sometimes companion on his rounds, an attractive young woman named Nola Queen, was seated in Vargo's gleaming black Cadillac Seville. They were obviously lovers, and Vargo enjoyed bringing her and the car around to show them both off as a set.

Donnie shook the business agent's hand. "They're paying me on time. That's all I ask."

Vargo's grin widened. "Kinda attitude we like to see, kid. Anything you need, any work problems come up here, you give me a call down at the hall."

"Thanks, Mr. Vargo, I'll do that."

Vargo made a sweeping motion with his right arm. "You get to know some of the monkeys around here, they're not so bad."

"I'm finding that out."

Vargo slapped him on the shoulder. "Good! You stay busy and keep outta trouble, the job'll work out for you." He turned and strode jauntily back to the Cadillac, trailing the faint, whistling strains of "Danny Boy."

Nola Queen stared straight ahead through the windshield, showing Donnie her perfect profile, slender neck, and swept-back blond hair. She looked like class all the way, but so did a lot of high-priced call girls.

Donnie restarted the forklift and watched Vargo drive the Caddy over to the yellow-lined parking area alongside the hangar. Nola Queen got out of the car and went inside with Vargo. It was something to see her walk. She was wearing a short mink jacket, tight red stirrup slacks, and heels. Her shapely long legs kicked out smoothly and the jacket didn't quite cover her hips and buttocks. She seemed to sense Donnie watching her and glanced over at him, then averted her eyes in a way that suggested disdain even from this distance.

There was nothing in his conversation that suggested Vargo might have a partnership with Roma and know Donnie's true identity. But Donnie didn't dismiss the idea or lower his guard with the business agent. These guys could put on an innocent attitude like a suit of clothes, and then put on a butcher's apron.

During the lunch break, Donnie went with Barkov and a Russian named Tomba to the Bonnaire Lounge, a combination bar and restaurant on Walker Road near the airport. Donnie figured Mako, who was watching him, would relay this sign of increasing camaraderie to Vinnie Roma, who would approve. Roma must love what he had going. Donnie Brasco, on the job for the Mafia.

The Bonnaire was divided in half by a wall of brass-framed glass panels with sports scenes engraved in them. To the left of the entrance was the bar, some booths, and a dozen bulky wooden tables with square tops and plastic overlays that covered assorted newspaper accounts of memorable sporting events. The tables in the restaurant side were the same, and there was a salad bar along the back wall. Dark red carpet flowed through both sides of the Bonnaire, and there were framed sporting scenes on the walls above oak wainscoting. Waitresses in dark slacks, white blouses, and frilly red aprons roamed the premises behind frozen smiles.

Donnie, Barkov, and Tomba took a table near the front by the window that looked out on a parking lot bordered by banks of gray snow and ice so imbedded with dirt and cinders that it had taken on a concrete consistency and wouldn't melt completely until spring.

Barkov was his usual cheerful self. "The Bonnaire Burger," he told Donnie. "That's what you want, my friend."

Tomba, a bulky, dour man with dark eyes and brows, and one of those fleshy chins that seemed to run like liquid down into his collar, nodded solemn agreement and repeated, "The Bonnaire Burger."

Donnie compliantly ordered the burger and a draft Budweiser. Barkov and Tomba asked for the Monday special, tuna melts.

"The tuna melts here are fantastic," Barkov said.

Tomba pulled a face and shook his head in disagreement. Now that he'd ordered it, he seemed not even to want to think about the tuna melt.

"If you like the burger so much," Donnie asked him, "how come you ordered the tuna melt?"

Tomba shrugged. "It's Monday. Tuna melt's always the Monday special."

Donnie looked at Barkov. "You didn't tell me about the tuna melt."

"You didn't know about the burger, my friend. You knew it was Monday."

Russian logic, Donnie supposed, as he watched Mako and three of the Italian workers from La Guardia enter the Bonnaire. They didn't seem to notice Donnie and the Russians, but they sat down at a table nearby. Donnie knew it wasn't a coincidence.

Barkov and Tomba were right about the burger. It was delicious.

Donnie had taken only his second bite when the remarks started wafting from the other table. The nearest of the Italians, a wiry, bowlegged man known as

Navy, grinned at Donnie with his mouth full, then said, "Fuckin' Russian army's over there with a defactor."

"That's de*fect*or," Mako said. "But Barns ain't that. He was never one of us. Or them."

"Gotta be one or the other, way I see it," Navy said, still spitting food as he spoke. He was in his forties but looked younger, with curly dark hair, a turned up nose, and a mouth that always showed a lot of teeth. "Hey, you, Barns! How come you're drinkin' beer and not a fuckin' glass of red wine? How come all you commies ain't drinkin' somethin' red?"

Barkov raised his beer mug in an amiable salute to the other table. "Iron Curtain's gone. You might have read about it in the newspapers. The only iron around here is in your head."

Navy started to get up, but Mako reached over and placed a big hand on his shoulder to settle him back down in his chair.

"No trouble, okay, fellas?" pleaded a waitress. She was a petite blonde woman with blue eyes that tilted up at the outside corners and she smiled when she spoke. She probably smiled when she slept. It was the job.

Mako reached out with his free hand and pinched her left buttock hard through her dark uniform slacks. The smile was gone as she winced and jumped aside. Mako and his buddies laughed up a storm. Navy spat some more food.

"I do *not* have to take that shit!" the blonde said.

"Trouble, Vicky?" A skinny guy with bushy hair parted in the middle appeared near the table. He was wearing a white shirt and tie. In the Bonnaire, that made him an authority figure.

Vicky said, "This bastard pinched me. I'll sue him. I'll sue this place if you don't do something about it, Warren." She was so angry she shoved her hair back away from her face violently with both hands. Donnie noticed a small blue and red butterfly tattoo near the base of her neck.

"That true?" Warren asked Mako.

"The pinch on the butt? Or the lawsuit?"

"The pinch."

"True, Warren."

"He better goddam apologize!" Vicky said.

"You should do that, mister," Warren said.

"But I ain't gonna, Warren." Mako took a bite of his burger and stared straight ahead. He'd known enough to order the Bonnaire Burger, not the tuna.

"Make him apologize, Warren!" Vicky said.

Mako smiled. Barkov nudged Donnie's leg with his shoe under the table. He was leaning back with his beer mug, grinning and enjoying this immensely.

"Do you need some help, Warren?" he asked.

The Italians bristled. "You try it and you'll need some fuckin' help brushin' your teeth 'cause you won't be able to find 'em!" Navy said.

Barkov seemed unperturbed.

Warren backed away about five steps and raised both hands. "Let's everybody stay calm here now."

"I want a goddam apology from this scumbag," Vicky said, "or I'll walk right outta here and phone the Office of Equal Opportunity Employment."

"I can give you their number," Barkov said. He

looked around and said to the room in general, "That's a federal agency, very serious people not to be fucked with."

Warren said nothing but glanced behind him at the bartender beyond a glass partition. The bartender nodded slightly to him. They were waiting for something. Donnie had a pretty good idea what.

"Gimme another beer, sweet thing," Mako said to Vicky.

She leaned forward at the waist and glared at him. "You are like the most fucked up human being I ever met!"

"Take it easy, Vick," Warren said. He didn't seem scared, but he knew the situation could get out of hand and ugly any second. This time he glanced behind him toward the door.

Vicky didn't want to take it easy. "This kinda harassment's gonna get every man in this place fined!"

Every man within earshot laughed. Even some of the women. At the table behind Mako's, a redheaded woman wearing denim work clothes said, "Cool your jets, dear. The guy is just another asshole. World's full of them. Forget about it, and next time he comes in put something in his food."

Mako swiveled in his chair to stare at the redhead.

The cold war between the sexes might have turned hot, but the door opened and two uniformed cops ambled in and looked around.

"We got a call," the larger of the two said. He had his right thumb hooked in his thick black leather belt near his holstered nine-millimeter and looked positively bored. Donnie thought he might look that way if he had to shoot you.

The bartender nodded, then motioned with his head toward the dining area. Warren had turned and was hurrying toward the cops.

He was still talking to them when Mako and the other three Italians got up from their table. Mako tossed some bills down next to his plate, and they all walked toward the door.

"We were leavin' anyway," Mako said.

The cops looked at Warren, who said, "That's fine, far as we're concerned."

"I didn't get my goddam apology!" Vicky yelled after them.

Mako grinned. "I'll put it in the mail."

Donnie, Barkov, and Tomba watched out the window as Mako and company climbed into a blue van, Navy behind the wheel, and drove from the lot.

Warren, the cops, and Vicky all left the dining area and went through a door next to the restrooms.

"Think they'll calm her down?" Tomba asked.

"I hope not," Barkov said. "She's got balls. I hope she sues the bastards." He looked at Donnie. "Think she's got a case?"

"Always," Donnie said.

"If she's got a bruise on her ass," Tomba said seriously, "she's got a case."

Barkov raised his mug high again and grinned. "Hell of a country, hey?"

When Donnie returned to work and tried to mount his forklift, the hand he'd used to grip the steering wheel and hoist himself up slipped and he lurched backward and almost fell. When he examined the forklift, he found that the steering wheel, gearshift lever, and seat had been smeared with grease. He didn't have to think hard to know who'd done it.

He got some rags and wiped most of the grease from the forklift, then went into the restroom and cleaned his hands and shirt as best he could with paper towels, soap, and water.

One of the stall doors opened and Mako stepped out.

He moved close to Donnie, flashing white teeth in his sharklike smile. Donnie could smell the onions from the Bonnaire Burger.

"We was just helpin' you out back there at the restaurant," Mako said. "Don't want the Ruskies to suspect you're really one of us."

"I was doing okay without you," Donnie said. "Didn't need this grease, either.'

"Makin' it look right," Mako said. "Au-fuckin'-thentic."

"Fuck you," Donnie said.

"Helpin' you out," Mako repeated, leaning closer to Donnie. "You an' your lovely daughter."

10

Donnie was in a dark room, sensing wide space around him in the blackness. He walked slowly, tentatively, his arms outstretched, his stiffened fingers eager for contact, awareness. He could hear a high, thin voice muffled by distance and walls, wailing, crying out for help. Suddenly he recognized the voice. He walked faster through the darkness, bumping unseen objects that seemed to move away so they were gone when he felt out for them, leaving him lost and directionless.

Something struck him hard in the right shoulder, but he kept staggering through the dark, confused and desperate to get a fix on the voice, to reach it and stop it.

Again something slammed into his shoulder. Something cold and hard.

"Wake up, asshole!"

Consciousness flooded his mind and he opened his eyes.

No voice crying for help, no darkness and sense of endless space strewn with obstacles.

He unclenched his fists as he stared up into the

lamplit faces of Vinnie Roma and Mako. It was Mako, on his right, who'd been prodding his shoulder—with the barrel of a blue steel automatic.

The barrel dug in again, in exactly the same spot, bruising the shoulder.

Donnie scooted up to a sitting position in the bed, leaning his back against the wood headboard. He glanced over at the clock on the night stand: 2:05 A.M.

"It's Friday night," Roma said. "Time for your first report."

"Actually, it's Saturday mornin'," Mako pointed out.

"Shut up," Roma told him.

Donnie rubbed his eyes, almost turning an eyelid inside out, and blinked at Roma. "A report? Now?"

"Sure. We wanted to catch you when you had some free time. When you least expected it. But keep your hands outside the covers."

"You call this free time?"

"Yeah, for us. All your time is free for us. You might say we're in charge of your time, how you use it, how much you got left."

"Looked like you was dreamin'," Mako said. "What about?"

"A rat with your head."

Mako moved to rake the gun across Donnie's face, but Roma reached out and touched his arm, and the big man relaxed. He lowered the arm and kept the gun aimed at Donnie. He held the weapon canted slightly to the thumb side, the way that was popular now to cut back on the kick and strain on the wrist when a round was fired. Either it was habit, or he was seconds away from squeezing the trigger.

"He's only trying to get to you," Roma said to Mako. "Grow the fuck up. Resist going for the bait."

"He can't resist," Donnie said. "He's too hungry."

Mako laughed. "You got some balls, I will say that."

"Donnie Brasco," Roma said, "brass balls. Better have a silver tongue, too."

"I've got nothing to tell you yet," Donnie said. "It's the kind of job takes time."

"We covered the subject of time," Roma said. "What goes on at the Westward Ho Club?"

Donnie shrugged. Perfectly relaxed in his Jockey shorts in bed, with two thugs in the room and a loaded gun pointed at him. Sure he was. "Drinking, weddings . . ."

"There must be some talk between when people guzzle booze and get married," Roma said. "What's it about?"

"About cars, what to drink, who's getting married. Just what you'd expect."

"Not what *I'd* expect," Roma said.

"Bet you was dreamin' about your little girl," Mako said. "I dream about her sometimes, too."

Donnie started to rise from the bed, but Mako shoved him back.

"Look who's snappin' at the bait now," Mako said with a grin.

"I want to talk to her," Donnie said.

Roma glared at Mako as if to censure him for bringing up the subject of Daisy. "That ain't possible," he said to Donnie.

"If you want my cooperation, make it possible. Goons like Mako have got her. How do I know she's still alive?"

"Point is," Roma said, "you don't know she's not. You'll cooperate."

"What have you got to lose if I hear her on the phone? Doesn't it figure I'll cooperate more if I know she's alive?"

"Fucker's got a point," Mako said.

"Shut the fuck up!" Roma told him.

"You're a big man now," Donnie told Roma. "A *padrone*. You mean you can't arrange to let me be sure my daughter's still alive so I know you got something to bargain with and aren't just bluffing?"

"You don't get where I am by bluffing," Roma said. "Or by getting bluffed."

"I bluffed people like you for six years."

"And look where you are. Pathetic piece of shit laying there in your underwear. Only reason you're still drawing breath is because I'm letting it happen. You're gonna have to take my word your daughter's alive."

"Would you take your word if you were me?"

"I wouldn't be you."

"You really wanna start gettin' Daisy pieces in the mail?" Mako asked.

"No," Donnie said. "But if I did, they wouldn't prove she was still alive."

"This hasn't been a productive enough conversation," Roma said. "You're not as much help as I thought you'd be. That's gotta change."

Donnie shrugged. "You don't always strike oil with the first well."

"Nobody here's in the oil business. And except for you, nobody here's in the bullshit business." He backed slowly toward the bedroom door. "Better learn something we're interested in, Donnie, then pass it on. We're not like the FBI pricks you work for. We do more than fire people who don't produce for us. First it'll be your daughter gets whacked, then you, then your whole fucking family, the dog, the cat, and the parakeet."

He disappeared in the dark, shadowed rectangle of the doorway.

Mako waited a few seconds then followed his boss, doing the same smooth backshuffle, light on his feet for a man almost big enough to be a horse.

From the darkness of the doorway he said, "I really do dream about her."

Donnie didn't dream the rest of the night, because he didn't sleep. He left the lamp on and stared at the cracks in the ceiling for over an hour, his mind feeling its way around his problem, finding nothing that resembled a solution.

At 4:30 he climbed out of bed and got dressed, then left the apartment and walked along damp sidewalks toward the corner deli. Whatever rain had fallen must have stopped recently; the air was still damp, and pungent with the sweet scent of garbage from the mounds of trash at curbside waiting to be picked up.

The deli, which Donnie had thought was an all-night operation, was dark and had a red-and-white CLOSED sign in its window. There was a handwritten note taped beneath the sign that said the deli was temporarily closed because of the death of the owner's daughter and would open in the morning. That shook Donnie. If other men's daughters died, for ordinary reasons, without being held by professional killers, what chance did Daisy have?

He walked another three blocks to a diner that was open and had a public phone back near a cigarette machine. He ordered an egg cream to go from the dreary-looking guy behind the stainless steel counter and carried it back to the phone. The sad counterman didn't so much as glance at him. He was disinterested in everything, simply waiting for one of life's arrows to pierce a vital organ and end his misery. Donnie had no advice for him.

Elana answered on the second ring. Maybe she wasn't sleeping, either.

"Yes?" She sounded sleepy, but eager and scared.

"It's me," Donnie said.

"There's news?" Instantly alert as fresh-perked coffee.

"No. I just wanted to talk to you, hear your voice, let you know things were still in control."

"Our daughter's been kidnapped by hoodlums who are threatening her life. Some control."

He took a sip of his egg cream through a straw. It tasted like nothing but carbonated water. "You alone?"

"What kinda goddam question is that?"

"I just wanted to know if you could talk freely."

"Yes, I'm alone, and it's none of your business."

"I know. Has the Bureau been in touch with you?"

"An Agent Lily Maloney, like you said. She's very nice and seems more than competent."

"She's both those things," Donnie said.

"Question is, are those things enough? How will they save Daisy?"

"Lily and others are working on that at the same time they're protecting you and Maureen."

"Maureen. If those bastards so much as—"

"Calm down, Elana. It won't happen. We won't let it happen, now that we're on our guard. And there's no reason for it to happen, as long as they have Daisy."

"If we're not in danger," Elana asked, "how come Lily Maloney's here?"

"We want to allow for every possibility."

"There's one you didn't allow for when you should have."

"I know," Donnie said miserably, "they already have Daisy."

Elana didn't say anything for a while. Then: "Sometimes I wish you were here, Joe."

He felt blood rise in his face. Why did she have to tell him that? They'd both long ago admitted the marriage was impossible, that they needed different things. Elana needed security and stability. Donnie needed to stay alive. These were not compatible goals. He'd known that leaving Elana and the girls was the best, the safest, thing he could do for them. Giving them up might save them. And now this had happened. Fairness wasn't part of the equation.

"You know what we decided," Donnie said. "Usually you're reminding me of it."

"I know. I'm sorry. But these aren't usual times. Anything that concerns the girls, especially something like this, you're a part of it whether I want it or not."

Donnie thought of Grace Perez, waiting for him in Florida. They were a part of each other now. He was sure he loved her. Most of the time. Living as he did, it was difficult to be sure if you could trust even your own heart.

"I just wanted to reassure you," Donnie said. Then he had to smile, alone as anyone could be in a city of eight million. "I mean, to reassure myself. To hear your voice, is all."

"Talking to you has made me feel better."

"I'm sorry I called, though, and woke you up. We could have had this same conversation four or five hours from now. Can you get back to sleep?"

"I think so. If I can't, I'll still be glad you called."

Neither of them wanted to hang up.

"Maureen's going to her dance recital tomorrow evening," Elana said. "Should I notify Lily Maloney?"

"If you get the chance. Either way, she'll know."

"Is Lily really that good? That dedicated?"

"She'd die for you."

Elana knew he wasn't joking. "I know that. Tell her I know that."

"You're my wife. She understands that you know it."

"Former wife," she reminded him.

Till death do us part, Donnie thought, but he didn't say it. The unspoken words made his heart feel small and cold. He did wish he were home in the house in St. Louis, lying next to Elana, knowing the girls were asleep in their own beds in their own rooms. All of the pieces for happiness in place. It was a longing that went back thousands of years, a human ache.

"Goodbye, Joe."

His lost name, his lost self.

She hung up before he could answer.

He left his egg cream on top of the cigarette machine and trudged from the diner.

The dreary-looking guy behind the counter nodded a goodbye to him. They were brothers.

11

Maybe Mako and Roma expected Donnie to visit the Westward Ho Club that weekend. If so, they'd be disappointed. Ten minutes after talking by phone to Elana, Donnie had called La Guardia for a flight to St. Louis the next day.

The earliest he could book was an afternoon flight, but he picked up an hour by switching time zones, so by six-thirty Saturday evening he was registered at a small motel near Lambert International Airport in St. Louis.

He knew the city. He'd rented a car at the airport and he made it to Maureen's recital at Miss Blistner's Dance Academy fifteen minutes before curtain.

Miss Blistner's Academy had an arrangement with the private middle school in the same block to use their auditorium a few times each year. Donnie took a seat near the back. The small auditorium was about half full, maybe a hundred people, mostly parents and grandparents, and a scattering of friends and neighbors.

It took Donnie a few minutes to locate Elana. She was seated in the second row and had a new hairdo.

Her brown hair had been lightened almost blond and was swept up in back to reveal her slender neck. It struck him in a way he didn't like that from behind with the new hairdo she somewhat resembled Sam Vargo's companion Nola Queen.

The lights dimmed, and a spotlight trailed Miss Blistner herself out onto the small stage. She was a tall, slender woman with the long, corded neck of an aging serious dancer. Maureen had told him once that Miss Blistner had danced long ago on Broadway. Didn't say which town, though.

After a short introduction by Miss Blistner, the curtain parted and a program loosely based on *Swan Lake* began.

That's when the trip became totally worthwhile to Donnie. Maureen was third from the left in a chorus of a dozen nine-year-old girls. She seemed taller and had lost weight, and actually had the poise and grace of a budding ballet dancer. He knew she'd soon grow out of the necessary body type to dance ballet, so he marvelled all the more at her youthful litheness and balance. She resembled Elana and she resembled him; the best of both of them. Her hair was skinned back and tied in a ponytail, and to Donnie she was the most beautiful girl on stage. A sadness swept over him; he was missing something invaluable by not living here, not being her full-time father. And he was losing even the difficult and remote possibility of ever having it. In another place, time was little by little taking it away from him. There was nothing he could do about it. Choices had been eliminated; that's what time was all about, choices lost.

Now, with Daisy's abduction, it wasn't only time that was limiting his options.

After half an hour of assiduous and sincere if not perfect dancing, Miss Blistner announced there would be a fifteen-minute intermission. The curtain swished closed and the auditorium lights brightened. People stirred then began to rise to walk up the aisles to the restrooms or to go outside and smoke.

Elana remained in her seat, as did Donnie, who was studying her from behind. She seemed to have come alone to the recital. The woman on her left, the man on her right, were obviously not with her.

"*Swan Lake* working for you?" a voice next to Donnie asked. Someone had moved along the aisle and was seated next to him.

He turned to see a compact, muscular woman in bleached-out jeans and a green sweater. She had a pale, freckled complexion, symmetrical, squarish features, direct emerald eyes, and generous lips set in a straight line yet somehow giving the impression they would smile easily and often. She wasn't quite beautiful, but she was something more. Lily Maloney.

"Best version I've seen," he told her, "and done completely without swans."

She smiled. There was no one immediately around them. A knot of people stood down the aisle and off to the side, taking the opportunity to be out of their seats for a while and stretch their legs. "They're safe," Lily said, nodding in the direction of the stage and the still-seated Elana in the third row.

"Who've you got with you?" Donnie asked.

"Rafe and C.J. are in town, on the job. We're going to

find out who's got her, Donnie, then we're going to find them."

"I know. The problem is that it might not be in time. And I'm scared about what you might find."

"She's still alive. She has to be. It's the only thing that makes sense."

He knew that people like Vinnie Roma didn't always make sense, but he didn't bother mentioning it. Lily knew it, too, and had merely been trying to comfort him.

"Witnesses saw Daisy talking with a man near the concession stand at the softball diamond minutes before she must have been taken. C.J.'s showing them mug shots, trying to get some kind of I.D. And we have a witness who might have seen the car the perp was driving, a dark green Taurus, possibly a rental." She touched his arm lightly. "You know how it works, Donnie: We find a thread, tug on it, try another, eventually it's the right thread and it unravels the secrets." She was a natural redhead and seemed to have more freckles than when last they'd met. They made her strong-featured face look even more Irish. Her voice sounded like someone else's, husky as a heavy smoker's, when she said, "We'll find her soon, Donnie, and we'll get the assholes who took her."

The elegant Miss Blistner was back on stage. The lights were dimming.

"We'll be around, Donnie," Lily whispered, and disappeared up the aisle in the enveloping darkness.

After the performance, Donnie saw that it was raining outside the heavy glass doors to the parking lot.

Shimmering puddles were forming on the blacktop, near the yellow lines where he guessed school buses parked to deliver and pick up the students. He stood in a corner near the doors, his back to the walls, watching the audience members who didn't have to wait for their kids to change clothes file out.

When the crowd started to thin, he moved farther away and took up a position just inside a doorway to a stairwell where he wouldn't be noticed. He watched Elana and Maureen leave. Elana looked worried. Maureen was poker-faced, carrying her dance bag by a strap almost long enough to allow it to hit the ground as she swung her arm with each stride. Donnie was sure Lily had instructed Elana not to tell Maureen what had happened to Daisy. Whatever Elana had told her, Maureen would eventually suspect it wasn't exactly true.

Donnie had four hours before his plane back to New York. He drove around for a while and eventually found himself in Elana's neighborhood, then on her street. His rental car seemed to turn into her driveway of its own accord, as if it knew its driver's loneliness and longing.

He sat for a few minutes with the engine idling, watching the wiper blades *thu-thump, thu-thump* across the rain-smeared windshield. Then he turned off the engine and climbed out of the car.

Elana didn't seem surprised to see him when she answered his knock on the door. Maureen, standing beyond her in the foyer, was surprised. She ran at Donnie and hugged him. It helped. It filled him up. Elana smiled and stepped back to let them both come all the way in through the door.

"Did you see me dance?" Maureen asked.

He rested a hand on her shoulder. "I did, honey. You were great."

"Miss Blistner says I'm making rapid progress."

"I'll just bet."

Elana took his rain-spotted coat and hung it in a closet, then led him into the living room. There was a pleasant scent in the house that he hadn't noticed before, as if the walls were permeated with the mingled smells of spicy meals that had been prepared over the years. The room looked the same as the last time Donnie had visited: early American furniture, comfortable plaid sofa, brown leather recliner, brass railed maple coffee table, the woven oval rug that contained every known color. Even looked like the same slick catalogs and magazines lying on a sofa cushion. Just as before, some of them had slid off to rest haphazardly on the floor.

Elana motioned toward the recliner and Donnie sat down, but he didn't tilt the backrest. Maureen sat on his lap and hugged him around the neck.

"Take it easy on your father," Elana said.

Donnie didn't care. Couldn't get enough.

Elana knew why he'd come, but they couldn't talk until an hour later, when Maureen had kissed Donnie goodnight and gone upstairs to bed. He'd gone up with her for a few minutes, checking the layout, the window that looked out over the yard and the house in the next block. Safe as can be expected, he decided, and closed the drapes before kissing Maureen a second time. She asked him if he knew Daisy had taken a trip. He told her not to let the bedbugs bite and switched off the light. He saw with satisfaction that a dim nightlight glowed in an electrical socket near the door.

Downstairs in the living room again, he sat on the opposite end of the sofa from Elana. The furnace was running softly, and the house felt all the warmer and dryer because of the regular drip of water from a gutter overflowing outside.

"Have you heard anything?" she asked.

"The men who have her assured me she's all right," Donnie said.

"What good are those assurances?"

"Better than none."

Elana gnawed her lower lip in the old way that told him she was fighting not to cry. "Damn it, this isn't fair! I want her back with me! I want the people who have her to die! I want to kill them myself!"

"I know how you feel. I feel that way, too. But the way out of this will take patience, and luck."

She bowed her head and closed her eyes. She wasn't crying, though, only breathing deeply, frowning as if concentrating. The two vertical parallel lines above the bridge of her nose deepened.

"I'm sorry," Donnie said. "It doesn't help to say it, but I am. This is what I brought down on you. Years ago I didn't plan on anything like this being possible, but little by little it happened. I'm not blaming bad luck. I made the decisions and some of them were wrong."

She didn't answer, didn't open her eyes.

He stood up. "I'll get my coat. My plane leaves in a little over an hour."

"Why did you come here instead of driving to the airport?"

"I didn't want to leave you alone with this thing. Or to be alone with myself. Visiting here was a mistake, and not my first. Usually my distance from you makes you and the girls safer. It didn't work out that way with the New York assignment."

"Anywhere in New York is too close to where you did your undercover work before."

"It's a big city, and I thought everyone involved was in prison or dead. That nobody would recognize me. Hell, I shave some mornings and don't even recognize myself." He didn't belong here. The feeling was strong in him now. This wasn't his house or his life. Wasn't his wife. "Goodbye, Elana." He moved toward the foyer and front door.

Her hand reached out and clutched his, stopping him. She was looking up at him, still not crying but her eyes were moist. He saw in them the same desperation and bewilderment that he saw in his own eyes when he looked in the mirror and thought about Daisy. Guilt grappling with dread.

"Stay," she said. "You can take a later flight."

He stayed.

She was, he realized later, the reason he had come here.

12

Sunday morning, back in his New York apartment, Donnie was awakened by a phone call.

He thought it might be Vinnie Roma and friends and was relieved to hear Jules Donavon's voice on the other end of the line.

Then not so relieved. Something in Donavon's tone.

"Any news about Daisy?" Donnie asked.

"Nothing," Jules said. "But you might know more about that than I do. Your trip to St. Louis yesterday wasn't smart."

"It was one I had to make," Donnie told him.

Jules sighed. "If you say so."

"Should you have called me here?"

"It's all right. As of right now your phone line's safe, but I can't vouch for it hour by hour, so let me call you rather than the other way around. And we better keep our conversations short."

"This one's growing lengthy," Donnie said, letting his head fall back on his pillow. He became aware that his hair and the pillow were soaked with perspiration though the room was cool.

"Tomorrow before you go into work," Jules said,

"you have an eight o'clock appointment with a Dr. Eams over on West 74th near Broadway—in the Almer Building."

"That won't go over well with the people I'm dealing with."

"You have a headache and assorted bruises from them using you for punching practice; they should understand that you might want to see a doctor. Besides, they take a workmanlike pride in their thuggery and won't like to think you're only pretending to need medical attention."

"I won't have to pretend hard," Donnie said.

"Eams will give you a prescription and a doctor's slip to take to work, make your story more plausible. He's safe, Donnie. He'll show you into his office, then into another room. Is Lily settled in okay in St. Louis?"

"She has a handle on things," Donnie said. He wasn't surprised Donavon already knew about their conversation in St. Louis. He probably knew about his visit with Elana, too, though he hadn't mentioned it. Maybe he'd mention it in Dr. Eams's other room.

"Save whatever info you've got for us until tomorrow," Jules said.

"I thought you told me the phone line and my apartment are safe."

"Safe is relative in our business. Forget about everything till tomorrow. Just relax the rest of the day."

"You think the mob is religious and takes Sundays off?"

"There's religious and religious," Jules said. "They like to watch pro football on television. The Jets are gonna play the Rams this afternoon. It'll be a one-sided game, so your new friends should enjoy it."

Donnie wasn't sure if Jules was serious, so he said goodbye and hung up. He really was developing a headache, and wished Dr. Eams had Sunday office hours. But Donnie experienced a vision of the doctor he'd never met, off playing golf somewhere while Roma, Mako, and Barkov sat around with their feet up, guzzling beer and watching football on TV.

Thinking it was some life, he climbed out of bed to search for an aspirin.

He'd expected trouble from Roma's men all day Sunday, but none materialized. Maybe they actually did take the day off to watch football.

Monday morning, after calling Lefty Ordaz and explaining that he had a doctor's appointment but would be in later, Donnie walked from his apartment over toward West 74th and Broadway. It was a cool but sunny morning and his headache from yesterday was a memory. Traffic was heavy. Bright sunlight glinted off the waxed limos and rain-washed yellow roofs of cabs. Families with kids in strollers were taking in the air, along with tourists. Even the panhandlers seemed to be invigorated by the day. Donnie was enjoying the walk, making better time than if he'd driven or taken a taxi in the snarl of morning traffic. The exercise sapped his body of some of the tension that had been stretching his nerves.

The Almer Building was fronted with those big white artificial stones that look like concrete pillows and had a faded red awning over the entrance. The lobby was an expanse of pink-veined gray marble and dark wood paneling, so spare and uniform that the elevators were hard to locate. Their doors were also paneled in wood, and the call buttons were recessed and didn't glow. It was as if the architect didn't really want anyone to get past the lobby; the building overhead might be as phony as Dr. Eams.

After a glance at the glassed-in directory, revealing that Dr. Eams's office was on the twentieth floor, Donnie rode an elevator up. It groaned and hissed as it ascended, as if submerged and fighting its way toward the surface and air.

The office was real, all right. There at the end of the hall was a door with the doctor's name on it. The stenciled black letters were chipped and worn and looked as if they'd been there for years.

Donnie opened the door and stepped inside. There was a real waiting room, with three patients seated far apart from each other on rows of orange plastic chairs that lined two of the walls. There was a table with old magazines fanned out near a slender crystal vase containing a wilted flower. A frosted glass window was set in one wall, with a nearby button to push to ring a bell and alert someone that you'd arrived. Donnie glanced at the three patients, two older men and a young, overweight woman, and pressed the button.

An elderly woman in a starched white uniform slid open the window and looked expectantly at Donnie. She had frazzled gray hair, a dime-sized dark mole on her chin, and blue eyes made incredibly huge by thick-lensed glasses. Donnie thought that if she was a nurse, he wouldn't want to see her first thing coming out of anesthetic. He gave her his name and said he had an eight o'clock appointment, and she instructed him to have a seat then abruptly slid the window shut.

Eams was a legitimate doctor as well as a Bureau operative, Donnie decided. The woman from behind the window came out and asked one of the older men to please follow her through an unmarked door.

About ten minutes passed before Donnie was summoned. The other two people in the waiting room stared at him, as if he owed them an explanation as to why he was being ushered in ahead of them. There could be dozens of reasons, he felt like telling them. He was a relative of the doctor; he was only here to pick up a prescription; the doctor had lost a golf bet with him yesterday; he was an undercover FBI agent.

No, not that last one.

Eams was a tall, thin man with a disproportionately large stomach paunch beneath his white smock. He had a face like an inquisitor and a lot of gray hair sprouting from his nostrils.

"Right through there, Mr. Barns," he said, smiling wickedly and motioning toward a door as if it might lead to a torture chamber. He didn't accompany Donnie, but he watched him until he'd entered the room and closed the door behind him.

Donnie stood still, astounded. He was in a torture chamber.

Wearing a gray suit, white shirt, and paisley tie, Donavon was seated casually on a bench that was outfitted with black leather wrist and ankle cuffs. Another man, a beefy, crewcut agent named Bert Clover who Donnie remembered meeting in Florida, was standing with his leg propped on a small steel cage that wouldn't allow its occupant to straighten up. Some sort of leather harness dangled limply from the ceiling, and various whips, clamps, and leather restraints hung from hooks on two walls. There was no window. The only light was from overhead fluorescent fixtures.

Jules smiled at the look on Donnie's face and said, "The good doctor's a member of a secret S&M club. That's one reason why we can trust him. Also, this room is conveniently soundproofed."

Donnie stood near a crude wooden chair that looked disturbingly like an electric chair.

"That's for using pins and clamps on the sickos," Clover said.

"This is—" Jules began, nodding toward Clover.

"I remember him," Donnie interrupted. He glanced again at the chair and decided not to sit down. "Hell of a world," he said.

Clover shrugged. "Keeps us working. Anyway, you oughta be used to moving among people who do this kinda thing. You're one of 'em, aren't you?"

"Knock off that talk," Jules said wearily.

"I remember our conversation in Florida," Donnie told Clover. "You still an asshole, jealous of undercover agents because you think we get all the glory?"

"Yes and yes. Maybe it's because they make movies based on what you UC guys do. You usually live well, make more money, get to wear expensive clothes, drive new cars, put up a front, work your own hours."

"We're free as larks," Donnie said. He wondered if Clover could ever comprehend what stayed with people after years undercover, the things they'd been forced to do that haunted them forever.

"Not this time, you're not free. You got the worst kind of jag-offs yanking you this way and that, you're doing real work, and your flash pad's a dump. You might not believe this, but I feel sorry for you this time around. I especially feel sorry for your little girl."

Donnie stared at him.

"Believe him," Jules said. "It'll make everything easier."

Donnie nodded. He believed Clover. For now.

"Bring us up to date," Jules said to Donnie.

Donnie did. The only thing he didn't mention was his visit with Elana.

Jules listened carefully with his head cocked to one side. Donnie knew that much of what he was saying, Jules already knew. Neither Jules or Clover commented when he was finished talking.

"Lily and C.J. are still working on getting some ID on whoever abducted Daisy," Jules said. "Clover is going to be your guardian angel for a while."

Donnie looked unsmilingly at Donavon. Usually it was someone from the EO Squad who did that kind of work.

"The Squad's spread pretty thin," Jules explained, guessing Donnie's thoughts, "what with the work in St. Louis and wherever that takes us."

"I'm the best at that sort of thing," Clover said. "You won't know I'm around, won't see me."

Good, Donnie thought, but he didn't say it. "I'm more worried about somebody else seeing you."

"They won't," Clover said confidently. He absently

reached down and scratched his testicles. Very unlike most people's idea of a guardian angel.

Donnie looked at Jules. "*Is* he the best?"

"Sure. He's not bragging, it's true. That's why he's here." Jules glanced at his watch and stood up from the bench. "Keep digging, Donnie. Give Roma some goodies now and then, but make sure we get them before or soon after he does. Call me from public phones, and if we need to meet, call Eams and make an appointment just as if you're a real patient."

Donnie nodded.

"I'll leave first," Clover said.

Donnie watched the bulky, crewcut agent button his suitcoat and lumber from the room. He was glad Jules hadn't asked them to shake hands.

Donavon handed Donnie two slips of white paper. "Your doctor's note and a prescription for some pills."

Donnie folded the slips of paper in half and stuffed them into his shirt pocket. "What are the pills for?" he asked.

Donavon glanced around and shrugged. "Pain."

13

Tuesday when Donnie got home from work and collected his mail from the bank of brass boxes in the vestibule, he found he'd received a letter-size yellow envelope with something soft inside. He waited until he got upstairs in his apartment before opening it.

Whatever the envelope contained was carefully wrapped in white cotton.

Bloodstained cotton.

He parted the cotton and revealed a neatly severed finger.

There was an accompanying typewritten note:

> Daisy's daddy should have taught her it's not polite to point.

The strength went out of Donnie's legs and he slumped into a chair. He was lucky it was there, or he might have hit the floor. His breathing was rapid and irregular, as if he'd suddenly found himself at a high altitude.

The rage that gave him his strength back started as a cold lump in his stomach that gained heat and volume. He stared at the note and wanted to leap up and immediately work out a way to kill Vinnie Roma, Mako, all of them, especially the ones who had Daisy.

They must have learned he'd traveled to St. Louis. They hadn't liked it because they thought he was going after whoever had taken Daisy. Donnie knew they hadn't been bluffing about sending pieces of his daughter through the mail, but the actuality of it was sickening and devastating, then infuriating. Maybe it would have its desired effect on him later, but right now he didn't feel more cooperative. He wanted Daisy returned, and he yearned for revenge.

He called Jules Donavon, and regretted it as soon as he heard the phone ring on the other end of the line.

He'd panicked, acted out of reflex and called out of the apartment. He hung up hard before the ring was answered.

Maybe the Mafia had known about his trip to St. Louis because his phone was tapped and they knew he'd called the airport. He hurriedly shrugged into his coat. Then, his hands trembling, he rewrapped the severed finger in its cotton, returned it to its envelope, and slid it into a side pocket.

Donnie watched Jules Donavon enter the Crispy Queen doughnut shop on West 72nd Street, where they had met before and where Donnie had called from. This time both men had only coffee.

There were no other customers in the far rear area of the shop, where they'd carried their cups. Donnie had explained the situation to Jules on the phone. Now he showed him what was in the envelope. This time his hands were steady.

Donavon's face was blank but his jaw was set firm. Donnie saw a vein pulse like a restless blue worm on the side of his forehead.

"Don't get stampeded into anything," Jules said tightly.

"I want to rip the bastards apart."

"Maybe later, Donnie. That's how they want you to feel, so your emotions overcome your judgment."

Donnie remembered the aborted phone call he'd almost made from his apartment. Emotion the enemy. He knew Jules was making sense, but he wanted to kill Roma and Mako anyway, even though he would also be killing Daisy and himself. He had to obey his reason and not his gut.

"Daisy's prints on file?" Donavon asked.

Donnie glared at him. "Are you serious? An eleven-year-old kid?"

"Okay, stay cool, Donnie."

"I am goddam cool! I could walk up to Roma and Mako and open them up without feeling a thing but satisfaction."

"That's not the kind of cool I mean and you know it. Listen, you want Daisy to survive, you do what I'm gonna suggest as your friend. You go back to your apartment and pretend this didn't happen, you haven't looked at your mail yet. Play it that way if Roma contacts you. If he or anyone else tells you what happened, keep your wits about you. Do what's best in the situation. Meantime, let me keep the envelope and what's in it."

Donnie nodded his assent.

Jules studied the envelope more closely, turning it over. "St. Louis postmark."

"The fuck did you expect? That's where they kidnapped Daisy."

But Donnie knew the significance of the postmark: it meant Daisy was probably still being held in the St. Louis area.

"The lab will get all of this and do a rush analysis, Donnie. We'll see if they find something we don't suspect, something that'll help us. You know how it works."

"Yeah, it works sometimes."

"Listen, I know how you feel—"

"Oh? You got a daughter somebody's chopping up, Jules?"

Donavon sat back and gave Donnie his dead-eyed look. "Be fair, Donnie. I'm trying. We're all trying."

Donnie felt some of the rage go out of him. He drew a deep breath.

Held it.

Released it.

Felt calmer.

"I know, Jules." He took his first sip of coffee. It had cooled but it didn't matter; he hardly tasted it.

"Go home," Donavon said. "Try to regain your equilibrium. Wait for me to contact you. I'll see what the envelope and its contents tell the lab, and I'll get in touch with Lily and let her know what's happened."

Donnie stood up and buttoned his coat. "This thing has reached a higher level, Jules."

"A very high level, Donnie, and you're working without a net."

Donnie nodded to show he understood. He jammed his fists deep in his jacket pockets and strode toward the front of the shop and the door.

Outside he kept walking, past Columbus Circle and along Broadway. People coming toward him who happened to see the expression on his face got out of his way. His feet grew cold and the wind picked up. He didn't care. He kept walking, thinking, looking for new answers.

But the answers were always the same. Roma had him in a vise and was tightening it. And Donnie knew no way to escape.

Donavon called him at ten that evening.

"This phone safe?" This time it was Donnie who asked.

"It's okay, Donnie, we checked the line. But remember, don't call out. For all you know they might tap into it ten seconds after we hang up."

"I won't forget. Haven't yet." Well, almost.

"I got some news for you. The finger's not a young girl's forefinger, it's an adult woman's pinky."

Donnie didn't know what to say, didn't know what this meant other than that Daisy might still be whole and well. He felt a flush of relief that made him unsteady on his feet.

"Still there, Donnie?"

"Here. Thanks, Jules. For pushing this through and letting me know so soon."

"I noticed in the doughnut shop the note didn't actually say it was Daisy's finger."

That was true. Something Donnie hadn't noticed. "What about the St. Louis postmark?"

"The whole package might have been mailed to St. Louis in a larger envelope or a box, then removed and mailed to you so it'd look like it originally came from St. Louis."

"A sick joke? The cat toying with the mouse?"

"More like a warning. To remind you you're being watched, and what'll happen if you cross the cat."

"If it isn't Daisy's finger, whose is it?"

"That I can tell you for sure. We ran the fingerprint through the computers and got a match. It's from the hand of a woman named Victoria Benning who lives here in the New York area and has two previous drug arrests in California, one conviction five years ago. We called her number and got no answer. We shoulda called the NYPD first. They had an unidentified woman they pulled out of the East River last night. She'd been beaten to death. Only identifying mark was a small butterfly tattoo on her neck, but the little finger of her left hand was missing. The body's been identified now; it's Victoria Benning."

"Petite woman, blonde and blue, late twenties, about five-foot-four?"

"How'd you know?"

"She was a waitress at the Bonnaire Lounge out near La Guardia. Vicky."

"That where you know her from?"

"Yeah. She had a run-in there with Mako Fazio,

called his bluff and embarrassed him. Looks like he got even."

"She's local, which means we should turn the evidence over to the NYPD."

"That'd make things more complicated for me, and for Daisy."

"I'll talk to Whitten," Jules said. "Since an undercover agent's life is in danger, we can keep what we know to ourselves. We can't give the locals Vicky Benning's pinky or the story about it being mailed to you, or any info on Mako. But keep in mind, us staying silent and holding on to physical evidence won't set well with them."

"It wouldn't be the first time they had a homicide case interfered with."

"The local law won't be able to pin the murder on Roma or his goons anyway. We can be sure there were enough manufactured alibis to go around even before Vicky Benning was killed."

"Maybe," Donnie said. "But a restaurant full of customers saw Vicky Benning lose her temper with Mako, call him what he is. That makes for motive."

"Not much motive, though, or nobody'd want to wait tables. Let the New York cops spin their wheels. The Mafia would expect them to ID the body and ask around. They won't tie it in with you or anything going on at La Guardia."

Donnie knew Jules was right, which was some comfort. There was always risk if the local law was mucking around in an undercover operation and didn't know the identity of the agent. Also risk if they did know his identity. The fewer people who held a secret, the better. Whispering it in the ear of just one person outside the necessary circle was like feeding a rabbit fertility pills. The number of people who knew would multiply exponentially.

"Can you be cool now with Roma and his friends?" Jules asked.

"For now. Since it wasn't part of my daughter in the mail."

"Is Barkov still being coy about what he wants to tell you?"

"Still is," Donnie said, "but I don't think he suspects me. He has a strong sense of drama."

"Must be a Russian thing. You were right about Gregory, the guy with the crossed daggers tattoo you met at the Westward Ho. Interpol says he's Gregor Mykovich, a Chechen who was involved with something called the Red Hand. In his homeland he helped to kill people with bombs, and did prison time once when he altered his M.O. and used a knife in a tavern brawl. Immigration has no record of him being in this country. Deportation might be a bargaining chip later on in this game."

If the game doesn't end suddenly before that, Donnie thought.

Jules assured him that any news about Daisy would be passed on to him immediately, then broke off the conversation.

Donnie's nerves were still taut, tightening his stomach muscles and trying to bend him forward at the waist. He went into the kitchen and drank a tumbler full of water with plenty of ice in it.

Feeling steadier, he walked back into the living

room, drifted over to the window, and looked down into the street.

There were almost always at least a few people on the sidewalk; it was that kind of New York neighborhood. Near the intersection, a stocky man in a dark topcoat might have glanced up at Donnie's window before moving out of sight around the corner. He might have been Bert Clover. Or one of Roma's men. Maybe even someone Barkov had sent to keep an eye on Donnie. Or maybe he was Yesa Marishov, the determined former KGB hitman who haunted Donnie's life.

Donnie saw it as an indication of how bad the situation was that he hoped the man was Clover.

14

Donnie awoke about midnight with the phone jangling near his right ear.

Why did people keep calling when he was asleep? But he knew why. The twilight between sleep and wakefulness was when people were most vulnerable.

He picked up the receiver and held it to his ear, saying nothing. A faraway siren that had been whooping like a drunk at a party became silent. He could hear the monotonous low hum of the refrigerator in the kitchen on the other side of the wall.

"That you, Donnie?" The voice on the other end of the line sounded like Mako Fazio's. "Donnie? I know this is your number. Hey, asshole!"

"It's almost midnight, Mako," Donnie said in a deliberately sleepy voice.

"Mako who?"

So that was how he was going to play it. "Mako the jag-off from La Guardia cargo."

"Don't know any Mako," Mako said.

"Lucky you."

"What I am is the post office calling to ask if you got your mail today."

"Do I get the post office in trouble if I say I didn't?"

"Don't be such a dickhead, dickhead. Be polite and answer the question."

"Now you're not only not Mako, you're Miss Manners."

"Couldn't be. Miss Manners never came over to somebody's roach preserve apartment late at night and kicked their head in."

"Not even allegedly," Donnie admitted.

"So'd you pick up your mail today?"

"No. If I got any, it's still down in the mailbox."

That seemed to strain Mako's mental resources, causing him to miss a beat. "How come you didn't get your mail outta the box after work?"

"Why should I? There's no rush. I've got plenty of time to read bills and ads."

"Maybe it ain't all bills and ads. Maybe there's somethin' there from somebody you know. And I mean that literately."

"Funny, you don't sound literate."

"Lis'en, fuckface—"

"No. You listen. You call at midnight and wake me out of a sound sleep to ask if I got my phone bill or my limited offer to buy a book or movie every month, and I'm supposed to humor you? Think again, Mako."

"Hey, you don't fuckin' get it."

"You forgot to deny you were Mako that time, shit-for-brains."

"You better listen, wise-ass—"

"I'll look at my mail when I'm damned good and ready."

"You don't under—"

"You expect me to do a job for you, then you make sure I don't get any sleep so I can't do it. Well, I'm going back to sleep, so don't bother calling again."

"Wait! I'm talkin' about your—"

Donnie dropped the receiver hard into its cradle.

Less than ten seconds passed before the phone rang again.

Donnie let it ring seven times before he unplugged it from the jack in the baseboard near his bed.

Then he stretched out again on the bed. He listened to the muted sounds of the city minutes past the bewitching hour, thinking that even if Cinderella had gotten home in time, she still shouldn't have come back here.

He didn't think about it for more than a few minutes after he closed his eyes.

It was the first time since Daisy had been taken that he slept well.

The next morning at La Guardia, Donnie saw that Mako was making it a point not to pay any attention to him. The big man diligently bent to his work, or stood around and bullshitted with his Italian buddies. That was fine with Donnie. He was afraid that if Mako ragged him today he might lose his temper, something he could no longer afford to do.

But Karl Barkov paid attention to Donnie. He deliberately knocked a crate of produce from a pallet Donnie was loading onto a truck trailer, then followed the forklift into the trailer as if to replace the crate so Donnie wouldn't have to climb down off the lift.

He hoisted the crate to shoulder level, crammed it

neatly back into place, then patted it and smiled up at Donnie. "How you feel today, my friend?"

"Not bad," Donnie said. He let the forklift's engine idle, loud in the almost empty trailer. It was obvious Barkov had followed him into the trailer for a purpose and had something more to say.

"You look better. Stronger." He moved closer. "Do you remember I have something to tell you?"

"I guess I do," Donnie said vaguely.

"You guess, hey? Well tonight I tell you. Come to the Westward Ho Club about nine-thirty."

"Is this a secret I'm not gonna want to know?"

Barkov flashed his white, crooked grin. "One you have no choice but to learn."

"Those kinds of secrets scare me. Am I right to be scared of this one?"

Barkov nodded. "You're plenty smart, my friend. Now you need to be enlightened."

Donnie went to lunch again at the Bonnaire Lounge with Barkov, Tomba, and two other Russians. There was no mention of his earlier conversation in the truck trailer with Barkov.

Mako and Navy were at one of the nearby small tables near a wall.

"What happened to that cute little blonde waitress?" Mako asked his waiter, a gawky blond boy not much out of his teens. "Nicki or Vicky or somethin'?"

"I dunno," the boy said. "I just started here. They told me somebody got killed, but I don't know nothing about it."

"Killed? Jesus! The food *that* bad here?"

"Just the specials." The boy laughed along with Mako and Navy.

"Kid's a joker," Mako said.

"Gotta like it," Navy told him.

"Not me," Mako said. Then to the boy: "Go get our order or I'll stick my fork in your fuckin' throat."

The blond boy stared at him, not knowing if he was serious. Mako sure seemed serious.

"A joke," Navy assured the young waiter.

"He don't get movin'," Mako said, "he's sure to get the fuckin' point of it."

Wearing a scared, confused expression, the boy hurried away toward the kitchen.

"I wonder if he got it," Navy said. "I mean, that remark about the point, right after you said you was gonna stick your fork in him."

"He did if you did," Mako said, gazing toward the kitchen.

"Yeah, he seems like a bright kid."

Donnie went to the men's room while the others at his table were waiting for their Bonnaire Burgers. The door with the Elvis silhouette above the word "Gents" was at the end of a short hall. There was an alcove with a pay phone out of sight near the door.

He called Dr. Eams's office. When he gave his name to the woman who answered, she put him through immediately to Dr. Eams. Donnie said he had a helluva headache and wondered if he could make an appointment for after work. The doctor said sure, he'd be in the office till seven.

In case someone had noticed him on the phone,

when Donnie got back to the table, he said he had a headache. "I called for some more pills," he added casually.

"You oughta work at not getting your head kicked around so much," Tomba said, gazing at him with his somber brown eyes. "That can cause headaches."

"The brain's like a muscle," Barkov said. "It's gotta be used or it starts to go bad."

Tomba nodded then raised his eyebrows. "Now you're saying Donnie don't use his mind. I thought you figured he was so intelligent."

"He is. That's why his head hurts—all that brain muscle not being used to full extent. In Russia they say the thoughts are the seed, the action is the corn. Donnie's sowing lots of seed but not doing much harvesting."

"You should read every night," Tomba said to Donnie.

"I'm not much of a reader."

"It's not what he does at home," Barkov said. "It's the job. There's not enough for him to think about. He's bored."

Donnie wished.

15

Clover wasn't with Jules Donavon this time in the room beyond Dr. Eams's office. Instead a tall man in a gray suit who looked like an elongated Harry Truman was seated casually in the torture chair with the leather restraints. He had his legs straight out and crossed at the ankles and was absently toying with the knot in his gray-and-maroon tie.

"This is Special Agent Frank Smith," Jules said. "From the New York field office."

Smith nodded from the chair, gazing at Donnie over his round, rimless glasses.

"We need to keep them informed," Jules said. He left it at that. Donnie knew better than to question the need for New York's involvement. Pressure from above, probably. Bureaucracy in action. He wasn't much worried about security within the Bureau; even Clover could be trusted in that regard. What he didn't like was complication, and the increased probability that the secret of his assignment would eventually find its way out of the Bureau. Then the danger to him would multiply every day. Secrets and rabbits.

"Sorry about your little girl," Smith said, seeming to mean it. His hand dropped abruptly from his tie knot, as if he'd suddenly discovered himself indulging in a bad habit. "We'll do whatever we can to help, all the way."

Donnie nodded. He didn't have to say thank you.

He turned his attention to Donavon and briefed him thoroughly, remembering to tell him about Mako's phone call.

"Vicky Benning's murder was in the papers this morning," Jules said. "Along with info about a missing finger. Roma and Mako are probably aware by now that you know the finger in the envelope wasn't Daisy's."

"The practical joke's gone sour," Smith said darkly. There was an edge of disgust in his voice. Donnie was beginning to like him.

"One of the reasons Smith is here," Jules said, "is because New York has been working a long time on the Italian Mafia's La Guardia operation."

"We've never been able to slip an informer in," Smith said. "We tried once and our man was almost killed before we could pull him. Now you've got a Russian who might tell you what we've been trying to pin down for sure."

Donnie absently took a long leather whip down from its wall hook and examined it. "Which is?"

"That the Mafia's been using Logan Air's flights in from Canada to smuggle drugs."

"Hidden in with the produce?"

"Maybe with all kinds of cargo," Smith said.

"I've kept an eye out for contraband and haven't

seen any. Most of the return flights from Canada bring in at least some produce, which seems the natural place to conceal drug shipments. I've 'accidentally' broken open several crates and found nothing but produce."

"If you weren't in place," Smith said, "we'd use drug sniffing dogs to try to find the stuff, maybe come up with something if we got lucky and timed it right."

"You'd have to be extra lucky," Donnie said. He used both hands to test the strength of the whip, making the black leather creak. "A lot of cargo moves through the place."

Smith smiled. "You're going to be our luck."

Donnie replaced the whip on its brass hook. "How," he asked. But he thought he already knew the answer.

"We want your conversation with Barkov on tape. We'd like you to wear a wire tonight to the Westward Ho Club."

Jules Donavon pushed away from the apparatus he'd been leaning against, something that looked like a gymnast's exercise horse equipped with shackles, and stood up straight with his arms crossed. "That gonna be too dangerous, Donnie?"

Donnie thought about Daisy. What could be *too* dangerous? "They trust me," he said. "Nobody's gonna look under my clothes." Actually he wasn't so sure of that. Nothing the Russians did would surprise him. These were people who drank Siberian Yellow beer and rewarded hit men with vacations in plush condos in Miami for contract killings. Who ate the tuna special simply because it was Monday.

"You gonna wear those clothes to the Westward Ho?" Smith asked.

"I can."

Smith dragged a brown leather briefcase around from the side of the chair. It was oversized and battered and looked like the kind that cheap attorneys brought with them to court. "Then we can attach the wire to you here and now."

"When you get back to your apartment tonight," Jules said, "put the transmitter, microphone, antenna wire, everything, inside some newspaper and put it in the recyclable bin outside the door at the end of the hall. It'll be picked up by us in a hurry. We don't want any recording equipment left in your apartment."

Neither did Donnie. He didn't even like the idea of leaving it in the recyclable bin for a short time, but he didn't have a better suggestion. After his conversation with Barkov, the longer he kept the wire, the greater the odds were he'd be discovered with it. Odds again. His entire life seemed to have come down to odds.

"Make it the *New York Times*," Jules said, "with the obituaries on top."

"Good choice."

"Agent Smith's a tech agent, expert at rigging a wire," Jules assured Donnie.

"I suspected he was."

Smith glanced at his wristwatch then bent over the briefcase and opened it.

"Okay," he said to Donnie, "get undressed."

Jules couldn't suppress a slight smile. "Plenty of people have in this room."

Donnie wished he hadn't said that.

When he parked across the street from the Westward Ho at 8:55 that evening, Donnie saw the same two heavies who'd been lurking near the door during his first visit. This time they were wearing expensive track suits, blue with gray stripes, and white and blue jogging shoes the size of canoes. Track suits were the uniform of the low-level Russian Mafioso—the soldiers in the enforcement brigades—so Donnie supposed they'd been dressed in suits during his last visit because of the wedding inside the club.

The two men looked just as big as last time, though, and just as dangerous. Both wore gold chains around their thick necks, one man a series of three or four, the other a single chain that looked as if it could double as a tire chain if it snowed. Nobody actually exercised or jogged through the park wearing jewelry like that. On the other hand, these two guys were hardly candidates for a mugging.

They looked at Donnie and said nothing as he walked past them. One of them was holding a lit cigar and aimed it at Donnie as if it were a gun. Didn't smile, though.

There were about a dozen men in the club, only one woman. Three men were seated at the bar, the rest in twos or threes at tables. The woman, a tall, husky brunette in a red blouse and tight Levi's, was perched on a stool near the end of the bar. Her eyes were half closed, and the glass before her, containing some kind of green liquid, seemed to emit a magnetism that barely kept her from toppling backward off her stool.

Donnie spotted Barkov sitting with Gregory at a table near the wall. There were two empty beer steins on the table, and two that were half full. The empty steins looked too clean to have been drunk from. Donnie felt the back of his neck tingle a warning. Barkov and Gregory might pretend to be drunker than they were.

"Donnie, my friend!" Barkov said, lifting his beer mug in a salute.

Gregory stared at Donnie from beneath bushy eyebrows then gave his gap-toothed grin. "Hi to you, tough guy."

Donnie said hello and sat down in the one empty chair. Within a couple of seconds the bartender placed a full beer mug in front of him on the table. Donnie took a long pull on the beer, figured it was Siberian Yellow, and centered the mug on a cork coaster. He wiped his mouth with the back of his hand and looked across the table. Barkov's hair was slicked back neatly and he was wearing a well-cut brown sport jacket, dark green shirt, darker green tie. Gregory was wearing a blue and gray track suit top, like the ones on the men outside the door, only Donnie remembered seeing that he had on blue dress pants and black shoes.

After another sip of beer, Donnie slipped his hand down and pretended to scratch his crotch, actually adjusting the miniature transmitter taped to the inside of his thigh. The microphone looked like an ordinary shirt button, replacing the third button down. A thin wire ran from the mike to the tiny transmitter. Somewhere outside the club, nearby, Donnie's conversations would be preserved on FBI tape.

"Too crowded to talk here," Barkov said, gazing around the smoke-hazed club. "Let's go in there, hey?"

Without waiting for anyone to agree with him, he stood up, still gripping his beer stein.

Donnie and Gregory stood also, and followed Barkov toward the double doors that led to the banquet room where the wedding reception had taken place.

Inside the doors, Barkov flipped a wall switch and the chandeliers and sconces along the walls came on. The room was cooler than the bar and looked vast in its emptiness. The round tables with their white cloths were still set up, some of them with glass ashtrays in their centers, but the chairs were stacked along one of the walls. Barkov grabbed one of the chairs and carried it toward a table away from the door. Gregory and Donnie did the same. The chairs weren't the kind that folded and they were heavy.

When the three men were seated around the table, Barkov set his beer stein off to the side and leaned closer to Donnie. "I think we got no choice but to trust you, my friend, so—"

He was cut off by a high-pitched yowling from the speakers set around the room.

"What the fuck is that?" he asked, wincing and twisting a finger in his ear.

"Some kinda feedback," Gregory said.

"What's that mean?" Barkov asked. There was more yowling from the speakers.

"Interference. A device."

"Device?"

Gregory glanced at Donnie, then back at Barkov. "Somebody here's got an electrical device."

16

Gregory stood up, his long arms dangling and his hands clenching and unclenching as if warming up to strangle someone. The speaker system in the banquet room screeched again. Donnie looked around as if trying to discover the source.

Barkov got up out of his chair slowly, glancing over at Donnie then beyond him. One of Gregory's big hands rested on Donnie's shoulder.

"A minute," Barkov said.

The hand didn't move as Donnie watched Barkov stride across the banquet room to the tiny raised platform where some music stands and a few pieces of electronic equipment sat near the dance floor. He went to what looked like a small black bookshelf and reached into it.

The yowling became even more piercing, then abruptly ceased.

"I saw a red light glowing," Barkov said when he returned to the table. "The stereo system was on, but there wasn't any disk or cassette in it."

"What about the radio part?" Donnie asked.

"That could have been what I switched off. Whatever it was, it cut the power and made the red light go out."

One of the banquet doors opened and a plump blonde woman in a too tight black dress and black pumps stepped inside. She didn't seem to notice the three men at the table as she walked toward the bandstand. Her high heels made her hips roll, but her stride was mincing and her shoulders sagged as if she were tired. Donnie didn't think she'd be walking that way if she knew she was being watched.

She bent and stared into the black case containing the stereo, then straightened up and stood for a moment with her hands on her ample hips. When she turned around, she saw that she wasn't alone and her entire body seemed to twitch slightly in surprise.

She smiled. Her face was round and pleasant, and the smile made her eyes squint up. Donnie thought he remembered her dancing at the wedding.

"What are you doing, Marie?" Gregory asked.

Her smile faded and she walked toward them. A different kind of walk now, practiced, more erect, seductive. "There's a speaker over the bar. I thought I heard the backfeed from the stereo system and came in to turn it off." She had a very slight accent Donnie couldn't place.

"How did you know what was making the noise?" Gregory asked. "You are an electronics expert?"

Something in his voice stopped her about ten feet from the table. Her expression became solemn and thoughtful; she knew she had to be careful here, not be caught in a lie. "I had the radio on earlier."

"Why?"

"I was in here dancing."

"By yourself?"

"Sure. You know how I love to dance. I was practicing, like. I thought I might have forgot and left the sound system on."

"You did leave it on," Gregory said, moving slowly toward her. He was working his fists the way he had a few minutes ago.

Marie stood still as if to hold her ground, but she began backing away when Gregory got within arm's reach.

"I'm sorry," she said. "I was careless." Her voice was an octave higher.

One of Gregory's long arms reached out slowly, but now the woman seemed paralyzed and didn't even try to avoid his grasp. His fingers closed and he had a handful of her blond hair. He used the grip to lead her to where the chairs were stacked along the wall. With his free hand he grabbed a chair from one of the stacks and set it down, then sat down in it and yanked the woman's head down at an angle so she was lying facedown with her stomach across his lap. Her skirt had worked up well above her knees. Gregory pulled it up higher to reveal thick pale thighs marked with dark bruises. Marie wasn't wearing panty hose. Gregory yanked her beige panties down, ripping the fabric as he worked them down her legs and over her feet, then wadded them and stuffed them in her mouth. Marie didn't resist. She seemed resigned to that kind of treatment.

Donnie found that he'd stood and moved a step toward Gregory and the defenseless woman. Barkov gripped his arm and pulled him back. He sat down again at the table and motioned for Donnie to do the same.

By the time Donnie had sat down, Gregory had removed his belt and was strenuously whipping the woman.

It was a brutal whipping. Gregory kept flailing with the belt, beating faster and faster, raising welts on the woman's buttocks and thighs, then drawing blood. She made no sound, didn't even move at first until the pain caused her to squirm in Gregory's grasp. Toward the end, she flailed her legs and one of her shoes flew off.

Finally Gregory released her and shoved her roughly to the floor. He was breathing hard as he stood up and worked his belt back through the loops in his pants and fastened its large silver buckle.

Tears were streaming down Marie's face. She averted her gaze from all three men as she removed the wadded panties from her mouth then modestly pulled her dress back down over her thighs. She removed her other shoe, retrieved the one that had flown off her foot, and slunk barefoot from the banquet room. A few dark bloodstains were already visible through the material of her dress.

Gregory returned to the table and slumped down in his chair, still taking deep breaths, huffing as if about to have a heart attack. "Hard goddam work!"

"She gonna be okay?" Donnie asked.

"Who gives a fuck?"

"It doesn't matter," Barkov said. "She's a *prasti-*

tootka—a whore. There are rules. She knows them. She almost caused some trouble."

Now Gregory was rubbing his right shoulder and working his arm back and forth.

"You need to be careful," Barkov said. "You're going to tear a rotator cuff one of these days."

Gregory showed his gapped teeth. "It'll be worth it."

"She didn't fight back or make a sound," Donnie said.

"She knows better," Gregory said. He threw back his head and sucked in oxygen, getting his wind back at last.

"Don't worry about Marie," Barkov said to Donnie. "Perhaps our attitude toward women is different from yours, but she knows what she is and understands, so we don't treat her as we would respectable women. Hers is the life she's chosen. She's all right. She'll probably be back at the bar when we leave here."

"Standing up, though," Gregory said.

Barkov leaned forward over the table again, assuming the same expression and posture he had before the speakers yowled and Marie entered the room. "You want to talk about the whore, or about business?"

"Business," Donnie said, thinking here was another side of Barkov. He was grateful to Marie for providing a reminder about the nature of the people he was befriending, and who sometimes were disarmingly easy to like. It might help him to stay alive.

Donnie was held by Barkov's hard, intelligent stare from across the table. "Here is why we decided to tell you about this," the Russian began. "We know you'll discover it on your own sooner or later, and when you do, we can't be sure what you'll do with the information."

"So you're going to trust me?"

"As much as we can. We Russians say it is wise to trust men so that you may gain their trust."

Donnie wasn't sure if he liked that answer. He knew he didn't agree with the proverb.

Barkov continued: "For a long time the Italians have been using Logan Air Express to smuggle drugs in among the produce sent by air from Canada. They haven't been caught for a number of reasons. One is that the method of shipment and concealment is effective. Two is that they've placed money in some hands, fear in some hearts. We became aware of their operation and decided we could use it to our advantage."

Donnie sat back and rubbed his temples with his knuckles, shook his head. "Whoa! Slow down. You're saying the Mafia is using those produce shipments to smuggle drugs into the country."

Barkov nodded. "Some of the shipments, yes."

"And you decided you wanted in on the deal?"

Barkov smiled. "I didn't say exactly that."

"No, you said 'we.' But who's 'we'? I mean, who do you represent?"

"Sometimes we're referred to as the Russian Mafia, but really that name applies to a number of criminal organizations that are in some cases only loosely connected. For years there existed in Chechnya an organization known as the Red Hand. It is still in Chechnya, but also in many other places. Like the United States."

Donnie stared at him. "Red Hand . . . Russian Mafia?"

"You've heard of us?"

"The Russian Mafia, yes. Here and there. Vaguely. Seen stuff on the news."

"Good." Barkov and Gregory exchanged looks. Barkov leaned back in his chair. "We don't care what you would do if you discovered one of the Italian Mafia's drug shipments. They would take care of you in that event. Probably they were trying to scare you into quitting your job when Mako attacked you in the truck." He grinned. "But you don't scare, my friend, hey?"

"Some," Donnie said.

"Modest Donnie," Gregory said.

"If you don't care about me finding a Mafia drug shipment," Donnie said, "what *do* you care about?"

"Ah!" Gregory said, as if Donnie had struck on something and pleased him with his aptitude. "An intelligent question."

"As I told you he'd ask," Barkov said. "He's a smart one, Donnie Barns is."

"Is there an answer to my question?" Donnie asked.

Barkov rested both elbows on the table and clasped his hands. "There is a story about a man who toiled in a large manufacturing plant and every day after work left with a wheelbarrow full of straw. The security guards searched through the straw, convinced that he was stealing, smuggling something from the plant. But they never found anything. Only later, when the man was long gone, did they realize he was stealing wheelbarrows."

Donnie was beginning to understand. He took a pull on his beer and grinned. "The produce is your straw, a diversion."

"In a sense. So is the Italian Mafia drug smuggling itself, which, contrary to their belief, we want no part of. The authorities might suspect drugs being smuggled in among produce shipments. And they might even suspect drugs being smuggled *out* of the country with the heavy equipment flown north by Logan Air."

"But they probably wouldn't take that third step," Donnie said. He already had.

Barkov's grin was wide and white as a toothpaste commercial. "Correct! We're smuggling stolen heavy equipment, earth-moving machinery, oil drilling apparatus, manufacturing systems, among the legitimate heavy equipment cargo moved by Logan Air. It's flown to Alaska, then to a point in Asia, where it is sold to various international customers. There is a huge market for such equipment among emerging countries. The police or FBI might search for drugs concealed in the heavy equipment, but they won't suspect that the equipment itself is the contraband."

Donnie pushed away from the table, leaning back with his hands still on the white cloth. "So now I know."

"Yes, you do. As you would have eventually, whether or not you were told." Barkov was still smiling. Donnie didn't look to see if Gregory was.

"You didn't try to scare me away, like the Italians," Donnie said.

"We didn't kill you, either," Gregory pointed out.

"That might have attracted suspicion where and when we didn't want it."

"You posed a problem," Barkov said. "But when I saw more of you, I liked you. I thought there was something that might be worked out."

They obviously wanted him to speculate. "You're going to cut me in?" Donnie asked.

"Not right away," Barkov told him. "We'll have to see about you. People beyond me have to learn they can trust you."

"What will it take to convince them?" Donnie asked.

"Time."

"What am I supposed to do in the meantime?"

"Mako, the rest of the Italian faction, haven't been bothering you as much at work. We want you to become more friendly with them, but not overly so because they'd become suspicious. We want you to listen to them, watch them, learn about them. Tell us if you think there's anything we should know."

"You want me to be your spy."

Barkov waved a hand in airy dismissal. "Not so much that, my friend. We want you to listen, remember, and if you learn something, share it. Meanwhile, I'll be talking to people, pressing your case. You're the first new employee we've seen in a long time in the cargo area. I know men. From the moment I saw you, I knew you had to be in or out—because you were going to figure out what was happening before anyone scared you away."

"Do Sam Vargo or Lefty Ordaz know about either smuggling operation?"

Barkov gave him a level look. "Don't disappoint me by starting to ask questions, Donnie."

"What you told me raises lots of questions."

"But only one is important, along with its answer, the one I mentioned earlier: You can be in, or you can be out."

Donnie knew Barkov was right about that. After what he'd just been told, *out* was another word for *dead*.

He lifted his half-empty beer stein in a toast.

"In," he said.

The other two steins at the table rose. There was a bloodsmear on one of Gregory's knuckles. Glass clinked on glass. The three men drank. Everyone at the table trusted everyone else. The toast had sealed their partnership.

But no one moved to throw their empty steins into the fireplace.

That made Donnie wonder if the toast was official.

17

After leaving Barkov and Gregory in the banquet room, Donnie made a detour to use the men's room before leaving the Westward Ho Club. The wiry young bartender with the red vest put down the glass he was polishing with a gray bar rag and directed him toward a door down a hall. As Donnie was making his way to it, he glanced sideways and noticed a woman's plump calf and a pale foot sheathed in a high-heeled black pump.

The women's restroom was beyond a door next to the men's, so he felt safe pausing and looking around the corner.

Marie was seated on some cardboard boxes in the hall outside of what appeared to be a small storage room. The door was wide open. Inside the room were cases of empty beer bottles along one wall, and some rickety shelves that held an assortment of glasses, a dusty electric blender, a spare vinyl seat for a bar stool. The room had no window; harsh light was provided by an overhead fixture with a bare bulb.

Marie's shoulders were rounded and her makeup was still marred by tears. She was staring glumly at the floor and seemed to have reached the point where exhaustion supplanted sobs.

Donnie glanced around to make sure no one could see them. "You okay?" He noticed the word PTERODACTYL scrawled in red ink on one of the cartons where she was seated.

She looked up at him, scared and puzzled, and nodded.

Feeling guilty because he was using her himself, making her an ally for possible future advantage, he stepped closer and patted her gently on the shoulder. "You didn't deserve what happened."

"Thanks for saying so," she said, not shying away from his touch. "But I should have remembered to turn off the sound system when I was finished dancing."

"Sure, but that rates a blue star instead of a silver, not a major beating."

She managed a laugh that was more of a sniffle. "That wasn't major."

"Why do you take it?" Donnie asked.

"There's no choice. I'm bruised, but I'm still breathing. Anyway . . ."

"Anyway what?"

"I come from a place where there's disease and hunger. There's none of that here. Most of the time I don't mind my work, what goes on around this place."

"Only most of the time?"

She looked suddenly frightened, remembering he was one of *them*. He felt small enough to climb into the blender over on the shelf.

"You don't have to answer that," he said. "I'm only making conversation, trying to cheer you up."

"Well, you have."

He absently reached down and lifted the free cardboard flap of the box where she sat. Inside the carton were silver metal cylinders that resembled steel thermos bottles. Casually, he dropped the flap back in place and used that hand to pat her shoulder again. "You take care of yourself, okay?"

"Yeah." She gave him a moist smile. "Thanks. Really."

"Gregory was wrong about one thing," he told her.

"What was that?"

"He was sure the next time any of us saw you, you wouldn't be sitting down."

He thought at first she was crying, then saw that she was laughing silently, dabbing her eyes with a wadded white tissue, as he left her.

After making sure the Honda wasn't being followed, Donnie stopped at a service station on the drive back to Manhattan and phoned Jules Donavon.

"Everything go okay with the wire?" Jules asked.

"I wouldn't be talking to you if it hadn't," Donnie said. "You get it all?"

"I don't know yet. Fill me in verbally in case something went wrong."

When Donnie was finished relating the details of his visit with Barkov and Gregory, Jules said, "We suspected drugs were being smuggled in with the produce. The DEA's raided the place twice on tips but never found any of it. They used drug-sniffing dogs, but maybe they're not so effective if the narcotics are frozen along with the produce."

"Or if the drugs are in air-tight metal containers," Donnie said, and told Donavon about his visit with Marie outside the storage room.

"Possibly that's what the containers were for," Donavon said, "but from what you say they're bulky enough to make any contraband a lot more noticeable. And, it's the Italians and not the Russians smuggling in drugs. We also have information they're using those Logan Air flights to smuggle in counterfeit bills, but that kind of contraband's even harder to find than narcotics."

Jules was better than anyone he knew at shooting down theories, Donnie mused. "I don't have to give the Russians anything yet," he said, "but how about me letting the Italians know the Russians are aware of their drug smuggling operation. They probably know anyway, and telling them might shore up my credibility."

"Sounds right."

"I want to take it further," Donnie said, "let them know about the heavy equipment racket."

"What's your thinking on that one?"

"Daisy. I've gotta make myself valuable as I can to the Italians."

"Yeah, I see your point. But be careful. And don't mention your conversation with the prostitute to the Italians. They might want to wring more out of her, or shut her up before the Russians discover she's talked. Remember what happened to Vicky Benning."

"Marie has more to fear from the Russians than the Italians," Donnie said.

"I believe it. Scratch the surface of any of these goons and you'll find the same thing underneath."

Donnie remembered Gregory beating Marie, and Barkov being unaffected by it. *It doesn't matter. She's a* prastitootka.

"Any mention from the Italians about Vicky Benning or her severed finger?" Jules asked.

"No, and there probably won't be unless I bring up the subject. To Roma and Mako the whole thing was like a sick joke that fell flat." A jet airliner flew over, low and loud, maybe headed for La Guardia. Its lights diminished and it sank from the sky beyond the buildings down the block like a multicolored meteor shower. "Roma or Mako are bound to contact me and set up a meet, Jules. I'd like to wear the wire there, too."

"Dangerous, Donnie."

"I know, but the tapes will be solid evidence when and if we go to court."

"I don't like to see you doubling the odds against you."

"Roma and his friends aren't going to keep Daisy alive forever, Jules."

"Yeah," Donavon said sadly, "time's a factor. Wear the wire, Donnie. Need a tech agent to set you up?"

"No, I can do it."

"Just let us know the where and when of the meet. We'll tape it in a mobile unit."

Donnie thought about suggesting he wear a recorder, in case Roma or Mako caught him off guard and began asking questions before he could contact the Bureau. But that didn't make sense. With a remote team taping, the evidence was preserved, and it would be evidence of murder if the Mafia found the wire and killed Donnie on the spot. Which they might well do. In men like Roma and Mako, rage easily outweighed reason.

"We meet the wrong kind of people in our business," Donnie said.

"Do we ever."

"Have we kept the preserved finger?"

"Sure. Why?"

"I don't know. Maybe I'll find a use for it later."

"Don't do anything stupid, Donnie. I hear that reckless quality in your voice."

"The last thing I'd be right now, Jules, is reckless."

"Right now," Donovan echoed.

The last thing . . . Donnie thought, but didn't say it.

18

They bought Donnie dinner the next night at Frannie's Italian Restaurant on Amsterdam Avenue. It was a dim place with red-and-white checked tablecloths, candles on the tables, lots of garlic in the air, and high wood partitions that made for private conversations.

Since it was only five o'clock there were only a few other diners in the restaurant. They wouldn't overhear. And it probably wouldn't matter if they did. The Bureau had listed Frannie's as a Mafia gathering spot for years.

Nobody spoke until the waiter had finished placing plates on the table. Donnie was wearing a gray sport coat and a white shirt with a band collar. He was using the button microphone again and thought a tie might interfere with it.

"You see we're not such terrible people," Roma said. "We do business, and we treat you to this nice dinner." He'd ordered lasagna and fettuccini and was slathering even more butter on his toasted garlic bread, as if to say what the hell, in his line of work he didn't have to worry about longevity anyway.

"It's like a date," Mako said. "First we feed you, then we fuck you."

"Your friend sure knows how to break a mood," Donnie said to Roma. It wasn't bad strategy to play these two guys against each other whenever he could. Divide and survive.

"Yeah," Roma agreed, "and if it's like a date, he forgot the conversation part." He shoved some fettuccini into his mouth and showed how that shouldn't slow down conversation. "So talk, Donnie."

"The Russians know you're using Logan Air's produce shipments to smuggle in drugs," Donnie said.

Mako grinned across the table at Donnie and began awkwardly winding pasta on his fork held against a spoon. "*We* knew *they* knew," he said with a conspiratorial wink. "Tell us somethin' we don't know, asshole."

Roma looked at Mako and shook his head; here was a project beyond reclamation. The tangle of thin pasta slipped off Mako's fork and plopped back onto his plate. He gave up trying to wind it and scooped it up with his fork and forefinger and sucked in the long strands.

Roma looked away in disgust. "Fucking animal."

"Probably got a tail," Donnie said, smiling at Mako.

"I could kick you in the leg under the table," Mako said, "break your fuckin' ankle."

"Only if you're told to," Roma said. "Have some of your supper, Donnie, and talk while you eat."

"The spaghetti's good," Mako told him. "It's angel hair."

Donnie had ordered the same special as Mako. He

wasn't hungry and hadn't been paying much attention to the unctuous waiter. But he deftly wound angel hair on his fork while the envious Mako looked on. He swallowed and took a sip of cheap house wine. "The cops and DEA think the Russians might be smuggling something out in the heavy equipment."

"Are they?" Roma asked, interested now. Then to Mako: "Shut up! You make too much goddam noise when you eat.'

"Just ignore him," Donnie said. "But they're not smuggling anything out in the heavy equipment. They're smuggling heavy equipment."

Roma and Mako stared at him. A strand of pasta dropped from Mako's chin onto his tie.

"Some of the heavy equipment cargo's legitimate," Donnie said, "and some of it's stolen. There's a market for it in countries with developing economies. Logan flies it to Alaska and delivers what's legitimate, then flies what's left to someplace in Asia where it's sold to buyers around the world."

"I'll be damned!" Roma said with grudging admiration.

"Clever fuckin' Ruskies," Mako agreed, and slurped in more angel hair.

"Why'd they tell you about this?" Roma asked.

"Because they figured I'd find out anyway, and they wanted to be sure ahead of time they could trust me not to talk. And because Barkov likes me."

"That wouldn't stop him from killing you."

"Of course not. But killing somebody who unloads Logan Air Express planes might attract suspicion. Besides, he thinks I might be useful alive, just like you do."

Roma grinned. There was a bit of oregano or parsley stuck between his front teeth. "You're worming in with them, just the way you did with us. That's your special talent, which is why you're still alive."

"Everybody's got a talent," Donnie said, "but I'd rather be musically inclined."

"You're gonna be *de*composin' soon enough," Mako said.

Donnie and Roma looked at each other in surprise.

"Smarter'n he looks," Roma said to Donnie.

"He does have an opposing thumb."

Mako fumed and angrily used his fork to flip a few strands of angel hair across the table and onto Donnie's shirt.

Donnie picked them off deftly, careful not to disturb wire or mike.

"Are you fuckin' nuts?" Roma almost yelled at Mako. "You think we're here to have some kinda high school cafeteria food fight?"

"I really wanna mess this prick up," Mako said.

"We got a good thing rolling here and I'm not gonna let you fuck it up 'cause you can't control your inner emotions, you got that, Mako?"

"What difference—"

"Shut up! Look at Donnie. He's not ever mad because of the things you do. He just thinks you're fucking stupid."

"Right and right," Donnie said.

Mako flushed scarlet. "He's fuckin' yellow, is what he is."

Roma looked at him in disbelief. "Don't shit yourself, Mako. A snitch he is, but yellow he's not. He had plenty of sand in that truck trailer."

"He cold-cocked me," Mako said, "or I woulda spread him around like Spam."

Donnie looked at Roma. "Does Spam spread?"

"Not easy, it don't. But Mako shuts up. Now!"

Mako glared silently and gulped down some of the Italian beer he'd ordered with his angel hair pasta. Donnie wondered how he'd react if he threw a meatball at him.

"There's a guy at that Westward Ho Social Club name of Zelensky," Roma said.

Donnie forgot about Mako. He knew he had to be careful here. "Yeah. I was introduced to him."

"What's his first name?"

"Mister."

Roma smiled and chewed some Lasagna with his mouth open. Donnie thought the table manners of the Mafia had definitely declined. "He a thief-in-law?"

A thief-in-law was Russian organized crime's version of the Mafia don. They were old-style Russian gangsters, middle-aged to elderly men who were just as arrogant and vicious as the Italian dons but better educated. Like Mafia dons, in emergencies or for special situations they had an elite advisory board, the *Bratsky Krug*, or Circle of Brothers, that was the supreme authority. And like Mafia dons, their authority was being increasingly questioned. They were gradually losing control to the younger and stronger hoodlums in their organizations.

"He could be," Donnie said. "He's treated with respect. And fear."

"Find out for sure," Roma said.

Donnie nodded. "Something I wanna bring up now."

Mako smiled, thinking he was going to hear about the finger in the mail.

"I'm going to St. Louis to visit my ex-wife."

"If we say so," Roma said.

"That's why I brought it up. She's upset because of our daughter, and it'd look funny if I didn't go there. The Bureau might wonder why I was staying away."

"You ever open your mail?" Mako asked.

"Naw. Kids get into the boxes, steal it some of the time. What the fuck do I care? All I get are bills. I pick up what's left of it every week or so."

"The man's made out of bullshit," Mako said.

"But he's got a point about visiting his ex," Roma said.

"Sure he's got a point—that's why the bull's asshole don't snap shut."

Roma put down his knife and fork and gave Mako a look that was harder than the crusted bread. Then he turned to Donnie. "You wanna go to St. Louis, you got permission."

"Want me to let you know when I go?"

"We'll know. Pass that bottle of wine."

Roma refilled his glass, looking thoughtful. Then he sat back, sipped his wine, shook his head from side to side and grinned. "Fucking heavy equipment smugglers. Ain't that something?"

"Something," Donnie agreed. "In this world, you

never goddam know." He shifted in his chair, making sure his shirt button was aimed squarely at Roma.

When they were finished eating and had left the restaurant, the three men stood outside on the sidewalk and looked around. It was a habit hard to break, taking in the lay of the land and making sure nothing had changed while they were inside, that there was no imminent danger.

After a few seconds had passed, Roma patted his full stomach and buttoned his suitcoat. Mako continued glancing around as they started walking north on Amsterdam toward where Roma's car was parked.

Donnie almost broke stride when he saw the traffic light change at the corner and half a dozen people cross the street and walk toward them. One of them was a tall man in a dark gray suit, white shirt, and red tie. Though the evening was cool, he had his coat folded over his arm. There was a chance he wouldn't notice Donnie, that they'd pass each other without a glance, lost in their thoughts like so many on New York's sidewalks.

But the man's gaze locked on Donnie when they were about fifty feet apart. FBI agent Dave Manders, who worked out of the New York field office and might know something about Daisy's abduction, had recognized his old friend Joe Pistone. They'd worked together collating evidence during the series of trials Donnie had testified in during his months after breaking cover. If Manders said anything indicating even slightly that he knew about Daisy, it might mean her death. And Donnie's.

Manders sidestepped out of the way of an old woman pushing groceries in her two-wheeled cart and veered toward Donnie, Roma, and Mako.

He was looking at Donnie and smiling, surprise and recognition bright in his eyes.

19

When he was a few feet away from Donnie, Manders extended his right hand and grinned. "Hey, how ya doin', J—"

Donnie's fist caught him just beneath the breast bone and knocked the wind out of him. Manders sat down hard, then fell back supporting himself with his elbows on the sidewalk. He was staring up wide-eyed at Donnie, working his lips soundlessly and trying to catch his breath.

But breath wouldn't come. As he needed it more and more, Manders turned onto his side and drew up his knees.

He was just beginning to suck in oxygen in harsh little gasps when Donnie bent over him. The gasps were louder when Donnie yanked Manders's wallet from his back pocket so hard the pocket tore half off. There was a question in Manders's eyes, but he couldn't voice it. Just working his lungs was hard enough for him.

"What the fuck you doing?" Roma asked.

Mako grabbed Donnie's arm but Donnie shook him

off and drew a fifty-dollar bill from Manders' wallet then tossed the wallet on the ground.

A crowd was gathering. Roma shoved Donnie's back hard. "Run! Run, you stupid prick!"

Mako gave him another shove that almost broke him away from his shoes.

Donnie started running down the sidewalk, knocking aside anyone who blocked his path. A big guy in a plaid coat dipped a shoulder and looked stubborn enough not to move, but at the last second he jumped back out of the way. Donnie was feeling good. He lifted his knees and picked up speed, then slowed down so Roma and Mako could keep up.

At the end of the block he slowed to a jog, turned a corner and began walking.

After a while he was aware of a rhythmic hissing behind him, then on each side of him. Roma and Mako had caught up. And his own breathing was ragged from running so hard.

A hand plucked at his coat sleeve. "C'mere," Roma said, drawing him to the side. "Wait up, dammit!"

Mako clutched Donnie's collar and forced him up against an iron rail near the entrance to a basement apartment. The top button of Donnie's shirt flew off; thank God not the mike button.

All three men stood still for a while, Donnie leaning back against the wall, Mako with his fists on his hips, Roma bent forward with his hands on his knees. They were all still breathing hard after their flight from the crowd and the man Donnie had knocked to the pavement.

"Why the hell'd you do that?" Roma asked. "Who was that guy?"

"Somebody who owed me twenty bucks from our bet on the Jets game. He didn't pay and said he wasn't gonna. I collected." Donnie held up the bill he'd taken from Manders' wallet and waved it around. "I hate a goddam welsher."

"That's a fifty," Mako said. "You told us he owed you twenty."

"Thirty dollars finder's fee," Donnie said. "I found the son of a bitch and made him pay."

"What's his name?" Roma asked.

"I don't know. Jerry something, I think. I met him in a bar when I dropped in to check on the game on TV, we got to talking and we bet. Then he pretended to go to the men's room and took off. Bartender said he did that kinda thing now and then, left a big bar tab behind, too." Donnie turned his head and spat off to the side. "Ol' Jer probably thought we'd never see each other again."

Roma had straightened up and was taking deep breaths. "You coulda drew the cops, fucked up our whole deal. Got you and your daughter killed and my balls in a vice."

"A welsher's somebody who deserves—"

"I don't give a flying fuck about that!" Roma said. "I got my own money in this project, ran up my own debt, and I'm not gonna have some dickhead like you screw this up! You goddam understand?"

Before Donnie had a chance to answer, Mako slapped the back of his head, making his teeth clack together. Donnie whirled and drew back his fist, then paused.

"He's only making sure you understand," Roma said to Donnie in a calmer tone, as if apologizing that his bulldog had nipped someone. He was still so angry he was trembling.

"I hope he don't understand," Mako said, "so I can help him see the light."

"I see it," Donnie said to Roma. "What you say makes sense."

Roma tucked in the front of his shirt, his tie along with it, and blew out a long breath. "Okay. Good. You realize you coulda got us arrested back there? I mighta got pinched for helping you steal a lousy fifty bucks. A mugging on a busy street is something draws attention." He buttoned his suit coat and used the flat of his hand to smooth the material in front. "At least you had the good sense to run."

"I had to jump start him," Mako said.

"We're going back up the street on the other side and get my car," Roma said. "You're not going with us, Donnie. You go the opposite fucking direction."

"But my apartment's—"

"Your goddam apartment's where you go straight to after you walk around the block and cool off, dammit! And don't cause any more problems for me tonight, you hear?"

"Sure," Donnie said.

"After a meal like we ate, I don't like having to run sixty miles an hour like some kinda fucking scared ostrich."

"But that Jerry asshole owed me—"

"Shut up, shut up, shut up!" Roma said.

"What he needs," Mako said, "is for me to get a pair of pliers an' pull his tongue out by the roots."

Roma parted his lips to tell Mako to be quiet, then gave up and simply shook his head and walked away. Mako followed.

Donnie watched them cross the street and walk back the way they'd come. They waited patiently and politely at the corner for the WALK signal, two law-abiding citizens.

Donnie didn't move until they were out of sight. The flight from where Donnie had punched Manders to ensure his silence had left the out-of-shape Roma winded and shaken, his heart still pumping adrenaline. He'd been careless and mentioned his own out of pocket expenses for the abduction of Daisy and the terrorizing of Donnie. That meant two things to Donnie.

The first was that probably no one above Roma in the Mafia knew about this operation. If they had, the money for it would have been supplied. Daisy's kidnapping was a bold move for Roma, a play for more power, and if it didn't work he'd be a goat instead of a hero. In his world, goats were mostly sacrificial.

The second was that if Roma was picking up expenses and going into personal debt in order to finance what was being done to Daisy and Donnie, then maybe he'd charged something or written a check.

Maybe he'd left some kind of paper trail, however faint or cluttered, that might lead to Daisy.

20

The next morning, Donnie was relieved to see that the wire he'd worn last night had been retrieved from the recyclable bin outside his apartment. Donnie thought Bert Clover had probably taken care of that task. Clover was right about his skill at remaining in the background unseen. Donnie wondered what he'd thought of last night's scuffle with Manders. Then he wondered if Clover had actually been nearby last night. How deep did his resentment of Donnie run?

No. Donnie caught himself. The possibility that Clover wasn't the pro he claimed to be was remote. Donavon was the best judge of agents in the Bureau, and he'd vouched for Bert Clover. That was good enough for Donnie. It had to be good enough.

During the next week at work, Donnie took every opportunity to check the produce shipments for drugs. He found none, but that wasn't too surprising. Narcotics would be well concealed in the cargo, and smuggled into the country intermittently to minimize risk. It would probably take a major DEA strike, or a careful search using dogs, to locate the drugs.

Friday evening Donnie quickly changed clothes

after work, then grabbed the suitcase h… morning and returned to La Guardia, this tim… passenger on a TWA flight to St. Louis.

Since he didn't have his Bureau ID with him, he had his Ruger 9mm automatic packed in the suitcase he'd checked through. It wasn't regulation Bureau ordinance; no undercover agent wanted even the slightest connection to the Bureau among his possessions.

After retrieving his suitcase from the baggage carousel in St. Louis, Donnie carried it with him into a restroom and in a stall removed the gun and tucked it in his belt at the small of his back. Then he returned to the area near the baggage carousels and went out the exit with the *Taxi* sign above it.

The cabs were lined up in the covered parking garage, which was a good thing. As Donnie's cab emerged into the night, snow began settling against the windshield and the driver switched on the wipers.

Donnie should have suspected something when the company voice on the cab's radio instructed the driver to stop at a pharmacy and pick up a package while he was in the vicinity.

"Sorry, buddy," the cabby said over his shoulder. "It'll only take a few minutes and we'll be on our way again."

Within a few blocks the cab slowed then turned into the parking lot of a large drugstore. Snow had layered most of the blacktop and the upper surfaces of the parked cars.

"Driving might get bad if this snow gets heavier," the driver said, climbing out of the cab. "Guess this package is important so they wanted it picked up now."

Grumbling about unpredictable St. Louis weather, he slammed the cab's door behind him and trudged through snow toward the drugstore's brilliantly illuminated entrance. He'd left the cab running with the heater and wipers on. It looked to Donnie as if the snow wasn't falling all that hard and might even convert to rain if the temperature rose only a few degrees.

That's what made him suspicious. There wasn't even an inch of snow on the ground, and only light falling snow. Hardly an emergency that called for detouring a cab with a passenger.

But his suspicion came too late. The cab's left rear door opened and someone slipped in to sit beside him so quickly and smoothly he hadn't had time to move.

"Cool now, Donnie," a female voice said.

He was relieved to be staring at Lily Maloney.

He realized instantly how she knew he was in St. Louis. Bert Clover. He'd contacted Jules, who'd contacted Lily while Donnie's plane was in the air.

"I'm on my way to see Elana," Donnie said, irritated. "Is there some reason I shouldn't?"

"Yes. Your reason's name Yesa Marishov. He must have learned you were here last time, and he figured you'd come back."

Donnie stiffened, his shoulders pressing into the cab's soft upholstery. "You know that for sure?"

"That's what our informers tell us. And C.J. thinks he saw someone in Elana's backyard last night." Lily looked hard at Donnie, her strong features only slightly softened by light reflecting off the snow. "You really think you should go there, Donnie?"

He let out a long breath. "No. And we need to move Elana and Maureen out." In some ways Marishov was more of a threat than the Russian or Italian mafias. A lone operator, brilliant, deadly . . . what might he do to Donnie's family for a clue to his whereabouts?

"We'll move them first thing in the morning. Meanwhile, they're safe tonight. Do you want us to let you know where they are when you get back to New York?"

Donnie knew what she was asking. If he had information on his family's location and the Mafia wanted it from him, they'd be able to get it. But only if he had it.

"No," he said, "not yet."

"You've got a reservation at the King West Motel off Lindbergh Boulevard," Lily said. "Go there now; then phone the airport and book a flight back to New York. Tomorrow morning if you can get a seat."

Donnie could see the cabby approaching the drugstore's automatic doors. He was still inside in the bright light, carrying a small brown package in one hand, turning up his jacket collar with the other.

Lily's pale hand was already on the door handle. "I'm sorry, Donnie."

"Don't be. Thanks." He reached up and cupped his hand over the cab's dome light. "What's in the package?"

"Headache remedy. It's on its way to me."

Light seeped faintly through his fingers as the door opened and shut, and she was gone.

The cabby crossed the lot, walking slowly with his knees locked so he wouldn't slip and fall. He climbed back in behind the steering wheel, sighing as if he were out of breath, and set the package next to him on the front seat.

"Some lady needs this stuff soon as possible for migraine headaches," he explained. "Least that's what the pharmacist said. Change of life or somethin', I guess."

"Change of destinations back here," Donnie told him. "I want to go to the King West Motel. Know where it is?"

"Sure. Back the way we came, not even a mile."

"Good. The lady with the headache will get her package all the sooner."

The cabby leaned forward and squinted out the windshield. "Don't seem to me it's snowin' so hard it oughta be such an emergency."

"I don't know," Donnie said, hearing the cab's tires spin momentarily in the snow as it pulled out of its parking space. "If you're in pain it makes sense."

The King West Motel was a block off busy Lindbergh Boulevard, not far from the airport. Plush it wasn't. Though there were only a few cars in its lot, a pudgy teenage desk clerk with "Angie" on her plastic name tag remembered her training, pretending business was booming as she agonized over an obsolete computer until she found Donnie's reservation. Finally she assigned him to a room at the west end of the U-shaped motel.

The squat, two-story structure embraced a drained

swimming pool covered by a sagging, snow-burdened tarpaulin. The King West's parking lot bordered another parking lot, and the window in Donnie's room afforded a clear view of a Dumpster behind a restaurant. The restaurant was called Ed's and had a red neon sign that cast a nice rosy glow over the snow. Angie had recommended Ed's.

The room smelled like Pine-Sol disinfectant and was uncomfortably cool, so Donnie had turned the thermostat higher as soon as he'd switched on a light. Now he stood listening to the reassuring whisper of warm air from the overhead vents and looked around. The furniture was phony oak with the exception of a tiny gray desk with stainless steel legs. There were a couple of ugly burn scars on the blue carpet near one of the desk legs. There was another near the head of the bed, as if a guest had fallen asleep and dropped a lit cigarette.

Donnie hoisted his suitcase up onto the low oaklike dresser so it lay near the TV. There was no closet, only a hanger bar in an alcove very near the washbasin, so it would be convenient to get water spots on your clothes when you washed up. He didn't bother unpacking.

Instead he drifted back to the window and stood staring outside at the snow swirling around one of the overhead lights in the parking lot. The white flakes resembled moths flitting about the glow in their persistent death dance, and they were larger and more numerous than when Donnie had checked in. He lowered his gaze to take in the red reflection of the *Ed's* sign, realized he was hungry, and decided to have some supper while his room's heating system was working to chase away the chill.

Ed's was a cozy place with a six-stool counter and high-backed wooden booths lining the opposite wall. Donnie seemed to be the only customer. A nervous-looking guy in his fifties, thin in the way of junkies and with watery blue eyes, shuffled out from behind the Formica counter and asked Donnie what he'd have. Without looking at the menu, Donnie told him a hamburger, fries, and coffee.

Only a few minutes passed before the skinny guy returned with the food on a tray. The burger and fries were on separate plates. He set them in front of Donnie on the table, then a white coffee mug and a chipped little white creamer. His fingers were trembling and he didn't ask Donnie if he wanted anything else. After hurrying back behind the counter, he stood with both hands visible and pressed to the Formica as he stared out the window at the falling snow.

Something wasn't right here, Donnie thought, as he shook ketchup from a half-full bottle onto his fries. Even as he thought it, a reflection in the dark window caught his attention.

He froze with the ketchup bottle then leaned to the side to see down the row of booths.

He wasn't the only customer after all.

A slim blond man was leaning out from the fourth booth down from Donnie's, aiming a handgun with a long silencer at him.

"He made me do it!" the counterman yelled, as wood splintered on the high seatback facing Donnie. The bullet missed his head by inches as it smacked into the seatback behind him, sending more splinters flying. Donnie could feel them bite into his left cheek.

Training ruled. Reaction was instinctive and immediate.

Donnie was out of the booth and reaching for the 9mm tucked beneath his belt in the small of his back. He took in everything in those few long tenths of seconds: the counterman ducking beneath the counter, his mouth open wide and contorted in another scream (*I ain't in on this!*); the slim blond man emerging from his booth and hesitating as his foot snagged on something beneath the table (slowing him down enough?), taking more careful aim with the gun with the long silencer; the frost patterning the wide window behind the gunman, who was smiling.

The name only, *Marishov!*, entered Donnie's mind as his hand came around with the 9mm and he saw the mouth of the silencer swing toward him and knew he wouldn't be in time, could never be in time, there would be no more time for him.

21

The pattern on the window was more than frost. Glass shattered behind the gunman with a tremendous roar.

"Mother fucker!" the counterman was screaming, oddly precise with his enunciation. He was standing up straight now, wielding the shotgun he'd pulled from beneath the counter. His blue eyes were wild and his entire body was vibrating.

"Mother fucker!" The shotgun roared again.

But the gunman was gone, out through the window whose glass had been blown from its frame.

Terrified that the counterman was out of control and would blast him in the back, Donnie followed Marishov out through the glass-sharded window frame, into the cold night.

Marishov's footprints in the snow were easy enough to follow. Donnie stayed low, trying not to lose his footing, too intent to feel the cold.

Ahead of him the dark prints curved toward the back of the building, where the Dumpster loomed like a military tank without a gun.

Donnie moved carefully. This was what he wanted,

Marishov in the open, on the run, not Marishov concealed and waiting in carefully thought out ambush. Not Marishov squeezing a trigger when Donnie least expected death. Open combat between two experts. Donnie knew it wouldn't be easy, yet he had faith that he'd come out the other side alive. His hard-earned skills, his dedication, were like religious convictions.

But a part of him knew Marishov was equally confident.

The spaces between the footprints weren't uniform now, and their direction wasn't so steady. Donnie brushed fallen snow from his eyelashes and pressed on.

Then he saw the red splotches on the snow. The shotgun had done its work. Marishov was hit!

His own blood racing, Donnie moved faster but even more carefully, to the corner of the brick building. He held his gun in both hands, arms high, his back against the wall, then twisted his body and exposed as little of himself as possible as he peeked around the corner.

More blood on the snow, but no sign of Marishov.

Was he in the Dumpster? Concealed with the lid raised a few inches, sighting down his gun barrel, waiting for Donnie?

Donnie saw now that there was a shallow dry creek between the two parking lots, running parallel to the back of the building then curving out of sight like a black scar in the snow.

And he saw something else. More blood on the snow—beyond the hulking dark shape of the Dumpster.

Sirens in the distance now, like banshee cries carrying in the crystalline cold night air. Someone, probably the counterman, had called the police.

But in this weather it would take a while for them to get here. Marishov would escape.

Donnie took the chance. Running in a crouch, he darted toward the Dumpster then past it, his muscles tensed for a bullet that never came.

Plenty more blood now, leading to the dry creek.

He followed the trail through bent, dead weeds, his feet crunching on last summer's frozen leaves beneath the snow, making too much noise.

He jumped down into the creek bed, holding the 9mm with both hands, ready to fire.

The creek stretched darkly before him. Moving to the side, he studied the snow-blanketed rough surface of the dry bed.

And saw a spot of blood.

Then another.

Marishov was using the creek bed as an escape route.

There was another spot of blood beyond the first two.

Handgun at the ready, Donnie began following the red splotches on the snow.

Sirens were drifting through the night from another direction now, still far away.

More bloodstains glistened vividly against the pristine white snow. But they were smaller, as if Marishov had found a way to stem the flow of blood. He was wounded, but Donnie reminded himself that the Russian hit man was still deadly.

Where the creek turned, Donnie's right foot slipped on an angled, icy stone and he almost fell. The heel of his hand stung as he caught himself against the frozen mud bank.

That's when his gaze took in something glittering in the snow off to his left.

Red, but not like a bloodstain.

Glass.

A ketchup bottle.

In an instant he knew what had happened. The realization caught in his throat.

A trap!

He scrambled back the way he'd come, around the bend in the creek, catching a glimpse of muzzle flash ahead and hearing a bullet snap past his ear.

Marishov had grabbed a ketchup bottle during his escape and faked bloodstains on the snow to lure Donnie into a trap. He wasn't wounded. Donnie knew that if he'd moved another few feet around the bend in the creek, Marishov's shot would have struck home. And Donnie wouldn't have been able to retreat fast enough to avoid being hit at least once or twice more. There would have been a coup de grace if necessary, and this moment wouldn't exist for him; he would be dead.

He ran back another ten feet then pulled himself up out of the creek bed, staying low on his stomach, gun aimed in the direction Marishov had gone. Something, maybe a bullet, kicked up dead leaves and snow on his right. He rolled away from the spray of snow and debris then stopped and lay still, gaze fixed on the curve of the creek.

For a moment he thought he saw a dark form in the

night, the arc of the long silencer against the snow. He fired twice, but he knew he was too far away for accuracy. Luck would have to enter into it if he hit Marishov.

And who knew what was beyond the dark figure? This was a crowded metropolitan area even if few people were out in the snow and cold. Donnie couldn't fire again, probably shouldn't have fired unless he was positive his target would stop the bullets. They were special rounds that did massive damage but had limited range, so the danger of injuring or killing someone innocent beyond the target was minimal—but it was there.

The sirens had growled to silence in the direction of Ed's restaurant. Marishov wouldn't stay in the area, and probably wasn't wounded. Doubtless he'd used the terrain wisely and had a car parked where he could easily get to it from the creek bed. He was probably already more than a mile away and driving fast.

And thinking about next time.

Donnie decided not to return to the restaurant or to his room. He'd make his way to another motel, phone Donavon, then retrieve his suitcase and check out of the King's West in the morning.

Brushing snow and dark, wet leaves from his clothes, he crossed the creek bed and skirted the snow-covered plane of the King's West parking lot. Beyond the skeletal branches of trees he could see the lights of Lindbergh Boulevard. He should be able to find a phone there, call for a cab.

Snowflakes settled coldly on the back of his neck, so he paused and turned up his collar. He was still alive, but his confidence was shaken now. Tonight had brought home to him what he was up against; *he might lose this game*. Marishov was like a relentless chess master biding his time in a death match. Donnie's luck had held, but maybe it had only postponed the fatal checkmate.

He was trembling, not from the cold. The snow was falling harder, silent as death, as he set out for the light beyond the trees.

22

Back in New York, Donnie called Jules Donavon from the corner deli. He was out of sight from the street and most of the rest of the store. Only customers who came to the rear of the deli to buy milk, juice, or refrigerated beer or soda could see him standing at the public phone. Business was slow today. Donnie was alone with the faint and indecipherable racket of rap music from the clerk's cassette player and the spicy scents of the buffet toward the front of the deli.

"At least I got my first good look at Marishov," he said, when he was finished telling Donavon about what had happened in St. Louis. "He looks like a kid." Marishov had in fact been trained when a teenager to be a KGB assassin, so Donnie shouldn't have been surprised. The KGB's intent had been to create a contingent of killers whose young, innocent appearance would allow them to get close to their targets without attracting suspicion. Still, the fabled hit man's youthful looks had taken Donnie aback and almost caused fatal hesitation.

"Are you sure it was him?" Donavon said.

Donnie thought about it. "Reasonably sure. I got a

glimpse of Marishov once in the Florida swamp. It was at night and didn't reveal much, but he was slender and might have been blond. My guess is he was the one I was dealing with in St. Louis."

"But you can't be certain."

"He was also very, very good at his work."

"Yet you're alive and talking to me on the phone."

Donnie had to admit that last was a convincing argument. Time to move on to another subject. "Are we getting good tapes?" he asked.

"Clarity and content are excellent. Can't wait to play them in court. We especially like the last one, with Vinnie Roma, the way he shot off his mouth when he was winded. We're applying for warrants to examine his charge and bank accounts. If his money left a trail, we'll find it."

"His type deals a lot in cash," Donnie said, hearing the frustration and despondency in his own voice.

"Don't let your hopes sag. They deal a lot in cash, but they're up and down when it comes to liquidity. Guys at Roma's level have been known to use up their own credit, then dip into the till to keep from coming up short."

Donnie couldn't think of an example, but he didn't disagree with Jules. He wanted him to be right. Then something occurred to him. "What about the possibility of Roma helping himself to some of the counterfeit money being smuggled in on the Logan Air flights?"

"Not much chance of that," Jules said. "He has to pass the funny money along to the higher ups in the Mafia, and none of it better be missing."

That made sense. Roma would never take such a

risk. Mob money, real or otherwise, was a sacred trust. The counterfeit currency was as unavailable to him as if it were miles away in a vault.

"How's Manders doing?" Donnie asked. "I hit him pretty hard."

"He's okay. A little pissed at you, though."

"He oughta know I didn't have any choice."

"Well, he's a little pissed at himself, too."

"Is there anything yet on the Ford Taurus the witness in St. Louis thinks might have been used to abduct Daisy? Any luck with the license number?"

"The witness had the number right," Donavon said. "It belongs to a lease car."

Donnie's spirits lifted. The leasing company would have records, someplace to start.

"The Taurus was leased at the airport by a businessman from Dallas, staying at a St. Louis Holiday Inn. It was stolen from the hotel parking lot a few hours before Daisy was taken."

Donnie almost punched a nearby display of Coke twelve-packs.

"It was recovered in a shopping mall parking lot after a security guard noticed it hadn't moved overnight. The lab techs have been at it since yesterday morning."

"The car yield anything?"

"So far only a few strands of human hair. They turned out to be Daisy's."

Rage welled again in Donnie.

"It doesn't sound like much," Jules said, "but it puts her in the car. And the techs are still working the vehicle over. Everything down to the lug nuts will go under a microscope."

Donnie was silent with his anger, but Jules homed in on it.

"Don't torture yourself over what you can't do anything about yet, Donnie. I can imagine the pressure on you, what with Daisy's kidnapping, being caught between the Russians and Italians, all the while Marishov on your trail. But we need to use what we have and concentrate our efforts where they'll do the most good right now."

Donavon's words caused some of the anger to fade, but not the resolve. When it came to giving Donnie perspective, Jules was better than a Bureau psychologist; most of those guys had never been shot at.

"If the Russians at La Guardia are only smuggling heavy equipment," Donnie said, "then they could just be fraudsters." That was the Russian Mafia's term for small, semi-independent organized crime groups, usually engaged in minor operations.

"I think they're more than fraudsters, Donnie. The Red Hand has roots in Chechnya, and the odds are your Mr. Zelensky, the occasional visitor to the U.S., is a high level thief-in-law."

"If that's true, then maybe something more than heavy equipment smuggling is going on."

"Maybe," Jules agreed. "Something more, and something much larger."

" 'Maybe . . .' " Donnie said. "I hate that word."

Donavon chuckled. "That's why you're such a whiz at what you do."

"Yeah. Working a job where *maybe* I'll still be alive at

the end of the day. Along that line, I think I should give the Russians the story on the Italians smuggling in counterfeit bills as well as drugs."

"Makes sense at this point. Another opportunity to gain credibility, and it might stimulate some useful conversation. You're providing some damned solid evidence, Donnie. You know how tapes impress in court. I hate to ask you, but how would you feel about wearing a wire again?"

"Eager," Donnie said. Which was true in its fashion.

"You know what'll happen if you get caught wearing one. Don't underestimate the danger."

"There's more danger in doing nothing while the clock's ticking away for Daisy."

"Look in your recyclable bin," Jules said, before hanging up. "*Times* again. Theatre section this time, big piece on acting."

The next night at the Westward Ho, Donnie sat with Gregory and Barkov at the bar. Barkov was as usual a snappy dresser, black slacks and loafers, gray sport coat with dark flecks in the soft material. Gregory was wearing an expensive jogging suit, black with artistic red and blue pinstriping. He had on the kind of over-engineered jogging shoes that looked as if they should perform functions far beyond those of mere footwear. Donnie had on his gray slacks, black sport coat, maroon shirt—and wire.

A bartender Donnie hadn't seen before—middle-aged, squinty eyes, seamed face, missing an ear—placed mugs of Siberian Yellow beer before them on the bar, then moved away. Near the end of the bar,

Tomba sat with a glum-looking woman whose nose had been broken and reset crookedly if at all. He smiled somberly and raised his glass in a greeting to Donnie. Donnie was becoming one of the regulars.

"I've been listening to Mako and his goons talk," Donnie said. He was seated between Barkov and Gregory. He saw the tops of their heads in the mirror, visible above a row of bottles, turn toward him, and knew he had their full attention. "I think they're using Logan Air produce shipments from Canada to smuggle in counterfeit currency as well as drugs."

Gregory took a long pull of beer. "Astounding."

"We've known that," Barkov said on Donnie's right, smiling. "The phony currency isn't smuggled that often, and it isn't very good. We leave it alone, as well as the drugs. Mostly they move drugs. They smuggle in, we smuggle out. It's a mutually beneficial arrangement even if they don't know about it. Have you ever seen any of these drugs?"

"I haven't looked," Donnie said. "I figure the stuff is deep inside crates of whatever, maybe frozen. It'd take the cops hours to break everything apart and find it, so I'm not gonna stumble onto it."

"Cops could use dogs," Gregory said.

"I dunno," Donnie said. "Would dogs be able to smell drugs if they were inside an iced case of lettuce or strawberries?"

"Dogs have got terrific noses," Gregory rumbled.

"They're wonderful animals," Barkov said. "In Russia they say, 'Dogs, vodka, women, in that order.' "

"Politically incorrect," Donnie told him. He thought about Gregory's treatment of the prostitute Marie.

"So's smuggling," Gregory said.

"What about the counterfeit bills?" Barkov asked. "Have you encountered any of them in the cargo?"

"Never."

"Probably in with the lettuce," Gregory said, grinning wide and ugly.

"What we'd like to know," Barkov said to Donnie, "is when the Italians expect their next large drug shipment. Can you get us that information?"

"I can try. But why do you want to know it?"

"Keep it up, your curiosity's gonna get you in deep shit," Gregory said.

"Being curious is simply a part of my friend Donnie," Barkov explained to him. "It goes with his intelligence."

"I never thought he was just a pretty face," Gregory said with his gap-toothed grin.

"We would like to know it," Barkov said to Donnie, "because the DEA might also know it. That's when they might stage a major raid. One or more of them—as curious as you are—might notice a piece of stolen heavy equipment."

"That makes sense," Donnie said. "You want to sit out during times of maximum risk."

"Ah, maximum risk," Barkov said. "Doesn't Donnie have a way with words?"

"Mmf," Gregory said into his beer mug.

Nothing there for the shirt button, Donnie thought. "Do you always try to time your heavy equipment shipments so they aren't on the same day as big drug shipments?"

Both heads turned toward him again in the back bar

mirror. Too hard, Donnie thought. I've pressed too hard.

"Fucking curious again," Gregory said. Sounding a lot like Mako.

"We might do that kind of timing if your information's good," Barkov said. "Might even let you in on the scam."

"I'm not looking to get rich as a smuggler," Donnie told him.

"You're a . . . how do you say, 'cohort' now. You might as well make some money. What's the difference, hey?"

"Maybe ten or twenty years behind walls."

"Still," Barkov said, "in Russia they say, 'Find a ruble in the mud, pick it up.' "

"We don't intend to get caught," Gregory said. "And if we do, there's people that'll take care of it."

This time curious Donnie kept silent. He recognized bait when it trailed past his nose.

"None of it is relevant anyway," Barkov said with a grin. "In our business people get dead more often than they get arrested. They get careless, then they get dead. Think about that, hey, Donnie? You want another beer, my friend?"

23

Donnie had been prying into produce crates since the day he'd gotten the Logan Air job, searching for proof of Italian Mafia drug shipments. Now he stepped up his efforts, and it wasn't long after his conversation with Barkov and Gregory when he discovered in a crate of iced lettuce something other than ice and lettuce.

With another forklift driver, he was unloading a Logan Air cargo plane, and he found himself alone inside the cavernous fuselage. As he often did, he hopped down off his forklift to snoop.

And there it was in the third case he examined. Half encased in ice was a metal cylinder like the ones he'd seen in the cardboard boxes Marie had been seated on in the Westward Ho.

Donnie tried to pry the cylinder out to examine it more closely but at that moment heard the roar of a forklift engine. The tone of the engine changed, became even louder, and he knew the driver of the other forklift was coming up the long ramp of the Hercules transport plane.

Donnie quickly shoved the thin wooden lid back

down onto the case, forcing metal brads back into the soft wood with his gloved hand. Then he moved to the rear of the forklift and pretended to be manipulating the valve on the propane tank.

Navy was driving the other forklift. Once inside the fuselage, the wiry little man braked to a halt. He waited patiently for Donnie, who would have to remount his vehicle, lift up a pallet with its long metal prongs, and back to the side and out of the way so Navy's vehicle could edge past.

Donnie gave the propane tank a whack with the edge of his hand, as if trying to adjust something by force, then climbed onto the forklift and resumed working. As he backed past Navy toward the ramp leading down to the concrete apron, he was looking the other way and couldn't see the expression on Navy's face.

Navy's job was to place his pallet on top of the one Donnie had removed from the plane then drive both pallets of produce into the hangar. While he was doing this, Donnie was to reenter the plane and remove another base pallet.

Donnie sat on his idling forklift, squinting against the cold breeze off the runways and thinking about what he'd found. This didn't make much sense. It was possible that steel vacuum containers were being used to smuggle drugs; it seemed logical that they'd render drug-sniffing dogs ineffective. That the cylinders contained counterfeit bills was unlikely. But most of all, Donnie was curious about why, if the Italians were smuggling in the cylinders, he'd seen them in the boxes at the Russians' Westward Ho Club.

The orange rear of Navy's forklift was visible as he began backing down the plane's cargo ramp. Donnie jerked his forklift's steering wheel to the right and maneuvered so he passed Navy at the base of the ramp, on his way back into the fuselage. He added the touch of gunning the forklift's engine intermittently so it sputtered and seemed to be misfiring. Navy might figure there was something wrong with the engine, or that Donnie was nursing a fuel tank that was running low on propane.

It was when the last pallet was removed and Donnie was driving toward the rack of propane tanks to replace the half-full tank, that he noticed something. As he was passing the nose of the big plane, he glanced up and saw black lettering and insignia on the fuselage, just beneath the cockpit. Nothing unusual about that; many of the planes had their pilot's name or the plane's nickname stenciled there, along with some sort of insignia that was sometimes in color.

But this time the stenciling caught Donnie's attention and held it. It was all in black, the unmistakable silhouette of a primitive flying predator along with identifying lettering: PTERODACTYL.

Donnie knew better than to play innocent and ask Barkov about the steel cylinders. Marie was aware that he'd sneaked a look into one of the boxes she'd been seated on that night in the Westward Ho. Donnie had formed a slight bond of friendship with the woman, but she seemed incapable of resisting the Russians and might even volunteer the information without being asked.

The logical person to share his information with was Jules Donavon.

Rather than wear out the phone in the deli, this time Donnie made his call from a pay phone in the lobby of an upper East Side movie theater that was running a classic film festival.

"The word *pterodactyl* mean anything to you?" Donnie asked. He looked down at the ticket he'd bought just to get far enough into the theater to use the phone. It was for an old Robert Mitchum movie set in Mexico, the one where Mitchum saves Jane Russell from a hit man played by Jack Palance. Donnie had seen it more than once and liked it. Everything was simple in that kind of movie. People were willing to die for love but didn't have to. Other people weren't willing to die for anything but had to. What a shame God wasn't a screenwriter.

"Big bird," Jules said.

"That's the one on *Sesame Street*," Donnie said.

"Different bird altogether. I'm talking extinct giant reptile with wings, cawed like an overgrown crow and scarfed down cavemen like worms."

Maybe in a movie playing here, Donnie thought. "That's the bird," he said. "Pterodactyl was printed on the boxes the cylinders were stored in at the Westward Ho. Today I unloaded a cargo plane named *Pterodactyl* and found one of the steel cylinders in a case of iced lettuce."

"You open it?" Jules sounded keenly interested.

"Didn't get a chance. Here's the thing: this plane had flown in from up north, place called Lang, Canada. I was looking for part of an Italian Mafia drug shipment. Instead I found something the Russian mob must be smuggling in."

"The Russians using the Italian Mafia's drug operation as cover for their own inbound contraband," Donavon said. "You think they're that devious?"

"Sure. There's probably even an old Russian saying that covers it. My guess is the shipments only come in on the plane called *Pterodactyl*, and probably when there's no conflict with a drug shipment."

"Sounds right," Jules agreed. "I guess I don't need to tell you we have to find out what's in those cylinders."

"Could be some kind of explosive," Donnie said.

"Yeah. They might be sophisticated pipe bombs."

"They look more like thermos bottles."

"Thermo-nuclear bombs," Jules mused.

Jules's train of thought had left the station, and Donnie knew better than to try to flag it down. Jules was intent on mulling over the possibility of devastating explosive devices being smuggled into the country and would stay on that track until he thought he had the odds calculated. Compact nuclear devices might not be an impossibility, Donnie thought. It was a microchip, miniaturized world.

"Take advantage of any opportunity to find out what's in the cylinders," Donavon said. "Meanwhile, see if you can figure any kind of schedule on the drug smuggling. Let us know if there's a date set for a major shipment."

"That's what the Russians want me to find out," Donnie said. "I'm not sure what they have in mind, but if the DEA decides on a raid then, it might be awfully crowded."

"Hmm. Lots of guests, drugs, vegetables for hors d'oeuvres, that could turn out to be a hell of a party."

"Don't forget thermo-nuclear devices," Donnie said. "To spike the punch."

"Be careful and watch your back," Jules said, ending the conversation, probably because he wanted to think some more about not-so-miniature mushroom clouds.

Donnie hung up the phone and made his way back through the red-carpeted lobby.

There were about a dozen people standing around now, holding soft drinks and popcorn, waiting for the first showing to end before filing into the auditorium. Donnie detoured slightly to peek in at the movie.

Mitchum and Palance were fighting on top of a cable car dangling above a dizzying drop. It was exciting, but Donnie didn't have much time or inclination to watch the rest of it. He knew who was going to win, who was going to live happily ever after or at least for a while with young Jane Russell.

Art not imitating life, Donnie thought.

24

Donnie dropped by the Westward Ho Club the next evening. Red-vested Bill, the wiry young bartender with the bushy mustache and weary blue eyes, gave him a grin and a nod, and Donnie ordered a Siberian Yellow on tap and sat at a table over near the far wall.

The Westward Ho was warm and smoke-filled, illuminated mostly by neon liquor advertisements. Nobody Donnie knew was around. Three thirtyish guys in jogging suits sat at a table about twenty feet away, nursing mixed drinks. Even in the dim light the gold of their expensive wristwatches and rings glinted as they lifted and lowered their half-empty glasses, sometimes using a free hand to gesture. They might have been upscale yuppies discussing how to buy bonds; more likely they were discussing how best to break arms and legs. Two older men Donnie had never seen before, wearing wrinkled gray suits, sat halfway down the bar. One of them was smoking a pipe with an elaborate curved stem. The other had a waxed handlebar mustache that looked like something from an old tintype. It didn't seem they'd have much in common with the three guys in jogging suits, but Donnie knew they did.

Donnie considered it fortunate to have come to the club when Barkov and Gregory weren't there. He wouldn't have to use uncommon guile or invite suspicion to try to check further on the boxes of steel cylinders in the hall near the restroom.

He sipped his beer and listened to some kind of Slavic music that wasn't half bad leaking from the speakers up near the ceiling. One of the men in suits swiveled down off his stool and walked unsteadily toward the restroom. Donnie waited until he returned before casually standing up from the table and moving toward the hall.

"You want another?" Bill asked from behind the bar.

Donnie nodded and pointed toward the empty beer mug on his table. "Sure. In and out, eh?" He grinned kind of stupidly; maybe he'd been drinking someplace else before coming here.

Knowing Bill would be moving around the bar and might have a line of sight into the hall, Donnie went into the restroom and gave the bartender time to have delivered a fresh beer to the table. Then he opened the restroom door and eased out.

He couldn't be seen by anyone in the bar. Staying to one side of the hall, he edged along a wall and around to the stacked cardboard boxes.

Immediately he saw that something was wrong. There were fewer boxes, and they seemed smaller. He pried up the lid of one of them.

It contained what looked like folded pullover shirts

in plastic bags. Donnie inserted his hand and felt lower in the box.

Nothing but more plastic-wrapped shirts.

He bent lower and searched through another of the boxes.

Same contents.

And none of the boxes was lettered PTERODACTYL.

To Donnie's left was the closed door to the storage room. It was an off chance, but the boxes of cylinders might have been moved in there. He had to look.

Voices drifted from the direction of the bar. Several more people had entered.

Donnie tried the door and found it locked. There was a deadbolt a foot above the knob lock. No give at all in the door.

He sighed and walked back toward the bar area, pretending to check absently with his right hand as if making sure he'd remembered to zip his fly.

Two men and a woman, none of whom Donnie knew, were now sitting at the bar. He dropped back into his chair and took a long pull from the cold mug of beer Bill had left on the table. It gnawed on him that he should have checked on the boxes sooner, that he might have let something important slip away. On the other hand, that the storage room door was now closed and locked suggested the boxes might be inside.

A shadow crossed the table, and Marie lowered herself into the chair across from him. She was wearing a tight red dress tonight, showing uplift and cleavage that made Donnie curious if he was looking at the result of breast implants or if she might be wearing one of those special bras. Maybe that was why they were called Wonder Bras. "How about company?"

"Sure," Donnie said. "What are you drinking?"

"Nothing right now," she said in her slightly broken accent. "I don't want to start too early. I need to keep my wits about me."

"Tonight something special?"

She smiled. "I have to make it seem special every night."

Donnie looked into her eyes, which were an odd color green made to look blue by heavy eye shadow. They were sad eyes, injured and defensive. "What Gregory did to you the other night, does it happen often?"

A sad smile to match the eyes. "Much too often." She lowered her voice a notch. "Thanks for what you said to me afterward. I'm not used to getting much sympathy from anybody else around this place."

"Then why do you come back here?"

She shrugged. "To stay alive."

Donnie nodded. It would be smart for him to ration his questions. This woman might like him, but she lay down regularly with men who might kill him. "Can't quarrel with that reasoning," he said.

He drank while she watched.

"Are you healing okay?" he asked.

"Yes, I always do."

Time was pressuring him. He knew he had to take a chance, despite the fact that she might reveal their conversation to the wrong person. One more question, phrased innocently. He couldn't ask too much of

Marie. "What was in those boxes you were sitting on when you were crying?"

Something happened in the green of her eyes, like an opaque movement in deep water. "Why do you ask?"

"They looked like they were full of Thermos bottles or something. I was gonna see if I could buy one. For work. Maybe I'm outta line, but I figured stolen merchandise moved through here now and then. Just now I saw some different boxes in the hall, with some new-looking shirts in them."

"What makes you think the shirts might be stolen?"

"You don't work in a sweatshop upstairs in your spare time, do you?" Donnie asked with a smile.

"No." She gave him back his smile. "I don't make vacuum bottles, either."

"Oh? So what are those things?"

"Golf shirts, I think. They're dorky looking and have little crossed putters embroidered over the pockets."

"No, I meant the steel cylinders."

"I don't know. Or care. Maybe they *are* vacuum bottles to keep soup warm." She looked directly at him. He knew the look; he'd been on both ends of it.

He said nothing. He'd done this before and knew when to stay quiet.

"They're in the storage room," she said.

He could feel trust and wariness emanating from her at the same time. She needed a friend, wanted hard to believe in him. He felt terrible using her, knowing she was aware she was putting herself in danger because of him. He felt terrible about a lot of things. "Storage room always locked?" he asked.

"Only when there's something in there nobody's supposed to see."

The temperature dropped a few degrees as the street door opened. Marie stood up, fast but not too fast. She didn't want to attract attention with a sudden move, so if whoever entered hadn't been looking right at them, she might have just stopped by the table to say hello to Donnie without sitting down.

"I have to meet Gregory later tonight," she said, and walked toward the bar.

Good luck, Donnie thought.

Barkov had entered the bar. Tomba was with him. They spotted Donnie and moved toward him, waving their greetings. Tomba was wearing a long black coat and looked like a mortician. Barkov had on his stylish tan topcoat. They removed the coats with slow deliberation and hung them on brass hooks mounted on the wall, then gestured for Donnie to join them at the larger table where they sat down.

Donnie got up and ambled over, then sat down across from Barkov. The legs of Tomba's chair scraped on the floor and he stood back up.

"I gotta go to the crapper," he said. "I'll order drinks on the way. You drinking beer, Donnie?"

"Beer it is."

Donnie and Barkov watched Tomba trudge over to the bar and talk to Bill, then head toward the back of the room and the hall to the restroom.

Barkov turned back to look across the table at Donnie. "So this place grows on you, hey?"

"Gotta drink someplace. Might as well be here."

Barkov studied him, squinting hard enough to make

the scar on his face crinkle the flesh beneath one eye. "You don't give much of yourself away, my friend. That's one reason I like you. You're quiet."

"Nobody ever learned much while they were talking."

"Yes, yes, there is a Russian saying to that effect."

"I'll bet."

"We all bet," Barkov said. "Every day in some way, we all gamble, don't you think?"

"In ways large and small," Donnie said, wondering what exactly Barkov was trying to say. Or was Barkov simply being cryptic, ruled by his Russian genes?

Tomba returned from the restroom. He plopped three plastic-wrapped shirts on the table next to the beer steins Bill had just delivered. They were dorky looking and had little crossed putters embroidered above their pockets. "You a large tall?" he asked Donnie.

"Usually."

"I thought so. Here's some shirts for us. They're designer label. *Daragoj!* The real thing."

Donnie prodded one of the plastic bags with his forefinger. "They look like good material."

Two of the shirts were blue, the third was red. They all had an underlying gray zigzag pattern that made him dizzy.

"They're all the same size," Tomba said. "Which one you want?"

"The red one. Especially if it's got a little hammer and sickle sewn over the pocket."

Barkov grinned at him. "That part of Russia is all over. Now we're all capitalists together, hey?"

"Like Bill Gates," Donnie said.

"A very rich man," Tomba said somberly. "Bill Gates, Warren Buffett. Very rich men. Like Rockefeller and J.P. Morgan used to be."

Donnie didn't think the Russians at the Westward Ho were much like American business tycoons. More like cogs in an Italian Mafia operation, stealing or raising money illegally any way they could, feeding the Family coffers. Maybe Zelensky was the equivalent of their Mafia don, as Jules suspected, the thief-in-law.

"Do I owe you for the shirt?" Donnie asked.

"No," Tomba said seriously, "you're with us, at the top of the capitalist food chain."

Barkov grinned handsomely across the table. "You think Bill Gates pays for his shirts?"

Donnie had no answer.

25

Donnie was tired when he entered his apartment that night after leaving the Westward Ho Club. It was almost midnight, and he no longer used any method for determining if someone had entered his apartment in his absence. He knew now that the people he was dealing with were beyond being fooled by that kind of thing. Still, because of his weariness he wasn't his usual cautious self as he keyed the deadbolt lock and pushed the door open.

As soon as he'd closed the door behind him and was reaching for the light switch he heard a faint rustling sound in the darkness of the living room.

He stayed his hand, right now preferring the dark.

After moving smoothly and silently to one side, he stood motionless. Who was waiting for him in the blackness of the room? Marishov? The stalker? As of now they might not realize he was aware of their presence. What did they have in mind? The prospect of another mental or physical working over by Roma and Mako seemed oddly desirable just then.

"Maureen's safe, Joe."

The voice that came to him through the blackness was Elana's.

Donnie felt relief, fear, anger, all at once. Tension released its hold on him.

"You shouldn't be here!" was all he could think to say, though a part of him knew her presence was what he wanted and needed most. The anger welled. "You could fuck up the job, get us all killed—including Daisy!"

"I was careful."

Jesus!

"I didn't have any choice. I had to see you. Had to come here. Don't you understand? I'm goddam suffering!"

"Not alone, you're not." He flipped the wall switch and the lamps on the circuit winked on.

She was seated in the worn armchair. Behind her the drapes were closed, as he'd known from the complete blackness they would be, and her legs were crossed gracefully and demurely, as if she were feigning ease and relaxation during a tense interview. But her delicate features weren't relaxed, nor were her hands, whose fingers clutched the chair's cloth arms. Her blond hair was mussed and fell in wisps over her forehead and ears. There were the two parallel vertical pain lines above the bridge of her nose, more pain in her eyes. She got up out of the chair slowly and stood the way she sometimes did, hipshot with her weight on one leg like a tired dancer.

"We're all suffering," Donnie said, and went to her and held her. He felt her body swell against his as she drew in a deep breath, then contract as she exhaled in a seemingly endless sigh. His own breath and body reacted, imitating hers. He understood why she'd had to come. It was emotion rather than reason, but it was powerful and he knew he had to accept it and make the most of the situation. He knew her, and she wouldn't leave New York.

"Are you sure Maureen's still safe?" he said, careful not to ask where she was, where Elana had traveled from in order to join him.

"She's still under guard," Elana said. "Lily, the others, know their business just like you said. She's safe with them watching over her."

"How did you know where to find me?"

"I knew you were in New York, and I did some eavesdropping on Lily Malony."

"Eavesdropping?"

She looked up into his face then lowered her eyes. "Spying, too, I guess you'd call it."

Donnie shook his head. Beyond the thick drapes the nighttime city rumbled and rushed like a black river. "Can you be sure nobody saw you come here?"

"I think so. I was careful without looking suspicious."

Donnie wondered how she'd accomplished that, but he knew he had no choice other than to believe her. "You have to get out of here. This apartment."

"I know. But does it have to be now?"

"Every minute you're here increases the risk."

"I want to help if I can in this nightmare. If anything happens, I need to know I did everything possible to help Daisy. That I was at least in the right spot."

"That's insane, Elana!"

"I'm sure it is. I'm sure that right now I'm insane with rage and grief and anxiety. But I won't lie to you—it's what I have to do, try to play a part in saving her. What I'm *going* to do."

Donnie moved away from her, then turned his back and walked to the closed drapes. But he didn't part them, didn't look outside and down at the dark street. He was afraid of what he might see, what might see him, like a child unwilling to peer under the bed.

"You don't understand the kind of people we're dealing with," he told her.

"How don't I? I know what they've done. They've taken my child instead of killing my husband, and they plan eventually to kill them both. Isn't that right?"

"More or less," Donnie said in a hoarse whisper. "But you can't help. You'll only hurt Daisy's chances by trying to help."

"I can't simply accept that. I at least have to be close."

"But she isn't here. She's probably still in or around St. Louis."

"You're here. Being close to you is being close to her."

Donnie didn't follow her reasoning and knew why. It wasn't reasoning, it was emotion. Emotion the enemy. He drew his hand down his face, trailing thumb and forefinger and rubbing them for a second into his closed eyes. He knew he was tired, not necessarily thinking straight.

"It would be safer if I stayed here with you and left

early in the morning," Elana said. "Between three o'clock and when the sun comes up."

He couldn't help giving her a dark smile. "Did you read that in one of your mystery novels?"

"Isn't it right?" she asked, not smiling back. "Isn't the time between three o'clock and sunrise when people are most likely to be asleep or off their guard?"

"If you know that, Elana, don't you think the people who might be watching this place know it?"

She raised her head and extended her jaw as if inviting someone to take a punch at her. "Even so, the worst you could say is that my leaving now or just before dawn doesn't make any difference."

He walked over to her and drew her tight to him, feeling the rapid rhythm of her heartbeat enter his body. "It makes a difference to me," he said.

They kissed, and when she pulled away she said, "Tomorrow I'll go to—"

"I don't want to know where you're staying," he interrupted, pressing a finger to her tense lips. "In case anyone asks me, I'd rather not answer no matter how insistent they get."

Saying that brought it home to her. Fear crossed her face like the shadow of something behind him. Her concern wasn't for herself, but for him. He couldn't look away from her, this woman he couldn't stay married to but couldn't exorcise from his thoughts. Was the magnetism between them love? Need? Mutual terror?

"Maybe I *should* go," she said.

Bullshit, he thought. She knew she had him.

"Stay," he told her, and kissed her again.

* * *

In the morning, after she'd gone out into the shadowed street and he watched from the window until she made the corner, Donnie sat back down on the sofa and finished his coffee. Then he made his way downstairs and to the deli and used the phone to contact a sleep-drugged Jules Donavon.

"Elana's here in New York," he said.

That seemed to wake Donavon completely. "Where? And why?"

"I don't know where and don't want to. As for the why, she needs to be close. It's a compulsion. In case she can help in some way."

"She told you that?"

"Yes. A few hours ago. She just left here."

"Here being your apartment?"

"Uh-hm."

"Donnie, Donnie . . . How'd she find you?"

"Did a little prying and spying on Lily."

"I guess it runs in the family."

"I hope not. She did it because she's desperate, Jules. She doesn't realize where it might lead, how she might blame herself."

"Is she desperate enough to do something dangerous?"

"She already has, just doesn't know it."

"I mean, something more, on her own?"

"I don't think so, but it's possible."

"Christ! This operation shows signs of spinning out of control."

"Tell me about it."

"At least with you wearing the wire, we're building a case."

Donnie wasn't thinking about the case just then. "Find out where Elana is, Jules, and watch over her."

"There's not much choice."

"Not much choice in any of this," Donnie said. "We have to keep taking chances. I won't leave the wire in the recycling bin tonight, Jules. I'll risk keeping it here in the apartment and use it more often with the mini-recorder so a mobile unit won't have to be nearby to tape."

"Are you sure you want to take that risk, Donnie? Roma and his friends, and the Russians, know how to toss an apartment. You better do a good job hiding the wire."

"I will," Donnie assured him.

"The other risk," Donavon said, "is that if they discover the recorder on you, they'll destroy the tape and the evidence after they destroy you. There probably won't even be proof they were anywhere near you at the time of your death. It'd cost us in court."

Ice water trickled down Donnie's spine. "Now you sound like a bureaucrat, Jules."

"You know I didn't mean it that way, Donnie. But you also know what we got here is a bureaucracy."

"Yeah, I know. 'Night, Jules."

"It's morning, Donnie."

"Not where I'm standing," Donnie said.

26

Donnie hid the wire and recorder in the back of the refrigerator. After pulling and shoving the old Frigidaire out from the wall, he removed the insulated fireproof panel that covered the motor and compressor compartment. He laid the disconnected miniature cassette recorder behind the unit's electric motor, covering it with the blackened, greasy dirt that collects from oil and condensation around the motor and coils. After tucking the tiny microphone out of sight behind a metal brace, he ran the wire itself alongside or intertwined with the wiring of the refrigerator, again using oily dust for cover, so that the recording device looked like part of the refrigerator's power and condensing units and electrical circuitry. Unless whoever looked there knew appliance repair, it wouldn't be found.

After snapping the panel back in place and making sure it didn't look as if it had been disturbed, he shoved the refrigerator back against the wall. Retrieving and replacing the recording equipment would be a lot of trouble each time, but it was worth it for the security.

The next day at work Mako approached Donnie as

he was changing fuel tanks on the forklift. The big man stood silently, close-set eyes peering around his bent nose at Donnie while he waited for the roar of a jetliner to subside.

In the reverberating silence he said, "There's a bar and restaurant near your apartment, over on West 83rd, name of Tastes Like Chicken. You be there tonight around eight o'clock, have yourself a drink, sit in a booth near the back."

Donnie blinked in disbelief. "Nobody calls their restaurant Tastes Like Chicken."

Mako gave his slow, sharklike smile. "Idea in this case is the owner's trying to discourage the restaurant business, concentrate on drinks."

Donnie understood. "The place is a front. For what?" He wished he were wearing the wire.

But it didn't matter; Mako wasn't talkative today. "You don't have to know. Nothin' you learn is long-term anyways. Just be there like you're told."

"Vinnie Roma going to be there, too?"

"Get fucked," Mako said, and turned and swaggered away toward the hangars.

"I'll take that for a yes," Donnie said.

He was wearing his wire as he approached Tastes Like Chicken, a squalid little place squeezed between a dry cleaner and a used-book shop. Taped to the inside of the window was a sun-bleached menu that was unreadable. It was impossible to see in. A faded fern that was obviously artificial seemed to have found life and looked as if it had grown explosively and was trying to force its way outside through the glass.

Donnie didn't blame the plastic plant. Tastes Like Chicken's interior was as rundown and depressing as its exterior. He saw little indication of any sort of restaurant business. There was a brass-railed bar beneath plastic shaded light fixtures on chains that disappeared in the dimness toward an invisible ceiling. On each of the pyramid shaped shades was the red silhouette of an axe-wielding man chasing a fleeing chicken above the letters TLC. The same silhouette and lettering was on the tattered awning outside, also stenciled on the wall above the back bar mirror. There was a large microwave oven, a cold grill, and a faded menu, twin to the one in the window, on the same wall—TLC was a restaurant, all right. But only nominally.

Donnie could guess the kind of place it really was, a front for minor transactions involving stolen merchandise or hot money, a safe haven where meetings could be held and criminal ideas could be hatched and explored before being put into action. He had been in places like it, dealing supposedly stolen jewelry to fences when he was living as Donnie Brasco.

The bartender was bigger than Mako but had a beatific Irish face that seemed to smile even in repose, and eyebrows and ears that marked him as a former boxer or wrestler. He looked at Donnie, his only customer, inquisitively, as if to ask why was he here; yet another unknowing citizen had wandered in from the street and had to be discouraged.

Then an expression of amiable comprehension brightened his features. Roma or Mako must have told him Donnie would be by this evening.

Donnie asked for a Heineken then carried the bottle and glass to one of the back booths. Though TLC was small, the wood booths were wide and could easily seat six people. Donnie settled himself on the booth's derriere-polished oak bench, staying to the outside. He didn't like being squeezed against the wall when seated in booths, but knew he probably would be when Vinnie Roma and Mako arrived. Near the paneled wall was an arrangement of condiments—half-full ketchup bottle, mustard jar, salt and pepper shakers; more evidence of restaurant trade that probably didn't exist. On the wall was a large framed black-and-white photo of a boxer in fighting trim and stance, his dark hair neatly combed and his left hand held high. He was smiling and looked as if he might be a younger version of the bartender with the angelic, thickened features and mangled ears.

It was 8:05 when the door opened and Vinnie Roma and Mako entered. They had Freddy with them. Freddy who yearned to open people with his carpet knife. Donnie didn't think this had the makings of an up evening.

The three men stopped at the bar to order their drinks, then advanced toward where Donnie was sitting.

Mako sat down heavily next to Donnie, scooting him over against the wall. Donnie held on to his glass and bottle so they came with him as he slid across the smooth oak. Freddy and Roma sat opposite them, Roma on the outside. It had warmed up a little tonight, and the other men were dressed like Donnie, in slacks and windbreakers, except for Roma who had on a light tan jacket with a tiny British union jack emblem on the chest. The jacket was trimmed all over with brown leather as if he were some kind of English sportsman. It even had a padded leather right shoulder patch to help absorb the shock of sporting rifle recoil should Squire Vinnie deign to pheasant hunt.

The bartender brought three more beers and placed bottles and glasses on the table, making sure each glass was centered on a cork coaster boasting TLC's distinctive fleeing chicken logo.

"Thanks, Ig," Roma said. When the bartender was back behind the bar and out of earshot, Roma looked at Donnie and said, "That's Iggy. He was the number twelve ranked middle-weight fighter about twenty years ago."

"He's a heavyweight now," Donnie said.

"And still packs a punch," Roma said. "Iggy got outta the fight game without his brains being scrambled. So don't take him light, if you get my meaning."

"Which is that he's reserve troops," Donnie said.

"Like a one-man army," Mako said. "And he ain't nearly so nice a fella as he looks."

Freddy just stared and grinned at Donnie. Tonight he looked more like young Richard Widmark than like Frank Sinatra. Crazy around the eyes like Widmark in the movie *Kiss of Death* and then a lot of movies afterward. Donnie wondered if Freddy was carrying his carpet knife.

". . . fucking look at me when I'm talking to you," Roma was saying.

Donnie looked.

Roma was frowning at him. "In my position," Roma said, "I gotta be able to weigh risks and values."

Where the hell was this going? Donnie wondered. He pretended to scratch his crotch, adjusting the voice-activated miniature recorder where it was taped to his left inner thigh alongside his testicles. A quick search by feel might not reveal it there.

"I mean," Roma went on, "how valuable are you and how much should I risk you?"

"You're asking *me*?"

"Not at all."

"You might notice, ass face," Mako said, "we don't ask you much. We tell you."

"What I'm saying," said Roma, "is that an operation is about to go down where it makes sense for me to risk losing you in the La Guardia scam."

Donnie looked at all three men, who dummied up and looked everywhere but back at him.

"It must be dangerous," Donnie said.

Roma sipped his beer and made a face. "Oh, it is that."

"Just the job for somebody already dead," Mako said.

Freddy giggled insanely. Donnie wondered if he'd seen *Kiss of Death.*

"Something else about it, I bet," Donnie told them. "The higher ups in the Mafia know about this one and are calling the plays, and they don't know about La Guardia."

"La Guardia's going to be a surprise," Roma said. "*I'm* going to be a surprise."

"The dons don't like surprises."

"Everybody don't like somethin'," Mako said.

"Don't try and get philosophic," Roma said to him. Then he leaned over the table and fixed his gaze on Donnie. "Remember that big construction crane fell in Times Square, killed a guy and fucked up the traffic for weeks?"

"Yeah, helluva accident."

"No accident," Roma said. "Business. Union business. Like the Arrington Hotel fire on the East Side. Business."

"Four people died in that one," Donnie said. "Not business—murder." He knew he was getting solid evidence on tape; the Mafia and factions within the unions putting pressure on companies and employees.

Roma smiled and shrugged. "In business, people get hurt. Like you might get hurt in the next business gets transacted."

"You expect me to cause another construction tragedy?"

"No. Don't need another right now."

"Burn down another hotel?"

"Been done, son," Mako said.

"Forget the hotel. This has more to do with a parking garage here on the West Side, gets most of its business from the theater district, people driving in from Jersey or wherever to see the latest hot ticket."

"You seen *The Lion King*?" Freddy asked suddenly.

The other three men stared at him.

"Owners of this garage need a lesson taught to them," Roma said darkly.

Donnie said, "*Cats.* I saw that one. *Cats* might run forever."

Roma kicked him hard in the shins under the table. "This is a fucking business meeting! Do not talk that kinda shit! Do not fucking fuck with me, fuckhead!"

Everybody at the table was silent for a moment, letting the reverberations of the outburst subside.

"Parking garages are mostly concrete," Donnie said. "They don't burn well."

"That's a true fact," Roma said. "That's why you're going into this one with a bomb."

27

It's this way," Vinnie Roma said, using a napkin to dab a beer foam mustache from his upper lip. "There's what you might call a dispute with the owners of the MetroMotor parking garage on the West Side."

"Takes two to make a dispute," Donnie said, keeping in mind he was wearing a wire. The more Roma talked, the closer he came to conviction and prison.

"All you gotta know is the party I represent wants a bomb to go off in the parking garage. But that's a dangerous thing to do, plant a bomb. A guy could get caught, might even get himself killed."

"We ain't the best technicians when it comes to bombs," Mako said with a sadistic smile. "Thing might go off in your hand if you stub your toe and jiggle it."

Roma looked a dagger at him. "What I figure is it's worth chancing losing you out at La Guardia to have you carry in the bomb."

Donnie thought he understood. Roma had gotten his Family orders to deal with the parking garage owners. The idea would be to scare them and get them in line with their protection payments or whatever part of their business the mob wanted. Probably Roma was the one who had come up with the details of the plan. Capos like him were given their instructions, then were expected to think for themselves.

Roma had decided it might look bad for him if a Mafia soldier was caught or killed. If Donnie was killed Roma would come up with a story about having figured out who he was and tricking him into carrying the bomb. The Family wouldn't know about Daisy, since the kidnapping was Roma's lone play. Roma might even get a pat on the back for using Donnie in such a manner, and collect the half-million-dollar bounty for his life. And with Daisy's life in the balance, Donnie had great incentive not to be caught. So Roma's risk wasn't as grave as he pretended. He knew Donnie would do the job and not bungle. He knew Donnie had the nerve. Maybe Roma wasn't so sure about the likes of Mako or Freddy.

And of course there was something more: This was a test. If Donnie went through with it they could be sure they had him. An active FBI agent wouldn't set off a bomb in a parking garage and possibly kill someone. It would take a broken FBI agent to do such a thing, and that's what they wanted to know for sure about him, that he was broken and he was theirs.

"Whose idea is this bombing?" Donnie asked, trying again to get information on tape.

"You're not working for the FBI now," Roma said. "They only think you are. You don't have to know anything other'n what you're told to do."

"This has gotta be union," Donnie said. "Sam Vargo's gotta be in on this."

"All that's gotta be," Roma said, "is you marching to your orders like a good soldier that's been drafted."

"So when do I do it?"

"Ain't he cooperative?" Freddy said from across the table.

"He knows his choices," Mako said, "which are none." He shoved Donnie hard up against the wall with his elbow for emphasis.

"You take in the bomb day after tomorrow, about three in the morning," Roma said. "There won't be hardly any cars parked there, so you got a chance to get in and out without being seen. It's not in my plan to lose you."

"That's reassuring." Donnie remembered what Elana had said about the early morning hours being ideal for stealth. "How much time will I have to get away after the bomb's planted?"

"Five minutes by the clock. That don't sound like much, but it'll give you plenty of time to get back to the car, where we'll be waiting to congratulate you."

"What kind of timer will the bomb have?"

Roma laughed. "That doesn't matter to you. You'll just have to trust it."

"Like you can trust us," Mako said.

"I'm worried the timer might have a loose connection, like you," Donnie said.

"You just be ready to go," Roma said to Donnie. "We'll be by your place about two forty-five to pick you up. You'll get the rest of your instructions then." He swiveled in the wooden seat and stood up from the booth, patted his stomach. "You got more questions, keep 'em to yourself."

The other two men slid out of the booth and stood flanking Roma.

"By the way," Roma said, "we know about your ex-wife moving in over on West 86th. We don't like you not telling us about it, but we don't much care if she's in town. She's just something else we can hold over your head. Keep in mind that if you screw up with this bomb or fail to go through with the job, she'll suffer."

"That'll be my job," Mako said. "I been passin' time thinkin' how I'm gonna do it."

"I was watching the night she spent in your apartment," Freddy said through his Widmark sneer. "You must be hard up, fuckin' your ex."

Donnie took a long pull on his beer, from the bottle rather than the glass, keeping his anger in check.

"Be awake and alert when we come to pick you up," Roma said. "I know I don't have to remind you to wear dark clothes." He headed for the door, trailing his lesser goons. "The drinks are on me," he called back over his shoulder.

Donnie decided to wait a while before leaving, finishing his beer.

He was in a box, all right. He couldn't detonate a bomb in a parking garage. He couldn't refuse. His stomach was arranging itself in complicated knots, and he saw that his hand was shaking as he poured what was left of the beer into his glass. He tried not to think about Daisy. Or Elana. His thoughts were jumbled, rattled. It would have been easy to panic. What he needed was a way out, but he knew he wasn't going to think of one sitting here.

Maybe because there wasn't one.

As Donnie went out the door, Iggy the genial giant bartender smiled and nodded good evening to him. "You take care."

28

Tucked between stamped, empty envelopes anyone watching would asssume to be letters or paid household bills, was the envelope containing the cassette of last night's conversation with Roma. Donnie dropped everything into a mailbox. Then, since the warm weather was holding, he walked to the address Donavon had given him over the phone.

Elana had phoned and wanted to see him, and they'd made a date to meet at a pancake house on Third Avenue. It was popular and would be crowded on a Saturday morning; usually on weekend mornings diners were clustered on the sidewalk waiting for available tables. Plenty of cover and diversion. Donnie and Elana wouldn't be very noticeable together.

The pancake house was on the East Side, and Donnie had decided to let Elana get there first. He wanted to see where she lived, to follow her from her apartment to where they were supposed to meet. Partly this was innate caution. And he wanted to know if anyone else might be following her.

As he watched from across West 86th Street, Elana emerged from a brick apartment building and buttoned her thigh-length gray coat with a fur collar. She stood in front of the door and glanced around, the breeze rustling her blond hair where it wouldn't stay pinned up. Then she squared her shoulders, tucked a strand of hair behind her ear, and began to walk.

Staying well back, Donnie fell in behind her. She walked to a subway stop not far from her apartment. It was crowded even for a weekend morning, so he had no trouble staying out of sight. When the train pulled in he boarded the car behind hers, standing where he could see her gray coat through the connecting doors. When she transferred to the crosstown subway, he rode in the same crowded car but at the rear. His gaze moved around the car, then the platform as the train pulled away. Only a few of the faces on the train were the same, had made the transfer. There seemed nothing suspicious about any of them.

When the train stopped at the Third and Lexington station and many of the passengers crowded out, Donnie looked to the front of the car. Elana hadn't yet gotten out. She was standing a few feet inside the car waiting for several people ahead of her to move.

Donnie waited until the last moment, then called her name.

She turned, surprised to see him, glanced at the still open door, then smiled curiously and instead of getting off moved along the car toward him. She'd taken only a few steps before the doors slid closed, the speakers in the car uttered an unintelligible announcement, and the subway began to move, picking up speed fast. Donnie watched the people on the platform outside the windows glide past.

"Would this be a coincidence?" Elana asked, holding tight to the same vertical steel bar he was gripping. There were only about a dozen other passengers left in the car.

"There really isn't a lot of coincidence in life," Donnie said, bracing himself against the subway's rock and sway.

At the next stop he touched her elbow, then led her out onto the platform.

"Is this because someone might have followed you?" Elana asked, turning her face away from the wind stirred by a westbound train arriving on the parallel track.

"Or followed you," Donnie said.

She seemed to think about that, then said, "Nobody knows I'm in New York."

"Except for the Mafia."

She stopped walking beside him and looked up at him. "How *could* they know?"

"They must have been watching my apartment when you were there, then followed you. They know where you're staying."

"You're sure?"

"They told me."

Now she seemed angry, walking again, so fast he had to hurry to keep up with her. "Those bastards!"

Donnie didn't contradict her. "They don't mind that you're here," he said. "They see you as added leverage they can use to control me."

She slowed momentarily and glanced up at him. "Is it?"

He nodded.

"I'm sorry. I have to be here. I still think I have to be here."

He smiled. "I wasn't trying to change your mind. But it'll be best if you're not in the middle of things."

"I know; leave it to the professionals. I can do that up to a point."

He wished she could stay out of the investigation altogether but knew better than to tell her so again. She might be devastated if she didn't think she'd done everything possible to help Daisy. But she might feel worse knowing something she'd done had caused Daisy's death. Donnie's mind recoiled. He wouldn't let himself contemplate the possibility that they'd both feel that way.

Instead of pancakes they had omelets and toast at a diner in Queens.

Over second cups of coffee, Donnie said, "I apologize for spying on you."

"That's all right. I understand. I wanted to meet you to ask about Daisy."

He cradled his steaming coffee cup with both hands, letting the heat seep into his palms and set up an ache in his fingers. "The people who have her might have screwed up," he said. He saw the flare of hope in Elana's eyes and hurried to explain so it wouldn't burn too bright. "They might have paid for things by credit card or check. That means we can trace the money, maybe find out where she is."

"You think she's all right?" She bowed her head, bit her lip. "I know it's a stupid question, and one you can't answer for sure . . ."

He reached across the table and rested his hand on

her wrist. Her flesh was cool. "I can't answer for sure, but there's every reason to believe she hasn't been harmed."

"Yet." She was struggling not to cry, or maybe not to scream.

"The folks looking for her are the best in the world at finding people," he reminded her.

"Speaking of which, do you think I should move? I mean, if the Mafia knows my address, maybe it doesn't make sense for me to stay there."

"It wouldn't make any difference. Once they're onto you, they stick. And even if you could sneak past them, they're pretty good at finding people, too."

"What if I moved in with you?"

"That'd be dangerous."

"Just for tonight?"

He squeezed her wrist. "I wish you could, but it wouldn't be smart."

She nodded and pulled her arm away, wouldn't look at him. "Anyway," he said, "this wouldn't be the night for it. There's something I need to do early tomorrow morning."

29

They were on time to the minute.

Donnie, wearing his wire with the button microphone, was standing in the vestibule at 2:45 A.M. watching the dark street when a white five-year-old Oldsmobile pulled to the curb. Mako, wearing black slacks, white shirt, and black windbreaker, piled out of the passenger-side door, ready to ring the apartment's doorbell and fetch Donnie. Instead, Donnie stepped outside to meet him.

"Hey, you eager to get shredded?" Mako said with a grin.

Donnie shrugged. "Why not get it over with?"

"Donnie Brassballs," Mako said. He got back in the car, and Donnie climbed in the backseat with Freddy. Freddy had on way too much cologne or deodorant and smelled like a department store perfume counter.

Vinnie Roma was behind the steering wheel. Donnie remembered he'd always fashioned himself a skilled driver. More than anything, Roma had liked to brag about narrow escapes and his driving finesse as he, Donnie, and some of the other Mafia soldiers played gin or poker to pass the time between criminal activities. Donnie, and a few of the others, had come to the conclusion that Roma was full of crap, but now Donnie wondered. Roma was driving tonight, which meant he thought he had the best chance for success with himself behind the steering wheel. Maybe it was Roma who'd been driving the night the black Bronco had matched Donnie's car move for move, then caught up with it in the park.

"You up for this?" Roma asked Donnie over his shoulder, as the Olds pulled away from the curb.

"I was already asked that."

"Watch your fuckin' mouth," Freddy said next to him.

"You mean follow your example?"

"He don't like our company," Mako said, sounding mock hurt.

"There's worse places you could be than with us here in this car," Roma told Donnie. "Like in a long box lined with plush velvet."

"Think of it that way," Mako said, "and we don't seem so bad."

"I would miss the camaraderie," Donnie said.

Roma ran a stop sign and turned a corner. Dumb. "What you don't wanna miss is any of your instructions," he said, heading downtown. Donnie hoped Donavon knew what he was talking about. The Olds hit a pothole and jarred the hell out of everyone. Its suspension was shot.

"This isn't your usual class of wheels," Donnie said.

"It was borrowed for the occasion," Freddy said.

Mako snorted. "Bet the fuckin' thing used to be a

cab, the way it rides. It oughta have new shocks. This was a nice car one time. What's wrong with people? Why don't they take care of their stuff?"

"Let's just concentrate on taking care of business," Roma said.

"Where's the bomb?" Donnie asked. "If I'm gonna blow up a parking garage, I need a bomb. You guys didn't forget it, did you?"

"It's in the trunk," Roma said, "where you're gonna be if you don't shut up and listen. I've had about enough of your wise-ass remarks. If you're scared, you got a right. But let off pressure some other way than with your tongue. Try'n do some serious listening so you don't fuck this thing up."

Talk away, Donnie thought, making sure his jacket was parted so it wouldn't block the button mike.

Roma could drive, all right. He shuffled the steering wheel expertly through his hands as he took a corner, then veered around a double-parked cab. He never took his eyes off the dark, damp street as he talked. "Pretty soon we're gonna be at the parking garage. You're gonna get out, go to the trunk, and get a black leather briefcase out. You bring it around to me and I'll reach through the window and arm the bomb inside it."

He drove on silently.

Donnie knew that once the bomb was armed he was in real danger of getting shredded by an explosion, just as Mako had suggested. Carrying an armed bomb in a briefcase given to him by these guys was already being halfway to heaven. When it came to bombs, they weren't exactly Unabombers with mathematicians' precision and skill. He imagined himself standing outside the car, hearing a soft ticking coming from the briefcase in his hand, coming from a timer that for all he knew was makeshift or set wrong.

"Then what?" Donnie asked.

"Then I'll tell you what to do next."

The garage was on a quiet side street of closed businesses. It was a drab concrete building whose entrance was blocked by pull-down steel shutters marked with years of graffiti. Above the first floor the building had open sides, where the ramps led to parking on the upper levels.

Roma let the Olds glide past the garage, then circled the block and parked on the other side of the street about a hundred yards away from it.

"The place looks locked tight," Donnie said. "How do I get inside?"

"There's a wood door to the left of the second overhead steel door. It looks locked but it's not. You go on in. Everything's been arranged."

"You parked back here so you don't get buried when the building comes down?"

"It's not coming down, 'cause you're gonna plant the bomb on the next to top level. We want lots of damage, but we also want the place to be able to reopen." Roma rested his elbow on the seatback and contorted his body so he could look Donnie in the eye. "Time for talk is over. Go back to the trunk and get the bomb."

Donnie climbed out of the car and stood in the

silent, deserted street that would be a bustling commercial avenue tomorrow—if it wasn't closed off due to bomb debris. The night was cool and clear, with plenty of stars. He had to ask himself, how could this have happened? Why was he going to do such a terrible thing on such a beautiful night?

He heard the trunk lid pop open as Roma worked the release inside the car. The right front window glided down. "Vinnie says get the fuckin' bomb!" Mako whispered harshly.

Donnie walked around to the trunk and raised the lid that was already up a few inches.

Inside the carpeted trunk sat a large black leather briefcase with a shoulder strap. Donnie picked it up by its handle, surprised by its weight, then shut the trunk and walked around to the driver's window.

Roma had the window down. "Hold that up here," he said.

When Donnie lifted the briefcase waist high, Roma opened it, reached inside, and seemed to press some buttons.

After snapping the briefcase shut, he looked up at Donnie. "You wearing a watch?"

"Yeah." Donnie let his jacket sleeve ride up and rotated his wrist. "Almost three o'clock."

"It should take you five minutes to plant the bomb and get back out here. We're gonna be counting from the time you enter the building. This is simple, so I'm only gonna say it once. The elevator's not running, so you take the stairs up to the fourth floor, orange level, and plant the bomb at the base of a concrete pillar. You come down the same way, then leave by the door, walk fast but casual back to us. Everything goes right, you oughta be getting back in this car at ten minutes after three."

"Sounds tight."

"Gettin' tighter all the time," Mako said through his vicious grin. "Like a geriatric pussy."

"The bomb's timer's ticking away," Roma said. "Go. Now. Fast but don't run."

Donnie crossed the street and hustled down the block toward the parking garage. He knew it was possible Roma had decided to end his plan to have him spy on the Russian Mafia. Or maybe his Mafia bosses had learned of it and ordered it ended. Ordered Donnie killed. There was no guarantee the bomb's timer wasn't set for five minutes, and not ten. Donnie might be scheduled to die in the parking garage explosion.

He saw the wooden door right away, painted a weathered green, traces of old notices and advertisements still stuck to it. Without hesitation he turned the knob, pushed in on the door, and it opened. Planning. At least something had gone right.

Donnie was inside and standing at the base of an angled flight of steel stairs. Each landing appeared to be lit by a single, yellow bulb dangling on a cord dropped from the landing above.

He slung the briefcase's strap over his right shoulder and began climbing the stairs. Fast. Praying this was going to work as planned.

By the time he reached the Orange Level he was breathing hard. There were actually a few cars still parked there, an old Caddie and one of those three-ton off-road vehicles that belonged out in the African bush someplace instead of in a city where there were no rhinos.

There was a damp coating on the concrete floor, and the night wind angled in every which way through the open sides where the ramp serpentined its way up.

Donnie didn't look around. Instead he set the briefcase down at the base of a concrete pillar, then spun on his heel and headed back toward the stairs. As he walked he let his eyes roam right and left, but he saw nothing moving in the darkness. He wasn't surprised.

It seemed to take longer going down the stairs than climbing them. Donnie let his body almost fall forward, catching his weight with quick little steps from stair to stair. But something seemed to slow his descent, like thick syrup he could barely move through. Seconds had to be passing like telephone poles zipping past the window of a speeding train.

Finally he was at the wooden door. He threw himself at it then remembered it opened inward. When he tugged at the paint-crusted knob, the door opened reluctantly.

He was outside in the crystalline cold air. Without bothering to close the door behind him, Donnie walked fast toward the white Olds parked down the block. Even from this distance he could see heavy clouds of exhaust fumes lying low as if clinging to the street behind it, blossoming out. The car reminded him of a space shuttle shot that was ready to go.

Staying controlled, his willpower keeping his legs

moving steadily and not too fast, he strode to the car's right rear door.

Freddy lost his nerve and flung the door open as Donnie approached.

Donnie lowered himself into the car and pulled the door shut. "Drive this sonuvabitch!" he said to Roma.

The engine was already running. Roma jerked the shift lever to Drive and started to make a tight U-turn so they wouldn't have to pass the garage.

That's when there was a thunderous explosion.

Donnie strained to see out the window of the canted car. Dense black smoke was rolling from between the layers of concrete at a corner of the building on the fourth-floor parking level. The explosion and smoke were nowhere near where Donnie had left the briefcase.

"That'll get your goddam fillings buzzin' in your molars," Mako said, using a thick forefinger to plug his right ear.

Sirens were sounding in the distance even before the Olds reached the intersection. Roma made a hard left, the centrifugal force sliding Freddy up against Donnie. Donnie shoved him away as the car picked up speed.

Suddenly the Olds's interior was infused with a dull red flashing.

"Holy fuck!" Freddy said, twisting around to stare out the rear window.

A car was on their tail, unmarked, sporting a flashing red rooflight.

"Better pick it up," Mako said calmly, and Roma stomped hard on the accelerator.

The car behind them fell back, but not far.

Roma made a right, then a left turn, almost hitting some kind of delivery van. If they were lucky the van would block the street and stop the pursuing car. Or maybe the car would hit it and end the chase.

They weren't lucky.

"Still sticking to us," Mako said, looking behind them and beyond Donnie out the back window. The ominous red cast still flickered in the Olds.

Roma made a right turn down a narrow side street lined with parked cars. Donnie's heart leaped.

The Olds gained speed, flicked an outside rearview mirror off a parked Cadillac, then burst out onto a wide avenue. Donnie thanked God there hadn't been any cross traffic. As Roma yanked on the wheel, tires screamed, and the Olds rocked into a two-wheel turn.

Now they were a block over from the parking garage, on a parallel street, speeding back in the direction they'd come from. Mako was peering out the back window intently. Donnie was aware of Freddy beside him swiveling his head every few seconds to look. Roma was hunched over the steering wheel, staring straight ahead. Donnie turned to look back.

The car with the red roof light broke from the side street, spun so that its headlights played wildly over buildings on each side of the avenue, and wound up on the sidewalk facing away from the Olds.

"Got 'em!" Mako yelled. "Dumb bastards spun out!"

"Turn! Turn someplace, for Chrissakes!" Freddy screamed in a high voice.

Roma made a left at the corner, then a right at the next intersection.

He dropped the speed a bit and wound through side streets, then they were on Park Avenue, where there was sparse traffic. The Olds slowed to the speed limit as two police cars sped past them in the opposite direction, sirens yodeling. As Roma turned off Park, a fire engine roared past with siren screaming and lights flashing.

"Some show, huh?" Freddy said, all man at slower speed. "Shame it's over."

The Olds slowed some more, and Roma veered to the inside lane to follow a cab.

"We're clear," Mako said, turning to face forward again.

"Beautiful driving, Vinnie," Freddy said.

Donnie saw Roma's right cheek crinkle in a grin. Freddy began to giggle.

Mako wasn't laughing. "You did all right, Donnie Brassballs," he said, swiveling his head almost all the way around to look back at Donnie. "Fuckin' FBI mad bomber."

"Amazing what somebody'll do when they got no choice," Roma said.

Showing off his wheel skills some more, Roma swung the Olds in a left with a flourish and headed back toward Donnie's apartment. "So you get to live another day," he said to Donnie.

And so does Daisy, Donnie thought.

At the lower edge of his vision he could see his shirt front vibrating with his shallow breathing. He doubted if the button mike was picking up anything but his heartbeat and Freddy's inane giggling. Sirens still sounded blocks away, like a distant wolf pack closing in on prey.

Donnie zipped up his jacket to the neck, suddenly cold. The hell with the wire.

30

It was five A.M., still dark, when Donnie walked down to the all-night deli to phone Donavon. The streets were almost deserted. Only a garbage truck and a few cabs passed him on his walk to the corner. The truck's taillights stopped halfway down the next block, and Donnie heard metal cans clanging around, then the grinding roar of the crusher.

The old Korean guy behind the deli counter was watching a black-and-white movie on a tiny TV with a screen about the size of a matchbox. A woman's bare leg filled the diminutive screen. The man hardly glanced up as Donnie nodded to him and walked toward the back of the store and the phone.

"They buy into it?" Jules Donavon asked as soon as Donnie had called and identified himself.

"Seemed to. I almost did, myself." Donnie knew that no sooner had he planted the briefcase bomb than concealed FBI technicians had hurried to disarm it. The explosion the four men in the car had heard was the detonation of several flash bang grenades, usually employed to stun occupants of apartments or houses about to be stormed by SWAT teams. Most of the dense black smoke had simultaneously been generated by devices designed to lay down cover for similar operations.

"Tomorrow morning," Donavon said, "the papers and TV news will report the bombing, say several cars were destroyed and a man was killed."

"The garage owners are going along with that?"

"They don't have much choice. They were in bed with the mob, now they want to climb out, and they need us if they wanna stay out of prison. Or worse."

Donnie knew what *worse* was: death at the hands of Mafia hit men. The garage owners would stay silent, then do as instructed. Just as Donnie had done when the Mafia had pulled his strings. It kept coming home to him again and again that nobody had much choice in his world.

"We accomplished our purpose," Jules said, "assuming you got good tape."

"I dropped it in the mailbox on the way to the phone," Donnie said. "It should be solid evidence to link Roma and the other two with the bombing. Some of it might not be clear, though. There was a lot of excitement in the car."

"I'll just bet. We laid back during the chase, could have had you a few times."

"Roma would be disappointed to hear that. He thinks he's Indy 500 material."

"He's on his way to where he'll be able to watch the race every year on prison TV. He'll trust you completely now, Donnie, because you passed your exam. You're one of them."

"You might think of another way to put it."

"You know what I mean. You've strayed outside your agent's role and broken the law, and they'll think you killed a civilian."

"Who'd I kill?" Donnie asked.

"Read the paper tomorrow—or later this morning. Be surprised, just like you would be if it was for real. Safer that way."

"Anything on Daisy yet?"

"No, but something'll break soon. It has to."

Donnie knew nothing had to; only some people had to. "I better get back, get some sleep before I go in to work."

"We're gonna build on their trust, Donnie. You tell the Russians about the bombing. Later, you're gonna tip off both sides about a DEA drug raid out at La Guardia. Tell Mako you learned about it from the Bureau so it'll be credible, then tell the Russians you learned it from the Italians."

Lies were what it was all about. Playing people against each other. "Let me know whenever," Donnie said.

"Will do. How about you, Donnie? You okay?"

"Sure." Donnie felt unsteady, and his eyes were burning. Tension flowing out of him. Weariness settling in. "Right now," he said, "what I'm gonna do is go back to the apartment and sleep."

"You can do that without worrying," Jules said. "I talked to Bert Clover just before you called. No one other than your guardian angel is watching you tonight. You earned your stripes with Roma."

"I'll try to think of Clover with a halo and wings," Donnie said.

"And a gun."

"'Night, Jules. Or morning."

"You did good, Donnie. They think they got you last night—you got them."

"Tell me about it," Donnie said, and hung up.

On the way to work later that morning Donnie stopped the car and got a *Times* out of a machine. The story of the parking garage bombing was front page. The man reported killed was Roger Beavers, identified as a medical supply salesman from the midwest. His wife and two teenage kids had been notified. Very impressive, considering Beavers didn't exist. Everything but a photograph.

As Donnie got back in the Honda and continued the drive to La Guardia, he experienced an unexpected feeling of satisfaction. It was sweet when everything went right. No one had been hurt last night, but as far as Roma and his thugs knew, they'd caused the kind of destruction they wanted, and soon they would be in negotiations with the weakened and subdued owners of the bombed garage. Even more weakened and subdued than Roma knew, because they'd be taking their cues from the FBI and helping to amass evidence. The only thing about the operation that bothered Donnie was that he knew this kind of secret could remain closely held only so long. Eventually someone—maybe the garage owners, the NYPD, whoever was playing along in the news media—would talk.

Later that morning he set more lies in motion. He approached Mako off to the side of the time clock just before lunch. "I got a phone call from the Bureau this morning with some information you oughta know."

Mako looked him up and down. "So share."

"There's gonna be a drug raid on this place soon."

"When?"

"That I don't know yet. And I might not be able to find out. It'll be DEA. They must have got a tip drugs were moving through here."

Mako faked a yawn. "Else it's just one of their nuisance raids they make every now and then. All they got's their suspicions. They ain't found nothin' yet."

"I thought Roma would wanna make sure they came up empty this time, too, so pass it along."

"You can bet I will."

"What the call was really about," Donnie said, "they asked about the bombing."

Mako perked up and looked more interested.

"Somebody got killed," Donnie told him.

"No shit?"

"It was in the papers and on TV. Didn't you see it?"

"I get most all my news from Geraldo. He covers broader issues."

"Some poor salesman, probably working late, or staying in a hotel nearby, and he went up to his car to get something he needed. Then *bang*!"

"And the poor jerk's dead," Mako said, grinning. "Who gives a fuck except another jerk-off like you? Way I see it, at that hour he was probably comin' back from boinkin' a hooker, cheatin' on his wife, got what he deserved."

"What about the wife?"

"She was probably cheatin' on him, an' now she lost her meal ticket. That's how the world really works."

"It's only how you think. Pathetic."

"Well, go ahead an' feel bad if it'll make you feel better." A cluster of workers who'd just knocked off for lunch was approaching. Mako touched Donnie's arm and guided him to face the opposite direction, then nudged him along. They moved farther away so the men clocking out were more surely beyond earshot. "So when you got this call about the bombin', what else did they ask?"

"What the fuck you think? They wanted to know who did it."

Mako chuckled. "You tell 'em you was the mad bomber?"

"I thought about giving them you," Donnie said, "but I played the innocent."

"You ain't that," Mako said.

You don't know how right you are, Donnie thought.

31

That evening at the Westward Ho Club, Donnie was sitting at the bar with Barkov and Gregory. Barkov was sharp in a tan sport coat and darker tan slacks, yellow shirt with solid mauve tie. Gregory had on his expensive gray-and-maroon jogging suit and complicated running shoes. Donnie was wearing black sport coat, gray slacks, blue shirt without a tie—and his wire.

They'd had several Siberian Yellows on tap, though Donnie hoped the other two men hadn't noticed he'd only drunk a little more than half of his before fresh rounds were ordered. Nobody seemed the slightest bit drunk. Donnie decided the Russian Mafia could hold its liquor better than the Italians.

There was no one near them at the bar. The little bartender with the squinty eyes and seamed face was working down at the other end, talking single malt scotch with a guy in a suit and tie. The scotch drinker looked like a straight citizen except for a scarred forehead and clouded left eye, and hands like a medieval peasant farmer's dangling beneath the white flash of his cuffs.

Donnie and Gregory were seated flanking Barkov, who liked it that way so he could bullshit at his best without raising his voice. He seemed to be an avid baseball fan and had been talking about spring training, how it really started in winter because the Major League season began so early. He thought the Yankees were on their way to another great season, building a dynasty. Donnie thought about asking him why he wasn't a Cincinnati Reds fan. Thought better of it.

Leaning in close so both men could hear, Donnie spoke to Barkov: "I got word there's gonna be a big drug raid soon out at La Guardia."

Barkov had been between breaths and about to take a sip of beer. He set his glass down and looked interested. "Word from the Italians?"

"Who else?"

"Why would they tell you this?"

"They didn't. I was with Roma and Mako when they were excited and not weighing their words. Also some little asshole named Freddy.'

"Carries a carpet knife?" Gregory asked, listening but not looking at Donnie except in the back bar mirror. "Looks like that James Woods actor plays all those creeps?"

"The one," Donnie said, thinking he hadn't considered James Woods for Freddy but it was true there was a resemblance. The jumpiness, the eyes and jaw.

"What was it that excited them?" Barkov asked.

"Some cops were chasing us in their unmarked car with a red light on the roof, detectives or something."

Barkov cocked his head to the side and looked curious. "Chasing you why?"

"The bombing. Parking garage on the West Side. You mighta seen it in the papers."

Barkov's scarred eyebrow rose sharply as he gave Donnie a quizzical smile. "That garage that was on TV, with all the smoke rolling out of it?"

"The one."

"The Italians did this? You were with them?"

"Sure."

Gregory said, "Holy fuck!" Still staring straight ahead at the mirror but looking at Donnie's reflection.

Gregory did take a sip of beer now, then lowered his almost empty glass. He stared at the real Donnie, not the reflection. "Explain, my friend."

"You wanted me to get in with them, learn some things that might interest you, like when they were gonna get a major drug shipment. Well, that's how I got in tight. The shipment *and* the drug raid's what I learned about, though I don't have the date yet. If I hadn't been with them last night, I wouldn't know anything about it. I got those scumbags trusting me. I'm even the one that planted the bomb."

Gregory looked at his own gap-toothed grin in the mirror, then shook his head. "This Donnie is a Publishers Clearinghouse prize."

"They'll change the date of the shipment," Barkov said.

"Sure, but the date of the raid won't change. That's when we don't want to have anything like stolen heavy equipment out at La Guardia."

No visible reaction to that *we.*

"Why did they bomb the parking garage?" Barkov asked.

"They wouldn't say, but it's not hard to figure. They were putting some kinda pressure on the garage owner for a payoff or piece of the business. He wouldn't go along, so they thought an explosion might be persuasive."

"Usually is," Gregory said.

"I figure it might be a union thing, too. They said something that made me think Sam Vargo might be in on the deal."

Gregory laughed. "The business agent out at La Guardia? He's too much of a pussy to shake down somebody."

"He could look the other way, though," Donnie said. "Take his cut later for keeping the union out of it."

"What union?" Barkov asked.

Donnie shrugged. "I dunno. Car parkers union, something like that." Playing dumb. "Unions are unions. They all talk to each other, got a kind of union of their own."

"Vargo's exactly the kind of guy would ask for a cut," Gregory said. "Gotta keep his girlfriend in furs and jewels."

"That's what I thought," Donnie said. "Why I bring it up. You ever hear anything?"

Gregory rubbed his chin. "Never. But that doesn't mean you're wrong. There's lots of business goes on between the companies and the union. Like that crane that fell in Times Square a while back. I heard that was a mob-union deal, got some work rules changed, some money paid in for workers health benefits. Only the benefits money will go someplace else, and somebody in the company'll get a kickback."

Barkov said, "There have been rumors about Sam Vargo, how he's working for the union and the company, and the hell with the people he represents."

"Lots of them union business agent assholes are that way," Gregory pointed out.

"Well, you do have courage," Barkov said to Donnie. Without his smile wavering, he asked, "How do you feel about killing that man in the garage?"

"I didn't kill him," Donnie said, "the bomb did."

"But you planted the bomb, my friend. You said so yourself."

"He wasn't there when I planted it. I didn't think anybody'd be killed or even hurt."

"So he's a necessary civilian casualty in a time of war, hey?"

"In a way," Donnie said, "you could say that. Wrong place, wrong time. He's a victim of his own rotten luck."

"And you have no qualms about what you did?"

Donnie lowered his gaze, then looked up at the reflections of both men watching him in the mirror. "I gotta admit I feel bad about it, but I don't see how I could have done anything any different. I needed a way to get in tight with the Italians, so when one came along I took it. Anyway, if I hadn't gone into the parking garage with the bomb, somebody else would have."

Barkov smiled. "That's what guilty men always say to themselves."

"We gonna moralize?" Donnie asked.

Barkov's smile turned slightly sad without seeming to change in any other way. "Too late for that, my friend. All I'm saying is this is a new side of you that I've never seen."

"Side I'm glad to see," Gregory said, hoisting his beer mug.

It took a while, but Donnie finally outlasted Barkov and Gregory. Siberian Yellow caught up with them, and they said goodnight and slid down off their bar stools. Gregory was weaving as he struggled into his coat and walked toward the door. Barkov's shoulders were slumped but he was walking a straight line.

When they were gone, Donnie asked the bartender with the squinty eyes for some black coffee.

"Good idea," the bartender said, when he placed a steaming cup in front of Donnie. "I hate to see guys leave this place the way your two friends did then get behind the wheel of a car."

Donnie nodded agreement. "They take unnecessary risks. It's a genetic thing."

When he'd drunk half his coffee, Donnie got down off his stool and made his way toward the restroom. He figured the bartender would be watching, so he put a little unsteadiness in his walk.

Still no sign of the boxes containing the steel cylinders.

Out of sight of anyone in the bar, he tried the doorknob on the storage room off the hall. The door was still locked.

Donnie knew he'd have to go in there soon one way or the other. He had to get his hands on one of those cylinders, either when it was shipped in or had been moved here to the club.

If they *were* in the storage room.

He didn't really know that.

The key to the room was what he needed. But he didn't know who might have one. How he might get one. He'd need help for that.

Back at the bar, when he'd finished his coffee and was settling with the bartender, Donnie said, "I haven't seen Marie around for a while."

The bartender squinted his eyes almost closed, crows' feet deepening and darkening. "Me neither. I heard she went back to the Ukraine, where she came from. Name's not really Marie, either. It's Katushka."

"I guess she wanted to sound more American."

"Less Russian."

Donnie wondered why the bartender was making the distinction.

"I liked Marie," the bartender said. "Liked her a lot."

"Me, too. Why'd she go back?"

"Family troubles, what I heard."

A cold suspision grew in Donnie. "So she's still got family in the Ukraine?"

"I guess you could call 'em family," the bartender said. "What I heard was, they were gonna take care of her."

32

Donnie's phone rang at six the next morning. He'd been dreaming about Elana, about Grace in Florida, about a horrendous explosion.

Could happen, he thought, as he rolled over, shook off as much sleep as possible, and answered the phone. He didn't like phone calls at odd hours. The caller might be Donavon, it might be Death, they might be one and the same.

Daisy?

About Daisy? The possibility jolted him all the way awake. He was suddenly aware of the dim gray rectangle of light rimming the closed blinds, the sounds of the city rousing itself outside the window, the soft, dim light that made the room look like it was hazed with smoke.

It was Lily, calling from St. Louis. *Christ!*

"Don't worry, Donnie," she said. "It's good news."

He exhaled, accidentally making a fluttering sound with his lips, like a winded horse. "I could use some of that. This about Daisy?"

"Yes, but keep in mind I said it was good news, not great."

"Right now I'll settle for good."

"Remember how we were going to see if we could follow the money, once you learned Roma was paying for his solo operation himself?"

"Yeah. I should have thought of it sooner," Donnie said. "It had to be that way; he doesn't want anyone higher than him in the Mafia to know what he's done until he's done it, or to find out about it if he fails. Gotta be his own money if he's acting independently."

"We didn't find any checks or credit card charges under Roma's name, but we did turn up an ATM transaction two days ago involving his card."

"A withdrawal?"

"Yes. For five hundred dollars. We put a trace on the ATM machine and got a break. It's built into the wall near the entrance to a Home Pride Depot store here in St. Louis. You know the chain. They sell tools, home repair products, building supplies."

Donnie said he knew it.

"We checked the store's security video camera tapes for the times just after the withdrawal, customers coming and going through the doors. Also the ATM security tape."

Donnie's throat was dry. "And?"

"C.J. thinks he made one of the customers who entered about that time, same guy who used the ATM card. A big man, early forties, bull-necked, dark eyebrows, thinning hair worn long on the sides. Bulky, pot-bellied, wearing a mustache."

The description made a connection in Donnie's mind but he couldn't quite grasp it, put a face or name to such a man. Someone from a time he didn't want to think about?

"We ran the description and came up with a name. Ever hear of a Charles or Charlie Farrato? Sometimes Chuck Faro?"

It came to Donnie. "Mafia soldier, Bonnano family long time ago. I knew him without the pot belly or mustache. Punk. Killer. Liked to hurt people."

"Him," Lily said. "There's a homicide warrant out for him right now in Phoenix. Beat up an old man last year after a traffic accident, then jumped bail."

"Sounds like him, killing an old man."

"Old man recovered okay, Donnie. But Farrato didn't learn that in time. So he decided not to stand trial. He financed his flight to avoid prosecution by killing his bondsman and cleaning out his safe."

"And now he's got Daisy," Donnie said. He actually shivered. He remembered young Charlie Farrato beating a kid about nineteen who wandered into a truck hijacking, beating and beating him even after the boy was unconscious.

"And we've got *him,*" Lily said. "Or we will soon. I swear it, Donnie."

He knew she couldn't guarantee it, but it was good of her to utter the oath.

"We questioned the Home Pride Depot clerks who were at the registers around that same time. One of them remembered Farrato. He bought lumber, nails, some tools."

A lumber purchase, Donnie thought. What the hell could that mean? What was going to be built? Not a coffin, thank God. He was reasonably sure of that. The people he was dealing with buried their victims like dead animals, not humans. If they bothered burying them at all.

"We figure they'd shop at the nearest place to make that kind of purchase," Lily said. "They might be holding Daisy somewhere in the vicinity of that Home Pride Depot. We're narrowing this down, focusing our resources. We'll locate her soon."

"Someone besides Farrato is holding her," Donnie said. "Someone had to watch her while he went shopping." Donnie prayed that whoever it was had some sense, some compassion, and could control Farrato.

"Probably," Lily said. There were ways to incapacitate a hostage when left alone. Neither agent wanted to talk about them. Even think about some of them. "Probably" would do. "We'll keep you informed, Donnie."

"Thanks, Lily. You make sure this line was clear before you called?"

"You don't have to ask. Nobody's listening in, at least right now."

"I shouldn't have asked. Sorry. I'm gonna use this phone after you hang up. To call Donavon."

"He already knows what I told you, Donnie. We talked last night. We tried to call you then but there was no answer."

"I was out carousing."

"We figured."

"I've got other reasons to call him," Donnie said.

"Early to be waking him up. He can be cranky."

"That's one reason."

"Wonderful."

* * *

He didn't even replace the receiver, just momentarily depressed the cradle button for a dial tone before he called.

Now it was Jules Donavon whose voice was thick with sleep. "Something wrong, Donnie?"

"Something else, you mean?" He wanted to keep this conversation short. He told Jules about Lily's phone call, then about his conversation with Barkov and Gregory last night at the Westward Ho Club.

"Good," Jules said. "Things are moving, Donnie. I've got some info for you. The DEA raid at La Guardia's set for Friday. Tell the Italians out there about it, that you learned it from the FBI. Tell the Russians you found out the date from the Italians. We wanna make sure both sides know, so nothing incriminating's found during that raid."

"Is the DEA in on this deal, Jules?"

"Donnie, Donnie . . ."

Jules hung up.

There was no way Donnie was going to get back to sleep before dressing for work. He went into the kitchen and made a pot of coffee, then sat at the table sipping a cup of it black. Thinking about ATM cards and lumber, about Daisy and Charlie Farrato.

Hating what he was thinking. Hating it.

33

Friday was clear but cool. There had been a light fog on the runways when Donnie showed up for work that morning, but by nine o'clock the sun had burned it off. Virtually everyone working in the Logan Air cargo area knew about the scheduled drug raid. Some thought it was only rumor. Some believed it. Everyone was behaving normally. Better than normally. As if they were actors playing cargo handlers in a TV commercial.

Lefty Ordaz was more visible than usual, popping in and out of the office and strutting around in a sleeveless T-shirt to show he wasn't bothered by the cold. Mako was working in a plane unloading a cargo of roofing material flown in from some company in Canada; it was a good place to be, considering that any minute the DEA might descend on the place and shake it hard, searching for drugs. Banded sheaves of shingles and nestled aluminum flashing weren't likely hiding places for smuggled narcotics.

A nagging tension clung to the area and grew as the morning progressed. Donnie wondered if anybody not in the know could discern it. If something didn't happen soon, some of these guys might start to howl.

At ten-thirty Barkov drove past on another forklift, glanced at his watch, and raised his eyebrows inquisitively at Donnie.

Donnie shrugged and continued working.

Not long after that, Sam Vargo arrived in his funereal black Cadillac and parked near the office. Donnie watched him climb out of the car, stretch and look around, then adjust the crotch of his dark blue suit pants and swagger into the office. Nola Queen was seated in the Caddy, barely visible with the sun on the tinted side windows. Donnie thought she might have turned her head to look at him but couldn't be sure.

At eleven o'clock they hit.

That was how the DEA worked—no time to flush drugs down the toilet, hide them, throw them away. Quick-freeze the scene then secure it, analyze it, they were taught. And they were good at it.

Suddenly there they were, right up out of the ground, guys in black outfits and carrying automatic weapons or riot guns, with nightsticks and leather-clad paraphernalia dangling from their belts. They looked bulky and dangerous in their bulletproof vests. They were dangerous, all right. And noisy.

"DEA! Hold it! Don't move! Stay as you are!" Yelling at top volume, spreading out all over the place, some of them waving government ID high in their free hands so they wouldn't get shot by accident and to make it all legal later in court if they had to shoot someone themselves.

Donnie had just backed down the ramp from a

plane and was driving toward the hangar with a load of crated melons on his forklift. He braked to a halt, lowered the load to the concrete, then turned off the lift's engine.

A DEA agent was immediately beside him, not exactly aiming his weapon at Donnie. Not exactly. He was a tall man about forty with a lean, pockmarked face and gray eyes capable of freezing the melons. "Climb down off the forklift, sir. Don't touch anything."

Donnie obeyed. The "sir" didn't fool him. It didn't take much to set these guys off. They dealt with people who'd rather kill them than not, who simply didn't care. Nothing was more dangerous than someone with nothing to lose other than a mandatory life sentence.

"What's going on?" Donnie asked.

"Just do as you're told, sir." The eyes not quite looking away from Donnie, the pupils sliding almost imperceptibly this way and that, never really still. Here was a guy who wouldn't be outflanked.

Several unmarked cars arrived in a rush. One of them veered right and parked crossways behind Sam Vargo's Caddy, blocking it in. Nola Queen didn't get out and inquire about what was going on. Half a dozen NYPD cruisers came on the scene, no sirens, only blue and red roofbar lights flashing ineffectually in the bright morning sun. They parked quite a distance away, guarding the perimeter. Donnie knew how it worked. This was a DEA operation; the NYPD was backup only, not responsible if anything turned to crap. Bureaucracies. Turf. Donnie smiled.

"Something funny?"

It was the DEA guy with the pockmarked face and icy eyes.

"Not at all," Donnie said, putting on a somber expression.

Five or six guys piled out of each of the unmarked cars that had just arrived. A few had on DEA action outfits, but most wore dress pants and black jackets or pullover sweatshirts with *DEA* lettered on the back. Some had on suits and ties.

They spread out from the cars, into the hangar, office, the planes on the concrete apron being unloaded, swarming the area like dark, hunched army ants storming the stronghold of their enemy.

Two agents in sweatshirts came over. One of them had Donnie lean with both palms against the forklift then searched him quickly but skillfully. As Donnie was allowed to straighten up, he saw Navy and two other men being searched in the same fashion near one of the planes.

The two agents hauled down three or four of the crates on the pallet Donnie had been transporting. They pried up the thin wooden lids and unpacked the melons, laying then in neat rows on the concrete. Icy Eyes helped by keeping a wary watch on Donnie while this was going on.

Donnie looked beyond Icy Eyes and saw that two dark blue vans had just driven up. DEA agents in combat gear got out and opened the side doors. Their bodies stiffened as they backed away, pulling on leashes and at the same time making room for the good-sized black-and-tan German shepherds that emerged from the vans and looked left and right like alert and curious lions in a Roman arena. Had to be Christians around here somewhere. Or narcotics.

One of the dog handlers let his charge lead him to the crates on the prongs of Donnie's forklift. For a second Donnie wondered if someone had planted drugs on or near him, for whatever reason. There were so many sides and motives floating around him, tugging him in different directions, anything seemed possible.

"Go to it, Hank!" urged the dog handler, a skinny man with a receded chin and short blond crewcut.

Hank the German Shepherd panted and twitched and nosed around the crates. His paws made frantic scratching noises on the concrete as he fought against the leash. Then he turned his attention to the opened crates and melons on the ground. One by one he poked his highly trained black nose at the melons, then at the crates. He made a lot of noise sniffing, sometimes whining in eagerness.

Then Hank backed away, wagging his tail, and looked around longingly for fresh challenges. His erect, pointed ears rotated on his skull like antennae.

"Hank's a handsome dog," Donnie said.

A fur ear rotated toward Donnie as Hank fixed watery brown eyes on him at the sound of his name. But his handler, not as friendly a creature, ignored Donnie. Hank seemed to be leading the way as they scurried off toward where another grim handler and his dog were examining cargo on the concrete near a plane's loading ramp.

"Better leave that stuff where it is for now," Icy Eyes said, and wandered off in the direction Hank and his master had gone.

"Okay if I go inside outta the cold?" Donnie asked.

"That'd be fine. But I don't want you driving a fork-lift till we're done here. It won't be much longer, sir."

Donnie left the forklift where it was and began walking toward the hangar. He could see Navy and another man also trudging toward the hangar, Navy talking and waving his arms, probably bitching about how the DEA agents treated him. There was an air of disappointment about the agents now. Their searching, the use of the dogs, none of it had turned up any narcotics. They might still find some, but usually, with dogs, if they didn't get it in the first few minutes of a raid, they were going to come up empty. It meant someone had probably tipped the smugglers. Donnie found himself feeling a little guilty. These DEA guys seemed genuinely distraught.

Ahead of him he could see one of them talking with Nola Queen, who was out of the car and leaning on a front fender. She could sure lean on a fender. She was wearing a short red skirt, black tights or pantyhose, black heels, black leather waist-length jacket. The jacket was open and the way she was standing made her breasts jut out beneath her sweater. The DEA agent was smiling and seemed to be enjoying talking to her.

"Fuckers are tearin' the place up," Lefty Ordaz was growling, as Donnie walked past the office. Lefty was standing in the doorway, gripping both sides of the doorframe. "How you s'pose to run a business with these guys droppin' in like an invadin' army and messin' up everything?"

"I dunno," Donnie said. "Anything you want me to do?"

"Lose yourself for a while. No way to get anything done with these DEA pricks here."

Sam Vargo appeared in the doorway behind Ordaz and rested a hand comfortingly on his shoulder. "C'mon in, why doncha? Get outta the cold. They'll be gone soon." He glanced at Donnie and winked, nodding. As if to say the two of them knew Ordaz was a sensitive soul and had to be babied.

Donnie walked across the hangar and went down the hall to the locker room.

The DEA was in there. Most of the lockers were hanging open. Two agents with dogs were examining the lockers at the far end, letting the dogs nose through the contents spread out on a bench and on the floor.

"Not a goddam thing here," one of them said.

The other agent scooped up the clothes and magazines they'd taken from the end lockers and stuffed then all into one locker. They left the louvered steel door hanging open like the rest of the locker doors. Neither of them glanced at Donnie as they stormed out.

Donnie was alone now, listening to the voices of the agents, the panting and paw scrambling of the dogs moving along the hall and away from him.

He went to his own locker. The sweatshirt he kept there, and a fresh undershirt and socks, a cheap umbrella, were inside. The umbrella had been shoved back in hard enough to bend one of its struts so the fabric was torn away.

"Looks like they busted that umbrella. The assholes aren't gentle, are they?"

Donnie turned around to see Nola Queen. Her

jacket was still unbuttoned, and her hair was nicely mussed by the wind. She was taller than she'd appeared from a distance. And better looking even beneath all the makeup. The real thing made up to look like a whore.

She moved toward him behind a wall of perfume that actually didn't smell half bad.

"They got their minds on their work," Donnie said, removing his jacket and draping it over a hook in the locker.

Nola stopped near the bench that ran the length of the lockers and smiled at him. It was a smile with voltage. "So much for their minds. What's on your mind?"

"You," Donnie said, turning to face her. "Wondering why you're here, why you're talking to me."

She shrugged in a way he liked, as if she were a billion-dollar movie star and had no problems. "I'm here, you're here, so why shouldn't we talk?"

"I guess because I work here and you don't."

"And you don't sleep with Sam Vargo."

Donnie smiled. "I'm glad you realize that."

"Sam said he thought you were a special kind of guy. I've been watching you. I agree."

"Special how?" Naive Donnie.

"Well, I think Sam and I might have different ideas about that."

"What's his idea?"

"I don't know, exactly. Also I'm not much interested." She moved closer to Donnie, giving him the electric smile. She could be a star, winning beauty contests, changing vowels on a quiz show. When she was about half an inch away, she said, "I notice things. I've noticed you noticing me."

"You're tough not to notice." He could actually feel heat coming off her, a sexual tension barely held in check. His heart was way ahead of the rest of him. Well, not all of the rest of him.

The half inch between them disappeared. He was breathing deeply. She saw it and smiled.

"You don't exactly play hard to get," he said.

"Life's short. I play get to hard." She glanced down at him, then quickly back up, doing something with her eyelashes, looking guilty about whatever she was thinking.

This is something, Donnie said to himself. This woman is right out of a movie.

Like maybe a Richard Widmark or James Woods movie.

Donnie had found in his time spent around movie sets that not much about actors was real. He liked them. Kindred spirits. "Is your name actually Nola Queen?"

"You kidding? Nobody's name is Nola Queen. But ever since I started using it I've had good luck. You should think of switching to another name, something jazzier than Don Barns."

"I'm used to it."

"Naw, that's not really you, is it?"

Donnie's chest tightened. What did she know about him? If anything.

" 'Fraid that's me, all right," he said. "Been my name all my life."

"Sure it has. Ordinary old Don Barns." Husky voice.

Still the movie femme fatale, troweling it on, making it work for her. "Like hell you're ordinary, Don Barns. I can recognize guys like you, guys that come in a plain brown envelope with something interesting inside." Her arm snaked around his neck like it was all in the script.

His cue.

A steel locker door clanged. In the next row, not ten feet away.

Scene over.

Nola's arm fell away and she stepped back.

Sam Vargo came around the corner. When he saw Nola and Donnie he looked surprised and stopped. Stood still.

Then he looked around at all the open lockers. His mouth was hanging open, as if the scene had suggested it. "Those bastards sure made a mess."

"That's what we were talking about," Nola said, "what assholes they are. They broke Don's umbrella."

Vargo looked at him. "That right, kid?"

"It was a cheap umbrella."

"Still, it kept the rain off, right?"

"Mostly."

Vargo drew his wallet from a hip pocket and peeled off a twenty-dollar bill. He held it out for Donnie. "You get yourself a new umbrella."

"I can't take that, Mr. Vargo," Donnie said, holding up both hands as if a gun were aimed at him.

"It'd make me feel better."

Nola snatched the twenty from Vargo's hand and stuffed it in Donnie's shirt pocket. "Now everybody feels better. Mostly."

"You ready to go, hon?" Vargo asked her.

"I been ready," she said, glancing at Donnie.

Vargo didn't seem to notice.

"Thanks," Donnie said.

Vargo turned and stared blankly at him.

"For the twenty. It's nice of you."

"You guys get shit on enough. You don't deserve to get rained on, too."

He took Nola's hand and they walked away like schoolkids with a mutual crush. Donnie almost liked Vargo then, felt sorry for him. His steady girl wasn't so steady.

Or was she?

It was odd how nobody else had come into the locker room for a while. And the way Nola had gone to work on him, like she didn't have much time. Maybe Vargo had sent her, then interrupted them too early. They might have wanted to see if Donnie would go for her when she laid it all out in front of him. If he would have, like many men, they could be sure he wasn't an undercover cop, a snitch. Undercover cops and FBI agents couldn't have sex with women involved in cases they were on. That led either to perjury or to lost credibility in court when they became the prosecutions' chief witnesses.

Donnie sat down on the bench, leaning forward and resting his elbows on his knees. There was no way to know for sure if he'd just passed a test, or failed one. He didn't like the way Nola Queen had singled him out. It meant something other than sexual magnetism. Vargo might suspect he wasn't genuine. Or maybe Vargo knew who he really was and knew about the parking garage bombing, but still wasn't convinced. Donnie didn't like the way this was going.

Didn't like the way his cover might be unraveling, and what that might mean.

Daisy, he thought.

Daisy!

"Donnie!" Lefty Ordaz was yelling. "C'mon and get up. Eliot Ness and the Untouchables are gone. You got a C-130 to unload."

Donnie stood up, shrugged into his jacket, and went.

34

Donnie hadn't worn his wire during the DEA raid, so he called Donavon that evening and reported. Nothing incriminating had been found and the DEA had retreated in a bad mood. Sam Vargo probably had something to hide and suspected Donnie wasn't the real item; he'd sent Nola Queen to see what she could find out. Donnie's position was becoming more precarious.

Overwhelmed by growing complications and helplessness, Donnie didn't go straight back to his apartment. The warmer weather was holding, so he walked past his building then turned the corner and wandered aimlessly, trying to work out his tension so he could sleep without the Benadryl he'd begun taking. Maybe Dr. Eams could actually prescribe something that would help.

Donnie walked for a long time at a good clip, his head down, his fists jammed into his windbreaker pockets so hard the material was strained. He looked up only occasionally to check traffic lights or avoid bumping into someone.

A few people were sitting at tables outside a restaurant across from Lincoln Center. Donnie thought that looked like a good idea. He asked a headwaiter for a table near the building, sat down where he could watch the street, and ordered a cup of hot chocolate.

Traffic was heavy and had to grind to an intermittent stop at the light, which gave a couple of panhandlers the opportunity to approach drivers. Donnie watched them. They were doing okay, getting change from about half a dozen drivers at each light change. Cab drivers seemed to be the most generous, and a few of them apparently knew one of the panhandlers. Watching this play out in front of him, Donnie thought it would be tough not knowing if each day's food and each night's shelter were going to be there for you. On the other hand, these guys' problems were basic. They weren't worrying about a kidnapped daughter, the Mafia, expert hit men, or living a life even more anonymous than theirs and maybe more lonely. This is a hell of a thing, Donnie thought, that I'm sitting here sipping hot chocolate and envying these guys begging for change. But it was true. At that instant it was true.

"Hello, fuckface."

Wearing his underslung smile, Mako sat down across the table from Donnie. He had on a three-quarter-length black raincoat with epaulets that made his shoulders look huge. Vinnie Roma, his tan double-breasted trenchcoat unbuttoned and its dangling belt almost dragging the ground, was talking to one of the waiters, who was listening attentively and nodding. The waiter, a thick-necked kid wearing a white apron over Levi's, hurried away as Roma turned around and walked over to the table. He sat down next to Mako, so both men were facing Donnie.

"They do serve liquor and'll make us some hot gin and root beers," he said to Mako.

Donnie looked at both men. "Hot gin and root beer?"

"You oughta try it," Mako said. "It'll warm you up better'n that pussy drink of yours."

"You too cold?"

"Don't quarrel, boys," Roma said. Donnie didn't know if he was kidding. Beyond Roma a man was seated reading the *Times* sports page. Baseball season started in less than a week, said a caption above the photo of a player leaping for a ball. Time was passing, all right, for Donnie, for Daisy. . . .

"Looka those fuckin' bums," Mako said; half turning in his chair and nodding toward the panhandlers working the street. "Somebody oughta run 'em down, discourage that kinda stuff. Damn parasites."

"They oughta get into honest stealing," Roma agreed.

Donnie wondered whose world was turned more upside down. "Is the three of us running into each other a coincidence?" he asked, knowing better.

"We were waitin' for you at your place," Mako said, "but you didn't come in. So we followed you here. We like to follow you. Kinda guy you are, you always go someplace interestin'."

"Like this place," Donnie said.

"Sure." Mako glanced around. "I might come back here with the family."

The thought horrified Donnie. "You've got kids?"

"Sure. Why the fuck not? My dick works. Got myself a good little wife out in the suburbs. You don't think I like dealin' with shit like you, do you? What I'm doin' now is sorta like a job, strictly business. It's great to get away from it all once in a while, go back to where things are peaceful an' safe an' orderlylike. Otherwise I'd go nuts."

Donnie was mulling that over when Roma said, "There's a purpose to this meeting."

"Is this a meeting?" Donnie asked. "I thought we were gonna chat about the PTA and whether pickup trucks and minivans should be parked overnight at the curb."

"Well, those are serious problems, all right, but you got one even more pressing."

Donnie didn't like the expressions on the faces of the two men across from him; the kind of anticipation he'd seen on the faces of boys about to torture a cat. "Am I gonna hear it and throw this hot chocolate on you?"

"Not unless you want hot lead for a chaser," Mako said. "I got a piece in my coat pocket, aimed more or less at your belly under the table. It's on full automatic and can fire a couple dozen shots before you can finish thinkin' about it. An' I'd love to watch you bounce outta your chair an' ruin everyone's appetite 'cause your guts are hangin' out. That thought bother you?"

"There's no need to be cruel," Roma told him.

"Oh, I dunno . . ."

"Whatever." Roma looked squarely at Donnie, smiling. "There's been a development about your daughter."

"No, she ain't pregnant," Mako said. "Least we don't think so."

Donnie held in his rage, clenching his fists out of sight beneath the phony marble table top. He found himself wondering if Mako really did have a gun pointed at him.

"She's someplace where she's perfectly safe," Roma said. "Plenty of food, warm enough clothes, an ample supply of air."

Donnie felt his heart contract. "Air?"

"It's supplied by a pump powered by a small gasoline-run generator on a timer. There's enough fuel to last about four days. Then enough air to last . . ." Roma glanced at Mako.

"Depends on how much she exercises," Mako said. "If she realizes she's runnin' outta air an' nobody's gonna come for her, she might start exercisin' a lot."

"Where is she?" Donnie asked, surprised by the hoarseness and hate in his voice.

"She's in a wooden box," Roma said, "something like a generous-sized coffin. Fairly roomy, though of course she has to stay laying down, and still as possible."

The lumber purchase at Home Pride Depot.

"There are no breathing holes in the . . . box?" Donnie asked.

"Wouldn't help," Mako said, " 'cause it's buried."

Donnie stood up, knocking over his chair. The half dozen other customers at the tables stared at him.

"Sit back down real calm," Roma said, his face and voice hard. "You're smart enough to realize your daughter's life depends on you keeping your cool."

Donnie set his chair upright, looked around and matched the stares aimed at him, and sat. Not a hell of a lot of choice.

"Don't worry so much about her," Mako said. "She's got food, water, warm clothes, and she's buried beneath the frost line in case there's a cold snap."

Donnie couldn't think about Daisy stretched out on her back in the cold with barely enough room to move her arms and legs, breathing stale pumped-in air, in the dark. *God, in the dark! With only her terror.*

Mako was watching Donnie's face, as if trying to figure out what was going through his mind. "Generator that feeds the pump also powers a twenty-watt appliance bulb," he said. " 'Course, current's not steady an' that bulb's gonna flicker now and again, maybe go out from time to time."

"Enough of that kinda talk," Roma said. "Donnie Brassballs gets the idea. Which is that he better start pushing his Russian and FBI friends for information. I wanna know what those Rusky bastards are really up to. I wanna know it before the FBI does, and if they already know it, I wanna learn it goddam soon after."

"Sorry it took a while," the waiter said. He'd arrived with the two warm gin and root beers on a tray.

"That's okay," Roma said expansively. "We'll enjoy them all the more."

No one said anything as the waiter left and Roma and Mako worked on their drinks. Donnie was looking beyond them, watching the traffic, the two persistent panhandlers. His mind bounced away from any thought of Daisy lying beneath the frost line, her only means of oxygen a hose hooked to a pump, her only source of light the kind of bulb used in refrigerators. He couldn't let the image, the emotion, all the way into his mind or he'd leap up from the table, maybe do or say something that would kill her for sure.

Roma finished his drink with a long swig and set the empty glass down. Mako's glass was already empty. He belched. Both men stood up.

"This one's on you," Roma said, tapping his forefinger on the bill.

Donnie sat looking up at them. "What if the spark plug on that gas-powered generator is bad? What if there's water in the fuel line or tank? What if something—anything—makes that motor kick out and die?"

"Then your daughter dies with it," Roma said. "The box becomes her coffin."

Donnie was gritting his teeth. He knew they could read the agony on his face.

"Don't worry about it, though," Mako said. "The guys who set it all up checked everything good and careful. We made sure of that." He shrugged. "What the hell, I got a daughter of my own."

"However it goes," Roma said, as they turned to walk away, "your clock is ticking."

35

Part of the time Donnie's clock was ticking, he slept. But he had the alarm set for 2:00 A.M., and by 2:15 he was in his car and driving toward the Westward Ho Club. There were only a few stars visible behind low clouds, and now and then a tilted sliver of moon put in an appearance. There wasn't much natural light. It was a good night for bad deeds.

Roma and Mako had been persuasive; Donnie knew he had to make something happen. Ironically, frustration and concern for Daisy might have been paralyzing him when he should have been forcing the action. No more. Not tonight.

When he was still in Manhattan, he pulled the Honda over to the curb near an all-night diner and waited while a compact, muscular Latin man in jeans and a dark green nylon jacket came outside and got in the car. He was EO Special Agent Rafael (Rafe) Acuna, and Donnie had phoned and gotten the Bureau to fly him up from St. Louis because he was an expert in what they were about to attempt.

Rafe placed on the floor between his legs the black Lands End canvas attaché case he was carrying, and the two men shook hands. The Latino's white, handsome smile flashed in the dim light, but his dark eyes were somber.

"You holding up okay?" he asked Donnie, without a trace of accent.

"Well enough," Donnie said, pulling the Honda away from the curb. "Did you have time to get what we need?"

"Sure. The way you described the alarm system, getting around it won't be a problem." No one in the Bureau knew alarm circuitry and bypass procedures more thoroughly than Rafe.

"The alarm system didn't look like junk," Donnie said.

"It's not. What you told me about's a solid operation, a combination of motion detectors and pressure plates."

Rafe didn't elaborate or tell Donnie how they intended to deal with the alarm and break into the Westward Ho Club. That was okay. For now.

During the rest of the drive, Donnie filled Rafe in on what they were going to do once they got inside.

Donnie parked the Honda in the block behind the Westward Ho and the two men walked to the club. This was primarily an industrial neighborhood, and the few people who did live here were asleep, so no one was on the streets. They ducked into a doorway while an NYPD cruiser glided past, but that was the only vehicle they saw. Donnie hoped the uniforms in the car wouldn't decide to circle the block. They might notice the Honda newly parked there and get suspicious. Nothing to do about that. He reminded himself there was risk in everything; you could break a leg in the morning getting out of bed.

Rafe grinned at him in the darkness and pulled a small cell phone out of his pocket. He dialed 911 and reported a prowler in a building about ten blocks south. He gave a fictitious name, said he was on his car phone and gave the number.

By the time the 911 operator called back to confirm the call and location, Rafe had the cell phone's ringer muted. Donnie saw the tiny red light on the phone go out, then heard Rafe tell the operator to hurry, dammit!

Within half a minute they heard the siren of the cruiser that had passed them set up a yowl a few blocks away. The ghostly wailing faded to the south.

Rafe tucked the phone in a pocket and said, "Was I right when I told you I brought everything we'd need?"

"Let's hope you stay right," Donnie said.

In the dark mouth of the gangway beside the Westward Ho, he waited while Rafe reconnoitered.

Five minutes later Rafe was back. "Just like I figured," he said, "they got a soft spot in the system."

"Which is?" Donnie asked.

"It's a good security system, wireless with a battery backup, probably plenty of sensor locations inside. Most alarms this sophisticated raise a racket on the site to scare away prowlers and alert anyone in the vicinity, and they also send a signal to the alarm company or police department. But not this one, because these guys don't want the police involved and nosing around the place even if somebody breaks in. They'd rather the burglar or whoever was just frightened away by the alarm bell. And that's what it is—your basic bell with a hammer beating on a toner. Two bells, in fact. One on each side of the building. Might be one or two inside, too. They make enough noise to rouse anybody around here."

"So what do we do, bypass the bells' wiring?"

"No need to. Ever see that foam insulation in an aerosol can? You squirt it into the cracks in your house like whipped cream and within seconds it sets up like concrete. I already squirted it into the outside bells. When they go off the beaters in them will hit sluggishly on the bells for a while then finally seize up in the coagulating foam. Only noise they'll make is a muffled clattering sound, and you'd have to be within ten feet of them to hear that."

"What about the alarm bells inside?"

"We get in through that side door you showed me, then I look around. I know how to find any other bells, or any electronic beams if they got other systems inside. Takes a little patience, is all."

I'm short on that, Donnie thought, as they moved toward the steel-core, locked door to the alley.

Rafe got a small but powerful portable high-speed carbide drill from his briefcase. Using candle wax to silence the bit, he drilled the locks out. Then he used something that looked like a misshapen screwdriver to turn the lock mechanisms.

He opened the door cautiously, then used an aerosol can to spray powder that would reveal a beam in case there was an electric eye or laser beam just inside the door. When he deemed it safe, he nodded and both men entered and closed the door behind them.

They were inside, in the silence and the smell of stale beer and tobacco smoke.

"What we want's down that hall and to the left," Donnie said. "We need to get to the cash register, too. Maybe the office, see if there's a safe." A safe would doubtless be locked, but that didn't matter. Donnie only wanted to scratch it around the keyhole or combination dial. The idea was to clean out the cash register and take anything else small and of value, make the break-in seem to have been an ordinary burglary. That way no one might look in any of the bottom boxes and discover that one of the steel cylinders was missing.

"Don't move," Rafe said. "I'm gonna clear the rest of this place, make sure we don't set anything else off."

It took him about ten minutes this time. While he was gone, Donnie checked the mechanism of the 9mm he had tucked in his belt in back. He was also carrying the compact .22 in its ankle holster. Gunplay wasn't in the plan, but sometimes it was the only way to forge a new plan in a hurry. He hadn't asked, but he was sure Rafe was carrying, that they'd have firepower if they got in trouble.

Rafe was back. "I found an LCD keypad. There's only one system in the place, wireless. An isolated system, all right. Two more bells. I shot foam insulation into them. We used to use shaving cream, but the insulation works a lot faster."

"If you found the keypad, why didn't you just turn off the alarm?"

"Can't do that. Some of them are set up with a backswitch so they'll go off if they're turned off at any but the set times. No way to know what those times are if they're inherent in the microchip."

"What's all that mean?" Donnie asked.

"Means lead on."

Donnie led the way to the storage room, using the thin beam of his small Mag light to find the way down the dark hall.

"Go ahead and see if you can pick the lock on the storage room door," he said to Rafe. "Is it safe to go behind the bar?"

"We can go anywhere," Rafe said. "If we break a beam or step on a pressure plate, the alarm bells will stay frozen or keep beating away inside the congealing foam insulation."

"I'll go clean out the register while you're working on the door. If you can't pick the lock we can just bust the door out of the frame, but it'd be better if that room looked undisturbed."

"I can pick it," Rafe said. "Won't even scratch it. Might make you a key while I'm at it."

"Now that I won't need a key," Donnie said. Was Rafe kidding?

Donnie played the narrow beam of his flashlight out in front of him as he made his way behind the bar and to the cash register.

It took him only a few minutes to open the register drawer and scoop out what looked like a few hundred dollars, which he stuffed into a plastic bag he'd brought. He slid the bag inside his shirt and started back to where Rafe was crouched at the storage room door.

In the dim light outside the flashlight beams, Rafe's lean face was serious as he manipulated the lock with what looked to Donnie like a dental pick.

"Got it!" Rafe said, and started to straighten up.

"You're gonna fuckin' get it," a voice said.

As he reached around behind him and wrestled the 9mm from his belt, Donnie was aware of Rafe diving to the side. The hall light came on. Automatic gunfire raked the hall, but Donnie had crawled into the storage room. He knew Rafe had been seen but wasn't sure he'd been spotted. He stayed low, scrambled around, and stuck his gun, then his head back out at floor level.

More gunfire. A round shattered the ceiling fixture and the hall went dark again. Donnie caught a glimpse of muzzle flash winking like an orange eye as he pulled back inside.

Silence then.

The hall became dimly lit as lights were switched on in the bar area. Donnie heard approaching footfalls, one person, soft-soled shoes.

Heavy breathing, with a faint whistling through the nose.

Donnie peeked out into the hall and saw a man wearing a white T-shirt, gray and maroon sweatpants, and gaudy jogging shoes. Gregory. His hair was mussed, one of his shoes was untied, and his T-shirt only half tucked in. He was standing over Rafe, who was on his back with his chest heaving, his eyes open wide, looking up at Gregory and not over at Donnie. A bright spot of blood glistened just below his armpit.

Rafe's gun was on the floor out of his reach. Gregory nudged it farther away with his foot. "Fuckin' burglar! I saw the open register drawer. You picked the wrong place to break into."

Donnie realized Gregory hadn't noticed the open storage room door. He assumed only Rafe had broken in, a petty burglar or a junkie trying to make a fast cash score, and now Rafe was lying wounded before him, helpless.

"So go ahead and call the cops," Rafe groaned. "I need a doctor."

Gregory laughed. "You're not going to see a policeman or doctor, *durahk*, you're going to see hell." He stepped back and lowered his automatic rifle so it was aimed at Rafe.

Donnie said, "Gregory."

Startled, Gregory turned.

His eyes widened and his jaw dropped when he saw Donnie. Saw the gun in Donnie's hand.

Donnie shot him.

Gregory spun as if he'd been clipped by a speeding truck. His momentum carried him out of sight from the storage room. Donnie heard him running down the hall toward the bar area.

But as he'd spun, Gregory accidentally kicked Rafe's gun over to where Rafe could reach it. Automatic rifle fire chattered, but not for long. Donnie watched Rafe take careful aim and fire.

In the ringing silence that always followed gunfire, Donnie lay on the floor and waited.

"He's down," Rafe finally said. "I think he's dead."

"Be careful of him."

"You be careful. I don't think I can get up."

"Don't try," Donnie said. He was sweating but he was cold; they must turn the heat down in the place at night to save on utility bills.

He got shakily to his feet, went to the door, and peered out and down the hall.

Gregory was on the floor. His lower body, the sweatpants and shoes, were visible. One of the shoes was off and lying on its side near a knee.

Donnie moved out of the storage room and stayed close to the wall as he edged down the hall. Keeping his gun trained on Gregory, he stepped into the bar area.

The left side of Gregory's head above his ear was blown away. Donnie stuck his gun back in his belt and went to help Rafe.

"That party made a hell of a lot of noise," Rafe said. He was seated leaning with his back against the wall now. "We better get outta here."

"How bad's your wound?"

"I don't know. Let's check on it later." He attempted to stand but started to fall back.

Donnie caught him, trying not to exert any pressure near the bullet wound in his side. "Can you walk?"

"Let's find out."

Rafe could walk, but only with Donnie's help. Donnie paused at the open storage room door.

"Get one of the cylinders," Rafe urged him.

"Not now. We can't. Let them think it was an ordinary burglary, and my cover might hold." Donnie reached out and swung the storage room door closed, hearing the lock click. It was a sound he didn't like, but Gregory had cut off their options.

Together the two men lurched toward the door they'd used to enter the building.

It had taken a while in this neighborhood, but someone who'd heard the gunfire finally called and the police were on the way. Sirens sounded, approaching from different directions.

Donnie strained to support Rafe as they made their way outside then down the gangway to the next block where the Honda was parked.

As they rounded the corner, Donnie was aware of a flashing red and blue glare behind him at the opposite end of the gangway. A police car pulling up in front of the club.

They hadn't been seen.

Not yet.

They had one chance. If none of the approaching cars used the next block as a route to the scene, Donnie and Rafe might make it to the Honda. If a police car did turn the corner, there was no way they could get out of sight in time, and the spectacle of the two men staggering along and supporting each other like drunks would stop a cop car cold.

Twice there was a crescendo of sirens and a brief display of red and blue light at the end of the block. It seemed a miracle to Donnie that no police car appeared.

"We'll get you to a hospital," he said, helping Rafe lower himself into the Honda's passenger seat.

Donnie closed the door and hurried around to climb in behind the steering wheel. The engine kicked over on the second try and he sped away from the curb, crossed the intersection then made a left turn and wove through side streets. The farther away they got from the Westward Ho Club, the less likely the car would be associated with what had happened there.

"Where'd that guy with the automatic rifle come from?" Rafe asked.

"Upstairs, I guess. I didn't figure on that. There's nothing up there but empty offices. He must have slept upstairs so there was somebody on the premises after closing time, a kind of night watchman."

Rafe was feeling around beneath his jacket. "I don't think I'm hit too bad." But his voice whistled with pain between clenched teeth. "Busted rib for sure, though."

"How about bleeding?"

"I'm already doing that."

"At least the bullet didn't hit your sense of humor." But Donnie wasn't fooled by Rafe's pass at a joke. The euphoria of their narrow escape had them both on a high that wouldn't last much longer.

"Bleeding's slow. I'm keeping my palm pressed to it."

"You hit anywhere else?"

"I don't know." The car bounced hard over a pothole and Rafe groaned. "We planned this job too fast, Donnie."

I planned it too fast, Donnie thought. Time was becoming more and more of an enemy.

"We didn't allow for shitty luck," Rafe said, "and we sure as hell had that."

"Tell me about it."

They didn't see another police car all the way into Manhattan. Luck mocking them.

36

"You bullshitting me?" Donnie asked.

They were in the washroom at La Guardia. Navy had just washed his hands and left. Donnie and Barkov were alone. Barkov reached to the basin and ran some water to make noise, as if worried the room might be bugged. It was a thought.

Donnie stared hard at him. "You saying somebody killed Gregory at the club Saturday night? You *are* saying it. What? He get into a fight?"

"With somebody who had a gun."

"Cops get the guy?"

"Cops might have been the guy."

Donnie felt the blood recede from his flesh. He controlled his face, not letting his alarm show. He hoped. "How do you mean?"

"Something isn't right, Donnie. Gregory was spending the night upstairs at the club. He does that sometimes, sleeps on a cot, acts as a night watchman. Somebody must have broken in. He heard them, went downstairs, and got himself shot."

"You mean by a burglar?"

"It could be that's what whoever did this would like us to think."

"Or maybe that's what really happened. The club's not in one of New York's low crime neighborhoods."

"The cash drawer was cleaned out."

"There you go," Donnie said.

"The guy got in by drilling out the locks with a high-speed carbide bit. The outside and inside alarms were silenced by somebody who knew what they were doing. Your average burglar doesn't have that kind of equipment or those kinds of skills."

"Maybe there were two or three of them."

"Two at the most, the way we see it. Possibly only one, with two guns. Lots of guns floating around this city, and the cops dug bullets out of the walls from three guns."

Donnie knew where the gun was that Ballistics could match with the bullet that killed Gregory. He turned around and levered out a paper towel from the holder so Barkov wouldn't see him swallow. "So it wasn't a burglar, what makes you think it was the cops?"

"The drug raid. They came up empty here, so maybe they were planning on raiding the club, but this time planting drugs so they'd be sure to find incriminating evidence. Cops'll do that."

"Cops will."

"Gregory might have heard them, came downstairs, and started blazing away. He had an AK47."

"Maybe the cops shot first."

"Doesn't matter now," Barkov said. "If it was them, they're all back on duty today protecting law-abiding citizens, hey? The police, they're the same everywhere."

Donnie dried his hands and tossed the wadded paper towel into a bin. "What about the Italians? Think they might have broke in?"

"I don't know. I've been thinking a lot of things. There is a Russian saying—"

The door opened and Mako swaggered in. Barkov reached over and turned off the water that was running in the basin.

Mako made a show of unzipping his pants and exposing himself while he walked to one of the urinals. As he urinated, he looked over his shoulder and grinned. "You two guys been hanging out a lot in here together, if you know what I mean."

Barkov casually walked over and punched him hard in the kidney. Mako was stunned. He bent over and his body twisted, causing him to spray urine all over the floor and walls. When he tried to back away he slipped on the wet tiles and fell to the floor. His hands pawed desperately at himself where his zipper had snagged loose flesh.

Barkov stood over him. "Perhaps you'll piss red for a while, my friend. Think about who you insulted."

Mako pumped his legs and scooted back against the wall. He didn't try to get up. Maybe it was out of the question, after a kidney punch like that.

Barkov turned around and strode from the washroom.

Donnie thought it was a good idea to follow him.

After work, Donnie phoned Donavon and told him what had happened, asked him how Rafe was doing.

A bullet had passed through Rafe, breaking a rib as

he'd said in the car, and taking some of the external oblique stomach muscle. He was in no danger but would be laid up for a while. Roma's ATM card had been used again, this time near a small hardware store where someone fitting the Home Pride Depot customer's description bought a battery-powered screwdriver and some wood screws. Lily was sure she was closing in on the specific area where Daisy was being held.

"We're running out of time, Jules."

"I know that Donnie. So does Lily. Everyone in St. Louis is doing what they can. We also don't have enough people. I'm pulling Bert Clover off playing angel for a while so he can stake out the Westward Ho Club. The Russians might try moving those cylinders, now that the place is a homicide scene."

Donnie thought Clover watching the club was a good idea. "My cover might be slipping away," he said. "Maybe it's time for me to go to St. Louis and do what I can to help."

"If you disappear from New York, Daisy will be killed for sure. You believe that, don't you? Donnie?"

He believed it, all right. There were times when even people like Roma and Mako could be counted on to tell the truth.

Donnie heard his teeth grinding and willed some of the tension from his body. "If this was your daughter, what the fuck would *you* do, Jules?"

"I can't tell you that, Donnie. I honestly can't. All I can guarantee you is everybody cares. We're doing everything possible and then some." Donavon's voice actually broke as if he might start crying. That was something Donnie had never seen and couldn't imagine.

"I know you are. I'm sorry, Jules."

When Donnie hung up the phone he knew he had to make another call—to Elana.

There was initial shock, a reaction impossible to read over the phone, then she took the latest news about Daisy with a calm detachment that scared him.

"I want to meet you," she said in a strange, emotionless voice. "We need to talk."

"I don't know what there is to say, Elana. I want to be with you, but time—"

"Let's meet, Donnie. The Paragon Diner on Second Avenue near 53rd Street."

"When? "

"Tonight about nine o'clock. It won't be crowded then and we can talk."

"Elana—"

She had hung up. The disconnected line buzzed like an angry insect in Donnie's ear.

He went into the kitchen and got a Heineken out of the refrigerator.

It troubled him, the odd monotone in Elana's voice. It was as if she was speaking to him from a vacuous, cold place beyond shock and terror, as if she'd become resigned to Daisy's death, to his, to her own. He didn't like her this way, with death at the top of her mind, philosophical in defeat, thinking in terms of eternity.

He told himself it was too early for that.

Made himself believe it.

37

The Paragon Diner was full of gray Formica, red vinyl, and angled mirrors. Because of the mirrors, three Elanas were waiting for Donnie in a booth near a window in back. It was well beyond the counter and near the doors to the kitchen and rest rooms. No one would overhear them there.

Donnie walked through a smoky haze and the scent of onions from something being grilled, chose the three-dimensional Elana, and sat down across from her.

A cup of coffee sat steaming before her. Donnie ordered the same.

When the waiter had brought the second cup, along with an insulated plastic coffeepot, then left, Elana locked eyes with Donnie across the table. She'd aged depressingly in the last few weeks. Donnie tried telling himself it was the harsh light hanging over the table, but he knew better. We're both getting older, he thought. That was something Elana probably regretted, but it was Donnie's aim in life. He wanted Daisy to get older, too.

"I can't stand this," Elana said, sounding not as detached as she had on the phone. Angry now. Agonized. "She's buried alive. Those animals have put her below earth in a box as if she's already dead."

"But she isn't dead," Donnie said. "That's what's important."

"All they have to do is walk away, forget about her. Don't you realize that?"

"*We* won't forget about her."

"Joe, this is pure crap. It's got to change."

He was getting irritated. He understood her pain, but did she understand his? What did she expect? What was the point in hashing over what they already knew, torturing each other with the facts while time slipped away? But looking at her, into her, he couldn't ask her those questions. "Have you got any ideas?"

"Yes. I'm going to do something about the situation instead of just sitting around while you and the Bureau get nowhere."

"We've been through that."

"And I've played along with you and Donavon. But what have you accomplished? Our daughter was above ground, and now she's below it."

"What could you do?" Donnie asked.

"I'm not sure. But tell me more about what's going on. Then maybe I can think of something. Dammit, I need to do *something*! Otherwise how am I going to feel . . . afterward? How will I be able to go on living?"

"What would that something be?" Donnie asked, still annoyed with her, pressing. They both had to wrestle with the same questions; did she have the answers?

"I don't know. How can I answer that? I look around

and see nothing but darkness. How could I know what direction I might take?"

Darkness. He thought of Daisy, with only a dim appliance bulb between her and a total darkness that might last forever. Even if she survived, what would that do to her mind, to the rest of her life? Donnie stared down at the table. Neither he nor Elana had taken a sip of coffee.

"You can trust me to keep it all secret," she assured him.

"I know I can, Elana." He meant it; he trusted her as much as he did anyone. But another part of his mind was turning it over, cautioning . . . one more person who knew the secrets, one more possibility that something would find its way out of the widening circle.

"I need this! You've got to tell me!"

Maybe she was right, Donnie thought. Did it matter now? His cover was slipping, time was running out, the operation had the feel of failure and death. Possibly it should have felt that way from the beginning.

"You owe it to me," she said simply.

Which was true. Daisy was more her daughter than his. He'd sunk into a life beyond home and family and relinquished some of the rights of fatherhood. She was the one raising their two girls. Alone. And if Daisy died, if he died, Elana had to continue living. *How am I going to feel afterward?*

He told her.

Everything.

The phone was ringing when Donnie returned from his meeting with Elana and entered his apartment.

It was Donavon. "Remember what I told you about assigning Bert Clover to watch the Westward Ho Club?"

"Yeah." Donnie somehow knew this wasn't going to be good.

"He was found dead ten blocks away in his parked car, a bullet in his head and a gun in his hand. It looks like he committed suicide."

"It would look like it," Donnie said bitterly. Now Clover didn't seem like such a bad guy. And whatever else he'd been, he was a fellow agent, a casualty in the same army. And there was no doubt he'd been killed by the enemy.

"Rough people," Jules said.

"Yeah. That's why it's us against them."

"The worst kind of trouble can pop up when you least expect it. You take special care, Donnie. Watch your back."

"I will, Jules."

As Donnie was hanging up the phone, there was a knock on the door.

He wasn't expecting company and didn't want any. Trouble in bunches.

38

Remembering what had happened to Clover, Donnie got his 9mm from behind him and held it low in his right hand, pressed tight against his thigh.

There was another, louder knock on the door.

Donnie moved close to the door, alongside it. "Who is it?" Making his voice sound casual, unconcerned.

There was no answer.

Maybe whoever was there had left.

He reached out with his left hand and unlocked the door, then backed away fast and crouched behind the sofa, aiming the 9mm at the door with both hands. Behind him was a corner, and his peripheral vision covered enough of the kitchen that no one could come in the back way without attracting his attention.

The doorknob turned.

He tightened his grip on the gun, arms forming a triangle whose apex was aligned with his nose. Where he looked his nose would automatically point, along with the apex of the triangle, along with the barrel of the gun. Geometric point shooting, it was called. It worked.

The door opened and Nola Queen stepped inside.

She was wearing her short mink jacket, high heels, and a tight red skirt that was modestly long but with a slit up the side.

She'd been smiling, but when she saw Donnie she gasped.

Quickly he lowered the gun.

She looked scared but she managed to retrieve the smile, not wanting the femme fatale image to slip. "This," she said, "is my idea of arriving at a bad time."

"I was expecting somebody else."

"I hope so."

"What do you want, Nola?"

Her smile held steady yet somehow grew warmer despite his curt question. "To see you."

"How did you know—"

"Lefty Ordaz gave me your address."

"You were right, it *is* a bad time. I'm sorry, but for both our sakes you better leave."

She studied him, then nodded and turned to go.

Then she turned back to face him. She glanced down at the gun. "Whoever you're expecting, maybe you oughta leave, too."

"Yeah. I was about to."

"Good. Let's leave together."

"Nola—"

"Why not? We're both on our way out, aren't we?" Nola was posed sideways near the front door, showing a gracefully curved calf. She must have watched a lot of film noir. "I'm waiting. It's an offer most men wouldn't refuse."

Most men in movies with the word *Death* in their titles. Danny tucked the 9mm back in his belt. There wasn't much choice. "I guess I'm most men."

She smiled again. "That's better. I'm spoiled, used to having my way."

"Easy to see why."

"Anything else is an inconvenience for everybody concerned."

"I'll remember."

"Do." She took a deep and attactive breath, broadening her smile. "What I like about New York is, you leave an apartment like this and there's everything out there waiting for you no matter what your tastes or compulsions. People should explore their compulsions."

"Even if the compulsion's name is Nola?"

"Ah, I guessed right about you, plain brown wrapper Don Barns."

He grabbed his windbreaker and slipped into it, then came around the sofa and went to the door. Nola moved aside to make room for him. She was a woman accustomed to having doors opened for her. Probably coats thrown over puddles.

"Let's go," Donnie said. "The city's a wondrous toy."

He wondered how he was going to get out of this. To be intimate with Nola would be to negate his future testimony and destroy the government's case. No FBI agent would do that. Which might be exactly why Nola was sent, to find out how Donnie would react to her invitation.

His problem was solved outside the building, when a white Lincoln limo pulled to the curb next to where he and Nola were walking.

One of the tinted rear windows sank slowly, and a beefy man with sleek black hair stared out at them with eyes as animated as dark wells. He said, "Get in the car, Nola."

"I don't think so," she said. "I'm not done here."

Donnie thought he knew what she meant. They hadn't had sex yet, the proof positive he wasn't FBI. She was supposed to have seduced him in the apartment, but when he'd answered the door holding a gun, she knew that was out and had quickly devised a Plan B. The goon in the limo assumed her mission was over.

"Don't goddam argue," the goon said.

"Listen to me, Gil, I'm not—"

"I ain't listening to shit." Gil the goon opened the limo door and seemed to inflate out of the back seat. He had to weigh close to three hundred pounds. With unexpected quickness, he clamped a big hand around Nola's wrist.

"Wait a minute!" Donnie said, moving in.

Gil tried to shove him away with his free hand, but Donnie slipped to the side and punched him hard in the jaw. Gil seemed almost to notice. He shoved Nola so she was half in the limo, then turned his full attention to Donnie and smiled.

Donnie kicked him in the testicles. That bent him over and backed him up, but strangely didn't remove the smile.

Then Donnie felt a sharp pain in the back of his left shoulder and knew why the smile had stuck. The driver had gotten out of the limo and come around behind Donnie, then stabbed him in the back. Now he was standing staring at Donnie, a tall, muscular blond man in a chauffeur's uniform, holding a long-bladed knife as if he were an expert. "Better back off," he said, "unless you wanna be dead meat."

Donnie didn't have a chance to back away on his own. Gil the mountain was up and shoved him down to the sidewalk so hard Donnie's head slammed into the base of a street light. While he was shaking his head, trying to clear it and deal with the pain in his shoulder, he saw Gil push Nola the rest of the way into the limo while the driver got back in behind the steering wheel. Smelling the limo's exhaust fumes, Donnie grabbed the street light and used it for support to help him gain his feet. Across the street, a man and woman had stopped walking and were staring over at him.

From where they were standing they wouldn't see the blood. Donnie knew that if they hadn't seen the knife, they'd probably assume he was drunk as he staggered back toward his apartment to use the phone. Just an argumentative boozer who'd gotten into a slight altercation.

The woman clutched the man's coat and tugged at it in an attempt to get him to start walking away. She'd decided this wasn't something to get involved in.

"You okay, buddy?" the man called.

Donnie waved him off and kept going.

39

They wanted to keep Donnie in the hospital a full three days, but on the second day he climbed out of bed, got dressed, and insisted. He had to swear by every religion to the hospital personnel that he wouldn't put any strain on his left arm. The knife blade had been deflected by bone, so the wound wasn't deep, more a gash near the point of the shoulder.

The problem was that sutures might tear, said the matronly blue-haired nurse who'd taken a liking to Donnie. The problem was that the dressed wound might begin bleeding, said the young intern who'd briefly thought of muscling Donnie into staying. The problem was the possibility of infection, said the doctor who'd treated Donnie when he'd been taken to the Emergency Room.

Donnie knew the problem was Daisy.

While he lay in his hospital bed, her time was running out.

When they'd given up trying to convince him to stay, they transported Donnie to the hospital's side exit in a wheelchair. It was a precaution that had to do with liability insurance, confided the gum-chomping teenage volunteer in the pink-and-white starched uniform as she pushed him along. Donnie told her insurance was a wonderful thing, and for some of us difficult to obtain. She looked at him blankly and didn't offer to wheel him to a line of cabs outside at the curb.

Liability stopped at the threshold, but not compassion. She stood watching and waved wistfully to him as the cab he'd climbed into drove away.

"Where the hell you been?" Roma asked, when Donnie phoned him from the apartment.

"Injured. I tore a tendon in my shoulder and couldn't go in to work." Donnie looked at the stain on the carpet where he'd dripped blood while phoning Jules Donavon for help. There was a red smear on the wall where he'd leaned against it.

"You didn't sleep in your apartment. I know because we called you."

"I was in the hospital."

"Some shoulder strain."

"It's more than a strain," Donnie said. "But it's getting better."

"So nice to hear it. When you going in to work?"

"I don't know. It's a day to day thing."

"You know what else is day to day?"

"Yeah. That's why I called. I want an extension."

"Why should you have that?"

"Christ! I been laid up in a hospital bed the last two days. My arm's still in a sling."

"So's your ass," Roma said. "The game goes on."

"Sure it does. All I'm asking for's a time-out."

"Sorry, not in the rules."

"*You* make the goddam rules!"

"So there's no appeal. Way I figure it, our planted Daisy's got about two more days before the generator runs outta gas."

"What do you want?" Donnie asked in exasperation. "I told you about the Russians, tipped you to a drug raid. What else can I give you?"

"More about the Russians. Every fucking thing about the Russians."

"They don't tell me every fucking thing!" And if you knew it all, Donnie thought, you'd kill me then let Daisy die for sure.

"Find it out," Roma said, and hung up.

There was a knock on the apartment door. Remembering what happened last time he'd answered a similar knock, Donnie stood motionless with the receiver in his hand, listening to the drone of the dial tone.

"Donnie? It's Elana!"

He slipped the receiver into its cradle and went to the door, then unlocked and opened it with his good arm and hand. He felt that he could use his left arm if he must, that it would be strong, but only briefly, and there would be a price. For now, let it rest in its sling.

When he opened the door Elana leaned forward and kissed him on the lips, careful not to let her body touch the sling. She was wearing tight brown corduroy slacks and a black sweater, no coat. It was getting warmer outside, tantalizing the city with the notion of spring. Donnie stepped back to let her enter, saw her gaze take in the bloodstain on the rug, the smear on the wall.

"Place needs paint," he said.

She smiled, but it might have meant anything. "Does being cool about it keep you from remembering you might have died here?"

"It dulls the recollection."

She walked over to the sofa and sat down, still wearing the smile.

"I guess you went to the hospital," Donnie said.

"No, I called there. They told me you'd walked out. I see they were right."

"Not exactly."

"I'm glad I found you here, because I've got something to tell you. I've been watching the Westward Ho Social Club."

He was aghast. She didn't know it, but she'd taken the place of the dead Bert Clover. Donnie wished now he hadn't confided in her. Always when he confided in those he loved he regretted it. "My God, they kill people at that place, Elana!"

"Around here, too," she said. "At least they try."

"You were watching the club. Were you watched back?"

"I'm sure I wasn't. I stayed in the car, kept my distance."

He hoped. "What did you see?"

"Two men loading some cardboard boxes like the ones you described into a van, then they drove away. I followed them to Greenwich Village, to a brownstone building that houses a doctor's offices on the ground floor, living quarters upstairs. They unloaded the boxes there. A tall, gray-haired man who watched them opened one of the boxes and checked its contents. I saw him halfway pull out a steel cylinder."

"You sure?"

"Sure enough to come here and tell you about it."

Donnie went to the chair where he'd tossed his windbreaker and worked his way into the jacket, letting the left sleeve hang empty.

"Give me the address, then stay here," he said.

"I'm going with you."

"That would be stupid of you." He immediately wished he hadn't said that; it wasn't the way to convince Elana.

"Stupid? Like watching the Westward Ho Club and following a van?"

He knew she'd dug in for a major battle.

"Anyway, with the useless arm, you need me to drive."

"It isn't useless. I can drive fine."

"So drive. But you're not going without me. I'm the one who knows the address."

She was right. He had no choice. Again. If there were any possible way to bargain with her, to change her mind . . .

But he knew there wasn't. About this there would be no compromise. She wasn't going with him—he was going with her.

"Come on," Donnie said, giving up and moving toward the door. "There isn't time to discuss it. There isn't much time left for anything."

Elana pushed herself up from the sofa, working her limbs stiffly and slowly. Donnie noticed her weariness, the redness of her eyes. She must not have slept for a long time.

In the hall, she hurried to keep up. "Don't be bull-headed and try to outrun me or get me to chase after you. If we get there a few minutes later, it won't be the end of the world."

"Won't it?" Donnie didn't slow down as he headed for the stairs. "The thing about the end of the world is that it happens to people one by one."

40

Seated beside him in the Honda, Elana pointed out the brownstone in the West Village to Donnie as they drove past. He parked half a block down and sat looking around.

They were on a typical side street for that part of town, with intermittent car and pedestrian traffic and lined with trees that would provide good shade but now bore only early spring buds. The buildings were old, most of them brick, with narrow concrete stoops and wrought iron railings, window flower boxes, wood shutters. The good life offered by Greenwich Village, where Donnie sometimes thought he would like to live in peace.

He and Elana got out of the Honda and walked down the block. On a brass plaque mounted near the brownstone's front door was lettered DR. NORMAN AQUASIAN.

Donnie glanced over at Elana and thought about asking her to return to the car. But he could predict her response.

When she sensed him staring and looked over at him, he said, "You don't feel well."

"Less and less well."

He held the brownstone's door open for her and they entered, finding themselves in what had once been a foyer but was now enlarged to be a reception room. While the building's first floor had been converted to serve as the doctor's office, touches of elegance remained. The beige ceramic tile floor was delicately patterned with glazed green maple leaves; the woodwork was enameled a light tan; flocked cream-colored wallpaper carried the leaf motif; a large crystal chandelier glittered like a galaxy above an ornate, curved mahogany desk that screamed Valuable Antique.

Behind the desk sat a narrow woman in her late forties. The lucite plaque near her phone said she was JOANI WINKLEMAN. She had a phony tan, skinned-back black hair, and even sitting down she appeared tall. Her prominent cheekbones, heavily mascared brown eyes, and slender figure gave her the look of an aging supermodel. Behind her were two tall, six-paneled walnut doors with a patina that suggested they were original to the building.

Donnie peeled off his windbreaker and draped it over a chair arm. Elana followed his example but stood with her coat folded over her arm.

Joani Winkleman had been bent over a notebook computer with intense concentration, occasionally pecking at a key with a talonlike lavender fingernail. Now she looked up as if just then realizing she wasn't alone. "Sorry, but I was in the middle of something. Can I help you?" Her smile was toothy and too wide for her face, and no more genuine than her tan.

"My wife isn't feeling well," Donnie said. "We're from out of town, and I'm afraid she got infected by whatever it is that's going around."

"Is something going around?" asked Joani Winkleman.

"So we heard on the subway."

"It's mostly my throat," Elana said hoarsely.

Donnie almost winced. *Don't overdo it!* "What we were wondering," he said, "is if maybe the doctor could take a quick look at her and prescribe an antibiotic."

"Oh, I doubt he would do that."

"Why not? Isn't he a doctor? Don't you take walk-ins?"

Still with the fashion show runway smile, Joani Winkleman stood up, all six feet plus of her, even thinner than she'd appeared sitting down. "Oh, he's a doctor, all right. And while he usually sees patients only by appointment, he might take walk-ins. But I don't think he'd be of much help to you. He's a fertility specialist."

Donnie glanced at Elana and grinned. "Nope, we don't need one of those. Not with our four kids."

"They're all great kids," Elana said with a catch in her voice. Donnie shouldn't have mentioned children.

"I'm sure they are." Joani Winkleman didn't sound even slightly interested. "There's a pharmacy at the end of the block, right around the corner." She motioned languidly with a long arm; she would never seem to be moving fast. "They're very good and would be glad to recommend something for you. Unless you'd like to have another child," she added, deadpan in a way that made Donnie think of the term heroine chic.

"No, no, sorry to take up your time." He backed toward the door, feigning embarrassment. Elana faked a cough and followed him.

"Be careful," said Joani Winkleman, "it's going around."

When they were outside and had taken the three concrete steps down to the sidewalk, Donnie said, "What do you think?"

Elana looked thoughtful. "Great cheekbones."

Donnie started walking back toward the car and she fell in beside him.

"There's really not much to think," she said. "We didn't even get to lay eyes on Dr. Aquasian. And what kind of name is that?"

"I think it's Armenian." They were passing the car.

"Where are we going?" Elana asked.

"The pharmacy."

"In case Winkleman calls them to find out if we really went there?"

"That, and to buy some flesh-colored bandages."

They returned to the doctor's offices ten minutes later.

Joani Winkleman favored them with her toothsome smile. "I thought you'd be back."

"Forgot my jacket," Donnie said, grinning awkwardly.

"I noticed," said Joani Winkleman.

Elana said, "Sorry we keep bothering you," as she stepped over in front of Donnie and lifted his jacket from the chair, letting it fan out as she straightened up.

Donnie took the jacket from her, slipped it on, then turned and seemed to struggle with the zipper for a few seconds before leaving.

"I hope you don't catch what she has," Joani Winkleman said as he was pulling the door closed.

"Slick," Elana said, when they were walking again toward the parked Honda. As she was retrieving his jacket, he'd used the opportunity to place half of a stick-on bandage over the strike plate of the door lock. It was the kind of lock that engaged automatically when someone turned it on the inside and closed the door. With the cavity for the latch capped by the bandage's adhesive strip, it wouldn't engage. With luck, whoever pulled the door closed when leaving wouldn't notice and would assume the door was locked behind them.

"It's worked before," Donnie said. "And the door frame and strip of bandage are close to the same color, so anyone would have to look closely to notice something's wrong."

"What if the lock pushes right through the adhesive strip when the door closes?"

"Not likely."

"What if there was another lock we didn't notice?"

"There wasn't."

"What if . . ."

"It won't, it can't, it never has, it isn't possible."

They were walking past the parked Honda again.

"Where are we going now?" Elana asked. "Back to the pharmacy?"

"To the hardware store farther down the block. To

see if they have a pry bar or a large screwdriver, in case something goes wrong."

While Donnie was in the hardware store buying a small steel pry bar, Elana went into the pastry shop next door and bought some cheese Danish and two coffees to go.

It was a few minutes past 11:30 when they returned to the Honda. They sat munching pastry, sipping coffee, watching the brownstone down the block.

Three patients came and went, opening and closing the front door, two women and a man. None of them acted as if they noticed anything wrong with the door.

"What are we waiting for?" Elana asked.

"Lunch."

"We're eating lunch."

"I meant Joani Winkleman's lunch. Dr. Aquasian's. It would be nice if he'd leave along with her, but even if he doesn't, he probably eats lunch upstairs in his living quarters."

"Maybe she eats in, brown bags it."

"Joani Winkleman's not the brown bag type. She'll go out someplace and get overcharged and pick at some lettuce."

"Maybe she doesn't eat lunch at all."

"She will."

"I'm not so sure. That body. Those cheekbones."

"You want that last Danish?"

"No thanks."

At 12:10 the brownstone's front door opened and Joani Winkleman stepped out onto the stoop. She was wearing a long leopard-skin coat that looked like a cape and made her seem seven feet tall, and black boots with leopard fur trim.

"Fur's back," Donnie said. He was suddenly feeling better, about to do something, shape the future.

"She looks ready to bring down an antelope."

They watched Joani Winkleman absently close the door and hang something on the knob. Then she took the steps to the sidewalk and strode away in the opposite direction from where they were parked down the block and across the street.

When she'd stalked around the corner, Donnie and Elana got out of the Honda.

What Joani Winkleman had hung on the doorknob was a small placard saying the doctor's office was closed until 1:00. Donnie didn't disturb the sign. He had the foot-long steel pry bar tucked in his belt beneath his jacket, but it wasn't needed. The adhesive strip over the striker had held and hadn't been discovered. He simply pushed open the door and they stepped inside.

Aware of Elana close behind him, he opened one of the tall doors behind the reception desk. It led to a hall lined with four more doors. Probably rooms the patients were shuffled between while undergoing preliminary procedures.

The floor creaked in the apartment above, startling Donnie, then reassuring him that Dr. Aquasian was upstairs.

Donnie began opening doors, seeing nothing but medical equipment, white porcelain, and examination tables covered by what looked like white butcher paper.

In the fourth room, he saw a second door.

When he opened it, there were the cardboard boxes with PTERODACTYL lettered on them.

He took several steps toward the stacked boxes.

A voice said, "Don't bother opening any of the containers. You'd be sorry. And they're empty, anyway."

Donnie and Elana whirled at the same time, as if they were doing a fast dance step.

A tall, handsome man with closely trimmed graying hair stood behind them. With his chalk-striped, double-breasted dark suit, white shirt, and conservative silk tie, he might have just stepped into a corporate board meeting, or out of the pages of *GQ*. In his right hand he held a long-barreled revolver Donnie recognized as a Smith & Wesson .44 Magnum, enough gun for any job. In his left he was clutching a letter-size white envelope.

He said, "Joani told me about your earlier visit."

Donnie reached out and clutched Elana's elbow, steadying her. It was a time not to move. Neither of them did.

Donnie met the doctor's unblinking gaze with his own. There was an old sadness in the man's expression, and at the same time something terrifying. "I take it you're Dr. Aquasian."

"Was," the doctor said, and inserted the revolver barrel in his mouth and squeezed the trigger.

The tiny room was all noise and scorched-stench and violent motion, much of it red. Someone was screaming.

Donnie pulled Elana tight to him and used both hands to cover her eyes.

He led her from the room and sat her down on one of the examination tables. The NYPD would be here soon, and he wanted to be gone when they arrived.

Careful where he stepped, he returned to where the doctor lay and plucked the white envelope from the dead man's hand. It was unsealed, so he opened it and unfolded the sheet of white paper that was inside.

On the paper was written a single sentence above Dr. Aquasian's scrawled signature:

Joani knew nothing about it.

Donnie replaced the envelope and its contents in the doctor's lifeless hand. He thought about grabbing one of the cylinders to take with him, then realized the phone call he was going to make to Donavon would assure that the boxes containing all of them would be in the hands of Bureau techs within the hour.

He went back to Elana, who was still seated hunched over on the examination table. She leaned heavily against him as they walked through the quiet reception room, then outside.

On the way out, he removed the adhesive strip from the brass striker plate and let the door lock behind them.

The street appeared normal, but the odds were good that someone outside or in the attached buildings had heard what might have been a gunshot. Donnie kept a firm grip on Elana's arm, making sure they didn't hurry, wouldn't be memorable.

As they were driving away in the Honda, he saw the leopard goddess Joani Winkleman come out of a restaurant two blocks down and stride regally toward her job. He remembered what Dr. Aquasian had taken the time to write before killing himself.

Cheekbones and luck, Donnie thought.

41

Donnie had called Jules Donavon at the first opportunity and told him what happened in Dr. Aquasian's office. The FBI would be on the scene soon after the phone call, which was brief. Both men knew the value of time. Jules told Donnie to sit tight in his apartment and wait.

Donnie sat slouched in the wing chair, working on a can of Heineken that had become lukewarm. He knew why it was taking a long time for Donavon to get back to him. Thoroughness. The Bureau would be all over Aquasian's office and upstairs apartment. They'd preserve and catalog evidence, carefully examine the empty steel cylinders. Later they'd talk to the patients the doctor saw today. And they'd question Joani Winkleman like she'd never been questioned before. The good doctor had done her a great favor by writing that note before killing himself.

Donnie had been sliding in and out of sleep when the ringing phone jolted him awake. He levered himself up out of the chair, the stale taste of beer still in his mouth, and crossed the room toward all the noise.

He simultaneously glanced at his watch and lifted the receiver: 9:05 P.M.

Jules Donavon.

"There was nothing in Dr. Aquasian's office or living quarters that provided any information," Jules said.

Donnie wasn't surprised. "What about Joani Winkleman?"

"She's all style and no knowledge. Been working for Aquasian since his wife died eight years ago. She and the doctor were good friends, maybe something more. The day the steel cylinders were delivered to his office, then moved on to another site, she was told not to come in to work, told the office would be closed. She said the doctor did that once or twice a year, when he'd drive up to Maine and visit his son."

"Think the son knows anything?"

"No. Guy's an orthodontist in some little town called Willow Walk, straightens teeth, supports a wife and four kids. Leads a life dull as Novocaine."

"So we've got nothing," Donnie said in exasperation.

"Yes and no. There's more news, good and bad."

"Give me the bad first."

"It's the same news. The metal cylinders are air-tight stainless steel with glass linings. Lab techs went over them and found traces of what they contained. Anthrax spores."

Anthrax. Terrorism. What he was involved in opened up wider and even more frightening in front of Donnie. It went beyond the personal to the catastrophic, to a place where people were sacrificed to save more people. *Daisy . . .*

"There was something else," Jules said. "Some of the cylinders and a few of the cardboard boxes contained faint traces of black powder."

"You mean gunpowder?"

"Something like."

"How do you figure that?"

"I'd like to think it's coincidental, that the people handling the anthrax containers had also been handling guns and ammo."

"It's possible."

"Donnie . . ." Something in Jules's voice, as if he were forcing out words he didn't want to say. "The anthrax means we have to move fast on the Russians. Find out what's going on. There are rumors about the tunnels leading into Manhattan. About the subway system."

"There always are," Donnie said.

"Maybe not just rumors this time. And remember when the toxic gas was released a few years ago in the subways in Japan. We can't sit on this. We have to lean on the Russians, try to stop whatever's planned before it actually happens."

There it was. Donnie felt weak, scared. "You move on the Russians, and Roma might see my usefulness as ended."

It took Jules a long time to reply. "I know. Daisy. But *anthrax*, Donnie! We've got to find out why it was brought into the country, where it was taken. We don't have any choice. You do see that, don't you? Don't you?"

"This is my daughter, Jules!"

"Dammit, that wasn't the question! You think this is easy for me, Donnie?"

"Fuck you, Jules! I'm not going to say it, not going to give you the okay! That's final!"

"Don't hang up, Donnie!"

Donnie didn't quite.

He slowly raised the receiver back to his ear.

"Roma's a loose cannon," Jules said in a new, cautious voice, "playing the game off the board. Maybe you've got no choice but to join him there."

"What's that mean?"

"Don't ask me that again, Donnie. But this anthrax thing, forcing the issue. It gives you a few options you didn't have before. I'm not suggesting any, just pointing out they exist."

Donnie stood holding the phone, not quite believing this.

"You did good work out at La Guardia, Donnie. That's one reason we don't need you there anymore."

"Jules—"

"Don't ask me about anything. I'm not asking you."

Donnie said nothing. Jules knew what had to be in his mind.

"Like you said, Donnie, she's your daughter."

42

As soon as Jules had hung up, Donnie phoned Elana.

"You all right?" he asked.

"Sure. Fine. I was sleeping." She didn't sound fine or as if she'd been asleep.

He told her about Donavon's phone call, about the traces of anthrax spore and of gunpowder. He didn't tell her about the move on the Russians, or about being pulled from the assignment at La Guardia.

"The important thing now is for the Bureau to find what was in those cylinders," he said. "And it has to be as soon as possible." Donnie had read how anthrax, airborne as mist or in powder form, could infect thousands in a heavily populated area. Inhaled like any other bacteria, it caused symptoms similar to a cold or the flu within about a week, and within twenty-four to thirty-six hours usually resulted in death. The fatality rate was over 90 percent, making it almost as deadly as Dr. Aquasian's bullet.

"How will they ever locate it?" Elana asked.

"That's one of the reasons I called. There's a good chance they transported it in the same van they used to move the cylinders from the Westward Ho Club. When you followed the van from the club to Dr. Aquasian's, did you happen to write down its license plate number?"

"It never occurred to me. Dammit! I should have, I know."

"This isn't your game. Don't flog yourself with guilt. Anyway, maybe it's not too late."

"What's that mean?"

"Close your eyes," Donnie said, "and put yourself back there parked on the dark street, watching the van being unloaded. Feel the steering wheel between your fingers. Smell the car's interior. Did you have the radio on?"

"No."

"Listen to whatever small sounds you heard that night." He waited. "Are you looking through the windshield at the van?"

"Yes."

"Now try to see the license plate. Lean forward. Concentrate."

Almost a minute passed.

"I can't. I'm sorry."

"It works sometimes."

She was silent.

"Elana?"

"Maybe it worked this time, too. At least partway. I do remember something, now that I've reconstructed it the way you said. Three numbers on the license plate: six, one, zero."

"Anything else?"

"No. Nothing."

"Were the numbers in that sequence?"

"Oh, yes, I'm positive of that."

Donnie wondered how she could be so sure.

"I remember because that's Daisy's birthday," Elana said, "June tenth. That's why I paid attention to the numbers, why I could recall them a few minutes ago."

"You remembered the numbers, but what about the van itself? Anything special about it?"

"I don't think so. It was a plain white van, a large one, not a minivan. It didn't look new, didn't look old. Ordinary work van, not banged up, an antenna on the roof, no lettering on the back doors or sides."

"What kind of antenna?"

"Not a big one. You know, one of those little aerials like some cabs have. Is any of this a help?"

"We're going to find out," Donnie said.

He called Jules Donavon and gave him the numbers and the fact that the van had a roof antenna.

"Three consecutive numbers is something, but not much," Jules said.

"Not by themselves," Donnie said. "But if the van has an antenna, there's probably a two-way radio in it and a license to go with it. Can the computers cross-reference commercial radio licenses with consecutive vehicle plate numbers six, one, zero, maybe come up with the registration for a late model van, color white?"

"Maybe," Jules said. "They can cross-check errors on my five-year-old tax return. Let's give it a try."

It took Jules half an hour to call back.

"The van's owned by Pyromagic, Inc.," he said.

"They got a warehouse over in Jersey. Thank God for the microchip."

Donnie knew that wasn't all they needed. He was afraid to believe. "Don't tell me what's next. The company reported the van stolen."

"No, it's not listed on the hot sheet."

"So what is Pyromagic? A cookware company?"

"Uh-uh. They're in pyrotechnics—the fireworks business."

Fireworks. *Gunpowder!*

"We're gonna drive out there tonight and see what's popping."

"I want to go," Donnie said.

"A car's already on the way to pick you up."

43

Pyromagic was on the eastern fringe of Newark, on a block of dim warehouses and small, mostly defunct factories. There was no residential or entertainment area nearby, so only a few parked cars lined the dark streets. They looked like the kind of cars the owners wouldn't mind seeing stolen.

The Pyromagic warehouse was a small, flat-roofed building colored a dusty gray. It had high, slitted windows and alongside it was a graveled parking lot enclosed on three sides by an eight-foot-high chain-link fence, and on the fourth side by the building's east wall. The fence had a chain-link double gate fastened shut with a padlock, and was topped with a jumble of coiled razor wire. Four vehicles were parked in the lot, three cars and a white van with the license plate number the computers had tracked.

Donnie was in the lead FBI unmarked Ford with Donavon, who'd told him Pyromagic was a legitimate fireworks business that was purchased anonymously by the Russians through a straw party six months ago. Since then there had been a complete employee turnover.

The car swerved to avoid a pothole but hit another, causing the driver to curse under his breath. He was a young, bespectacled agent named Favorall. Jules Donavon sat next to him. Donnie was in back. All three men were armed with stubby and deadly 9mm Heckler and Koch MP5A5 submachine guns and wore bulletproof vests and dark jackets with orange FBI lettering on the back. Newark PD's SWAT team had met them half a mile back; six combat-equipped officers in a beat-up Dodge van disguised as a work vehicle. The team's commander, Lieutenant Barry Engleman, was a wiry, restless man in his fifties who made Donnie nervous.

The battered old van had turned right at the last intersection and was circling the block, giving Engleman the opportunity to size up the warehouse from all sides. He'd said the van was confiscated six months ago in a drug raid and had proved useful to both the SWAT team and Narcotics. The name of a nonexistent exterminator service had been lettered on it; maybe somebody's notion of humor.

The other FBI car, containing two Organized Crime Squad agents and the ADIC from the Bureau's New York Field Office, was tailing the car driven by Favorall.

Half a block down from the warehouse, the van passed the FBI cars going the other way. Engleman, in the front passenger seat, raised a fist with a thumbs-up signal. The van continued to the end of the block, then turned the corner to drive back to the rear of the building. Favorall led the two FBI cars in a U-turn, then pulled over so they were parked down the street from the warehouse, out of sight. The plan was for the SWAT team to storm in through the back of the building. The FBI would delay, apprehending anyone who tried to make their escape out the front.

There was a sharp, loud report—the flash-bang, or percussion grenade the SWAT team used as a diversionary device before charging the building. Donnie removed his left arm from its sling. Favorall stomped on the accelerator. The operation was underway. Since this was a fireworks warehouse, the diversionary grenade had been detonated against one of the outside walls. Donnie hoped it would be diversion enough.

Both FBI cars screeched to a halt at the curb across the street from the building, where they would be used as cover if a firefight erupted. The agents had strict orders not to shoot if a bullet might find its way inside the warehouse.

After the initial explosion, which Donnie figured should have scared the hell out of anyone working in a fireworks warehouse, nothing seemed to have changed. The SWAT team had to be inside by now. At least there was no gunfire. Maybe whoever was in there had decided not to resist. Crouched low next to Favorall, forearms and automatic weapon resting on the car's warm hood, Donnie waited.

"Whadya think?" Favorall asked.

Thunk!

Donnie knew the sound. A bullet striking the car.

"That we're being shot at," he said.

"I was afraid you were going to say that."

Someone had screwed up. Donnie saw several dark figures in the fenced-in parking lot. There must have been a door in the side of the building, one painted the same color as the wall, and no one in the raiding party had noticed it. The occupants of the warehouse, at least four of them, were out in the parking lot, armed and shooting. Well armed. Automatic weapons rattled loudly in the night. The dark figures were dashing around and firing crazily and inaccurately, trying to use their weapons while at the same time attempting to pile inside the parked cars. One of the cars was already started. It looked like an old black Lincoln. In his panic, the driver had switched on its headlights.

Favorall was standing up, craning his neck, blasting away with his submachine gun. Donnie stayed down but also fired, aiming low to blow out tires, keeping his shots well right to stay clear of the warehouse full of fireworks. The gun bucked in his grip, sending needles of pain up his left arm to his shoulder and probably popping stitches in the stab wound sutures.

Tires growled on gravel and the car with the headlights was speeding toward the closed chain-link gate. The driver was going to try breaking through it even though it was chained and locked. Donnie aimed at the bright headlights, which were now directed at the FBI cars and agents, making them easier targets. Return fire whined and ricochetted off the bricks behind him, and there was the crash of broken glass as bullets took out a soaped over shop window. The Lincoln's headlights suddenly winked out, but not because of Donnie's gunfire. The car had slammed into the chain-link gate, which gave but didn't open. The fencing had simply formed a steel net to catch the car.

The big Lincoln backed away about twenty feet then came at the fence again.

Same result. But its engine continued to roar above the rattle and bark of gunfire.

The SWAT team was positioned at the back of the lot now, firing through the chain-link. The men fenced inside the parking lot were caught in a crossfire. Donnie saw one of them break into a violent dance then suddenly drop.

Then with a roar the Lincoln was through the gate. But the driver wasn't trying to escape. He was steering the big car straight at the parked FBI vehicles, picking up speed. The engine was revved so high it was screaming and one of the headlights was blinking like an angry, sightless eye. It took everyone by surprise, and there was a lull in the gunfire. The Lincoln charged across the street at an angle like an enraged and blinded beast.

There was no way, no time, to get out of its path. Guns were blasting and chattering again. Favorall was standing straight up, pouring fire at the car's windshield, trying to take out the driver or get him to swerve. Donnie could think of nothing else to do. He was up and firing, as were all the agents. No way to know which way the car might veer. No choice but to stand their ground. Favorall threw up his arms and fell back, his left hand striking Donnie's forehead.

The Lincoln crashed into the Ford Donnie was using as cover, shoving it with two tons of momentum. Its right fender was coming at him. Instinctively he leaped onto the Ford's hood to avoid being crushed against the building behind him.

He was crouched low on the hood, traveling backward, knowing it was no good, that both cars would hit the building and fold up into him.

Then he was hurled off the hood into darkness, landing hard on his back and sliding.

Time seemed to slide with him. In the darkness above, vague shapes were rotating.

When he realized his motion had ceased, he wasn't sure how long he'd been lying on his back.

Something was choking him, a strap up tight against his chin. He grabbed it and yanked it away. Then he struggled to his feet, feeling and hearing broken glass crunch beneath his shoes.

He was looking past both wrecked cars at the world outside. They'd gone through the broken-out shop window, taking only part of the brick wall.

Donnie started to raise his submachine gun to cover the driver, then realized he was holding nothing but air.

Get it goddam together! he told himself, lowering his arms. Something was very wrong with his left one.

He saw Donavon behind the two crash-merged cars and struggled in his direction. There was just enough room to squeeze between the smashed FBI car and the damaged wall.

As he wriggled his way outside, Donnie peered into the Lincoln. The driver was looking back at him with one eye in half a face. Stupid fucker, you had a fierce heart, Donnie found himself saying silently to the dead man through his shock. And he experienced a sense of shame and rage for admiring such a man. The admiration joined them in a way that made him feel guilty.

"You okay, Donnie?"

It was Jules. "I think so. Landed on my back, and the Kevlar vest broke my fall and protected me from shattered glass."

Jules looked over at the dead man in the car. Donnie couldn't help it and looked again himself.

"Stupid fucker," Donnie said.

"Had some balls, though."

Donnie didn't answer.

Sirens were sounding now, and Jules and someone else were helping Donnie out of his jacket and vest. His left arm and shoulder still hurt, but not as much.

"You got some blood there," Jules said, holding out the vest. It glittered with glass shards, and there was a dark stain on the left shoulder.

"It's from the old wound," Donnie said. "Far as I know."

Donavon grunted and tossed the vest down in the street, which was littered with 9mm shell casings.

Donnie kept waiting for pain but felt none, only a dull throbbing. Across the street SWAT team members were standing near three men who were leaning at a sharp angle with both hands against what was left of the chain-link fence. Beyond them a man lay facedown in the parking lot. Sirens were wailing now, close by. Police cars. Ambulances.

"How's Favorall?" Donnie asked.

"Dead."

Killed by the guy with the balls, Donnie thought.

"One of the SWAT team's dead, too. And three from

inside the warehouse. None of us noticed that side door; it was painted the same color as the wall so it wouldn't be an invitation to burglars." Jules put his fists on his hips and looked around him. "I hope to hell we get something out of this when we search the place and ID and interrogate the three warehouse guys who survived." He angrily kicked aside ejected shell casings, sending them clattering across the concrete. "Shit! Didn't this turn into one hellacious mess?"

"Tell me about it," Donnie said.

An ambulance glided down the block, polished chrome glittering, lights blazing, a jukebox on wheels. Donavon stepped out in the street and waved it over. "Here!" he yelled as the vehicle slowed and the driver lowered the window so he could hear better. "Over here and help this man!"

The Bureau taking care of its own.

The paramedics tended to Donnie's shoulder wound, then put a fresh dressing on it and outfitted his arm with a new sling. An overweight paramedic with hair that made him resemble Moe of the Three Stooges told Donnie it looked like he had no other injuries but that he couldn't be sure. And his new dressing was only temporary. He was going to be transported to the hospital ER for further examination. But when Moe and his partner were occupied talking to someone from another ambulance that had just arrived, Donnie slipped away unnoticed.

An hour had passed since the shootout. Donnie walked across the street to the warehouse, which was crawling with agents and lab techs, searching for any sign of whatever might now contain the anthrax spores.

Jules saw Donnie enter the warehouse and came over to him.

"We haven't found anything yet."

"Not that big a place," Donnie said. "If it's here, we should find it."

"You'd think," Jules agreed.

"Maybe it's mixed in with the powder in the fireworks."

Jules shook his head. "Doesn't look like it. We spot checked for that and didn't find any traces." He gazed out at the agents working among the racks of boxed fireworks. "This place isn't a factory, just a storage building. My guess is the Russians only used it for that."

"What about the three prisoners?"

"Nothing there yet," Jules said. "And it's gonna be time-consuming. They've already got expensive attorneys and nobody's talking." He took a closer look at Donnie. "You won't go to the hospital, why don't you go home and rest? You look worse than that guy in the Lincoln."

"Couple of differences between me and him," Donnie said. "One of them is there's something I need to do."

Donvaon squinted hard at Donnie as if his eyes were burning, then hitched his thumbs in his belt and turned and walked away.

If Donnie had anything else to say, he didn't want to hear it.

"You! With your arm in the sling!"

Donnie turned around. It was Moe, looking as angry as if Shemp had just poked him in both eyes.

"Get back to the ambulance! We gotta get moving!"

Donnie figured this wasn't a guy to argue with, and besides, he was feeling a little queasy.

Moe grabbed him by the unslung elbow to support him.

That was okay with Donnie.

44

Once they have you they don't want to release you. They transfer you from department to department, room to room, sedating, testing, probing, observing. Donnie was afraid they were going to reinjure his arm and shoulder just by vigorous examination.

It was almost noon when he finally got out of the hospital. He met again briefly with Donavon, then he phoned Roma from the deli near the apartment.

Roma was obviously aggravated. "I'm sitting here in a restaurant, just ordered lunch, taking this on my cell phone. You better have a damned good reason to be calling."

"I was hoping you hadn't had lunch. We need to meet."

"You calling from work?"

"No. Didn't make it in. I'll explain later. I'll buy lunch."

"Let's make it dinner. This evening at Frannie's."

"Gotta be sooner. Something's happened I don't want to talk about on the phone."

Long sigh. "Give me a goddam clue!"

"How about a shooting war outside Newark, should

be in the news by now? Five dead, including an FBI agent."

"Well, I'm not up on the news. You tell me about it. This has to do with you?"

"Me, you, the Russians."

"Tell me some more."

"Not on the phone."

"Five dead, huh? I hope one of 'em's that goddam— No, never mind. What I'm gonna do is postpone lunch. We'll meet. You at your apartment?"

"Close."

"I'll have a car pick you up outside your place in half an hour."

"I'll be—"

But Roma had hung up, demonstrating who was in control of the conversation. The kind of thing you had to learn if you wanted to move up in the Mafia. And you had to take a chance and show some initiative. Like moonlighting by kidnapping somebody's daughter and making it pay off big.

Mako was driving the car, a gray Mercedes 500SL with tinted windows. It glided to a halt near Donnie in front of his apartment building and the passenger side door opened. Mako, leaning over from behind the steering wheel, motioned Donnie inside. He was wearing dark green work pants and a gray shirt. His work outfit. Roma must have called him away from La Guardia.

"Some set of wheels," Donnie remarked, settling into the soft leather upholstery.

"What's in the bags?" Mako asked, pointing to the white paper sacks Donnie was carrying.

"Lunch. From the deli down the block. Roma told me he had to postpone his, so I thought I'd bring some."

"You tryin' to get in good with your keepers?"

"That, and I'm hungry."

Mako looked straight ahead and took the car up to forty in a blink. "Hold onto those sacks an' fasten your seatbelt, fuckface. It's a dangerous world."

"Don't you ever lighten up?"

"My first wife used to ask me that all the time. Seemed to think I oughta be giddy just like her. Then one day she asked me once too often and I stuck her hand down the garbage disposal."

"She was pretty far out of line," Donnie said.

"More'n you think. Bad part was, it was the hand with her expensive wedding ring."

"Bet she caught hell for that."

"Naw, we had one of them modern marriages. Doctors saved that finger but not the ring, so I bought her another one."

"A marriage like that, I'm surprised it ended in divorce."

"I didn't say nothin' about a divorce."

They were on the East Side, not far from the Queensboro Bridge. The Mercedes slowed on Second Avenue and turned a corner, then pulled up to the basement garage entrance of what looked like a tall condominium or apartment building in the final stages of construction and partly occupied. Mako used a card in a machine, the garage door opened, and the Mercedes purred inside.

The parking spaces were unmarked. Mako drove the Mercedes to the far side of the garage, where there were no other cars parked, and braked it to a halt alongside a thick concrete pillar.

"What is this place?" Donnie asked, as they got out of the car.

"Place where you better come up with a damned good reason for getting us to drive into the city."

The garage was deserted, and their footsteps echoed as they walked toward an elevator. So far, no one had seen them arrive, which was undoubtedly the way Mako and Roma had planned it, why they'd brought him here. No witnesses. Donnie wondered if anyone else would get on the elevator on the way up, or happen to see them in the hall.

Not to worry. Mako used a key in a slot then punched the "Penthouse" button. They rose without stopping. The smell of pepperoni on the deli sandwiches was overpowering inside the small elevator.

The elevator opened directly onto a foyer containing glitzy gold wallpaper and a bust of Adonis on a marble pedestal.

"Guy was a Roman emporer or somethin'," Mako explained, noticing Donnie looking at the bust.

"I thought it was Napoleon."

Mako used a card key on a gilded white door then stepped aside so Donnie would enter the penthouse ahead of him.

The drapes were closed and it was dim at first. A gold chandelier and wall sconces came on automatically, triggered by a sensor. The penthouse had white walls, gold carpet, and hardly any furniture. There were four chairs around a marble-topped table, and not far from them a cream-colored sofa and matching easy chair. Next to the sofa was a brass floor lamp and a small end table with a phone on it. The air was stale, as if no one had been there and disturbed it for a long time.

"Who owns this place?" Donnie asked.

"It's Family owned. We bring clients here now an' then, people we wanna talk with about important matters. Like you better wanna talk to us about, if you don't want some bones broke."

Donnie knew what kind of family owned the penthouse. He glanced around.

"Vinnie'll be here soon," Mako said. "Sit at the table and we'll wait."

Donnie placed the deli bags on the table and sat down. There was little or no furniture in the other rooms he could see into. In the nearest were a few paint buckets. A thick, plastic-coated drop cloth was spread over the carpet.

"You sure are nosy," Mako said, catching him looking.

"That's okay, I'm not insulted. It's my job."

"They're redecoratin' this place. Gettin' ready to put it on the market."

Donnie didn't think so.

The door opened and Vinnie Roma stepped inside and peeled away his light raincoat and tossed it on the sofa back. He was wearing a navy pinstripe suit, white shirt, red silk tie. There was a dark stain, looked like a gravy stain, on the tie.

"I heard some news on the car radio driving in," he said to Donnie. "All hell broke loose at some warehouse in Jersey last night. That the subject of our conversations?"

"More or less."

"You know something about it?"

"I was there."

Roma sat down at the table, opposite Donnie. Mako remained standing. He pulled a revolver from his suitcoat pocket and checked to make sure it was loaded, then replaced it, mostly for show so Donnie would know he had the gun at the ready.

"What's all this?" Roma asked, looking at the paper bags from the deli.

"Fuckhead brought lunch," Mako said.

Donnie nodded. "Sandwiches." He opened the bags and got out three hoagies half-wrapped in thin waxed paper. They smelled great, looked tasty. The other bag held three cans of beer.

"So how's that little war in Jersey figure in with us?" Roma asked, grabbing the nearest sandwich.

"It changes things." Donnie unwrapped a sandwich, then opened a can of beer. "This'll be a little warm, but I think it's okay."

Roma chewed a bite of hoagie and looked at him. Something was going on here, the look said, that maybe he didn't understand. Time to walk a little careful. "Changes things, huh? Way I see it, far as you're concerned, things haven't changed for the better."

In the corner of his vision Donnie saw Mako slowly

draw the revolver back out of his coat pocket. He placed it on the table next to his can of beer. "Go ahead an' talk free," Mako said. "This place is soundproof. Hell, you could fire a cannon off in here an' nobody'd hear it."

"The important change," Donnie said, "is I'm now playing where you are, off the board."

Roma smirked. "FBI agents don't play off the board."

"They do if their daughter's been kidnapped."

"I don't follow."

Mako suddenly coughed, choking. "What the fuck is this?"

Donnie and Roma looked. He was holding in his palm the half-chewed food he'd spit out, along with something slender and dark that he'd bitten into in his sandwich.

Donnie glanced at the mess in Mako's hand. "Looks like a finger."

Mako stared at him, then stood up and began to gag.

"I got it in the mail, thought you might want it back," Donnie said. "Thought you might wanna meet Vicky Benning again."

Mako tried to speak but couldn't.

Roma's face reddened and he looked horrified. Then he began to laugh. Loud, uncontrollably. "Donnie Brassballs!" he said. He slapped the table with his palm. "Practical fucking joker!"

The sickened Mako glared at him in rage.

Roma laughed even louder. "Looka the expression on the poor fucker!" Roma was laughing so hard his eyes were watering.

"What's changed for the better," Donnie said, "is I don't have to stay tight with the Russians anymore."

Roma gradually stopped laughing, grasping what that might mean, why Donnie was pushing this thing.

"There's a certain Family tradition," Donnie said. "Remember? Like this is a date. First you get fed, then you get fucked."

Donnie lazily reached into his windbreaker pocket. Mako, still hunched over and hugging his stomach, noticed and lunged for his revolver. Not fast enough. Donnie's arm snapped to the side with the speed and suddenness of a striking snake. His hand at the end of the straightened arm gripped his 9mm automatic. He shot Mako through the head.

Mako dropped straight down as if a trap door had opened under him. All his circuits had gone dead at once.

Roma jumped up and backed away, knocking over his chair. Mako had become nothing more than a mess on the carpet.

"I would have shot him in the other room on the drop cloth," Donnie said calmly, "where you were gonna shoot me. But I thought I'd make more of an impression this way."

Roma's eyes were wide. One of his hands started to tremble. He held it with the other to make it still, pressing both hands to his crotch as if he were a schoolboy who had to go to the bathroom. "Why'd you do that?" Terror had turned him into a soprano.

"To show you I'm not always a joker. I can be serious."

"So you're fucking serious," Roma said. There was a

touch of the old hollow bravado, what he was made of. "Just what the hell do you want?"

"You're going to make a phone call to whoever took Daisy and tell him to go dig up that box she's in. And make sure she doesn't get hurt. Tell him the deal's over and you want her set free."

"You really think I'm gonna do that?"

Donnie shot Roma through the left arm. "I think." He motioned with the gun toward the table by the sofa where the phone sat. "Make the call."

Bent over, his face screwed up in pain while he clutched his left wrist with his right hand, Roma shuffled over to the phone. "I'm not Mako. You know if you kill me you're good as dead yourself," he hissed in a voice vibrant with pain.

"You forget two things," Donnie said. "Nobody above you in the Mafia knows about our reaquaintance. And I've already got a Mafia contract out on me. Another one wouldn't mean much."

"You stupid asshole! You really think you got nothing more to lose?"

"Freedom's just another word. Make the call. If you have any reservations, take another look at what Mako did to the carpet. It's way beyond spot remover."

Roma lifted the receiver and laid it next to the phone. Using the forefinger of his good hand, he pecked out a long distance number. He almost dropped the receiver when he picked it up and pressed it to his ear. Pain could make people awkward. So could fear.

"Don't screw this up," Donnie warned.

Roma glared at him through his agony. But there

was defeat in his eyes. "Hymie, it's Vinnie Roma. We got what we wanted on this end, so drive over and set the girl free. . . . That doesn't matter. I'll explain later." Almost a minute passed. "Dammit, Hymie, you do it and do it right and do it now!"

Roma hung up the phone.

"What happened to Charlie Farrato?" Donnie asked.

Roma didn't seem surprised that Donnie knew about Farrato. "He wasn't there. Only Hymie." His left hand was still resting lightly on the receiver. And there was something about the set of his shoulders, the way he was standing.

Donnie knew what he was going to do and could have stopped it, but he decided to let it go. Off the board.

"So what now?" Roma asked, but the question was only to divert Donnie's attention while Roma's good hand reached out and wrestled the gun from the pocket of his coat slung over the sofa back.

Taking careful aim, Donnie waited until the gun had cleared the pocket then shot Roma through the chest. Roma screamed shrilly and collapsed backward, dropping the unfired gun on the sofa cushion. He grabbed his coat on the way down, pulling it off the sofa and halfway over him like a blanket. He was still alive. Both his hands were visible, even the one on the injured arm. Donnie kept an eye on both of them.

Roma was sneering up at him. "You woulda shot me one way or the other."

"Maybe," Donnie said.

"Dumbfuck."

"What?"

"Dumbfuck. What I said on the phone was code to tell Farrato the operation's blown."

"It didn't sound like code," Donnie said. "You're lying."

"All it took was one word. A signal we had worked out."

"Bullshit."

"That wasn't the word. But don't worry, we're not gonna cut off your Daisy's air supply. Never were gonna do that. The plan is she's gonna get dug up and used to recoup the money I spent on this deal. Damn near broke me."

"She's going to live?"

"Sure is. For a while longer, anyway. There's a big market in certain Middle East countries for real young blonde virgins. And I got the connections."

Donnie knew that what Roma said about the Middle East market was true. It didn't happen often, but it still happened, and for a lot of money. Oil money, usually, spent by men above the laws of their own countries. Men who made the laws. Young girls, teens and preteens, disappeared, became prime California blondes even if they were picked up hitchhiking in Vermont. "You actually telling me you're gonna sell my daughter?"

"Damned right, I am. It's only fair, the money I spent on her. The buyer's all lined up."

Donnie stared down at the dying man who was still feisty, still playing the game even though he was about to cross over. "You got balls," Donnie said, "but you're lying."

"Oh, yeah? You ever hear of anybody in the Mafia

name of Hymie?" Roma's good hand darted for his coat's other pocket, disappeared into it like a pale rodent scrambling for cover. He could fire through the fabric, maybe get off an accurate shot, close as they were to each other.

Donnie had no choice. He squeezed off two shots and killed Roma.

The hand, holding nothing, slid out of the coat pocket and lay limply palm up.

Donnie went over and felt inside the pocket.

It was empty.

Donnie stood numbly. Smelling the acrid stench of shots fired at close quarters. Smelling spilled blood, like an old copper penny held close beneath his nose.

Smelling his own fear.

Hymie.

Off the board.

45

Donnie made himself calm down, tried to will himself to stop sweating so much. He could almost feel time running through his fingers like hourglass sand. He had to figure out something, then act on it. Every move seemed a step into the abyss. Choose one, choose one! The tiger or the tiger?

He went over to Mako's body and felt in the pocket where he remembered Mako putting the elevator key. When his fingers closed on the cold metal of the key, he withdrew it along with the car keys on their Mercedes remote control fob and backed away, avoiding the area of blood-soaked carpet.

No one saw him when he took the private elevator down to the garage, got the cell phone from the Mercedes, then went back upstairs with it to the penthouse.

He used the cell phone to call Jules Donavon and tell him what had happened. Then he told him the number of the phone in the penthouse and asked him to put a quick trace on the last call from it.

"You need help where you are, Donnie?" Jules asked. "You in control?"

"Nobody's in control. Not in this goddam mess."

"Hang tough and we'll see about that."

Bureau resources were something when all the stops were pulled. Donavon called back in less than ten minutes.

"The call was received in the St. Louis area, but the number belongs to a cell phone. Bad luck, Donnie."

"Maybe not. If I call the number, would you be able to trace its exact origin when the connection's made and I get a ring?"

"I think so, sure. But if Roma was telling the truth, the guy he talked to is gone from where the phone'll be. Unless—"

"Right. Unless it's a mobile phone he was supposed to stay close to all the time. Which means it's a cell phone he's been living with, in his car and wherever he's been staying. He won't just abandon it even though it's served its purpose. He'll take it with him when he gets into his car to drive to where Daisy is."

"It'd be on the move," Jules said. "If the guy gets a suspicious call on it, he might tumble to what's going on and toss it out the car window."

"He's got to drive for a while, then do some digging. I'm gonna wait another twenty minutes, give him time to reach his destination. Then I'll call. If he's outside the car digging, and the car windows are up, he might not hear the phone."

"*If* he parked far enough away from where he's digging."

"They probably chose an isolated spot to bury the box, well away from where anybody might drive past and see the earth's been disturbed or spot the air hose or electrical hookup. Or it might have been buried inside a shack or storage building with a dirt floor. Remember there's a gas operated generator and an air pump. I'll let the phone keep ringing, give us plenty of time to trace the location, then Lily and her team can move in fast."

"It could work. Better wait a half hour, though. Give the guy going for Daisy plenty of time to reach his destination and start his digging."

"That won't be easy, but you're right."

"It's five-oh-seven, Donnie. Start counting down your thirty minutes. After you call the cell phone, make it look like you were never there and get out of the penthouse. What happened can pass for a mob killing. I'll call you later at your apartment. I'm going to hang up now and give the instructions, get everyone on standby."

"Thanks, Jules."

"Later."

After Donavon had hung up, Donnie went around with some tissue from the bathroom and wiped down everything he remembered touching. Then he replaced the Mercedes keys in Mako's pocket and recovered his own 9mm shell casings from the floor and put them in his pocket wrapped in the tissue. Everything he'd brought from the deli he stuffed back into the bags, including the sandwich with Vicky Benning's finger. He didn't see it as evidence any longer, since Mako wasn't going to stand trial.

Then he sat with the dead bodies, looking away from them, trying not to glance at his watch so often.

He had never sat in a quieter room.

* * *

At 5:37 he picked up the receiver of the penthouse phone and used a knuckle to punch the redial button.

The phone on the other end of the line rang.

And rang and rang.

Donnie couldn't ask for anything more. In his mind was an image of a parked car with the cell phone ringing inside, and the driver, maybe Charlie Farrato, off in the distance, bending and straightening with a shovel, bending and straightening, unaware of anything but his digging. Donnie worked hard to hold that image.

He didn't hang up. He wiped down the receiver and laid it on the table next to the phone. Then he went back down in the elevator and walked out of the garage and kept walking until he was several blocks from the building.

The evening was cooling and there were scudding gray clouds that looked as if they were only inches above the buildings. Donnie wondered how the weather was in St. Louis. Was it raining? Was the spring earth soft, making digging easier and faster?

As he passed a ripe-smelling Dumpster, he tossed the elevator key and the cell phone from the Mercedes into it, along with the deli sacks.

Now he could do nothing but go to his apartment and wait for Donavon's call.

The center hadn't held, and this was the day when everything was flying apart. Full of surprises.

When Donnie opened his apartment door and stepped inside, there was Barkov.

46

Barkov was sitting in the same chair, wearing what seemed to be the same clothes he had on when he'd first appeared in Donnie's apartment: Dark brown slacks, camel hair sport jacket, oxblood wingtips. He looked prosperous and relaxed, Mr. World-by-the-Ass. His legs were casually crossed. As before, a tan topcoat lay neatly folded in his lap. His right hand was out of sight beneath the coat.

He was also wearing his crooked, handsome smile. "You're not what you seemed, hey, my friend?"

"Nobody is," Donnie said. He removed his windbreaker, careful of the arm in the sling.

"You were injured at the warehouse last night?"

"A kind of accident," Donnie said noncommittally. He sat down on the sofa, facing Barkov. The Russian seemed concerned but calm. This might as well have been a social call, prelude to an evening of quaffing Siberian Yellow at the Westward Ho Club.

"There would be people searching for me," Barkov said thoughtfully.

"There would be. You want something to drink? A beer?"

"No, I don't think so."

"Want to surrender to me?"

"In a way. I'm here to negotiate."

"With what?" Donnie asked, keeping an eye on where the hand was under the folded coat.

"*Sprahvachnaye*. Information."

"In exchange for?"

"Immunity."

"I can't promise anything except to try."

Barkov sat looking at him. While waiting for Donnie in the dim apartment, he'd been reading. The *Times* was on the floor by the chair, folded to the sports section, and the lamp was on, sidelighting his strong, scarred features. The yellow light that filtered through the lampshade lent his face a brutality not usually part of his handsomeness. "All the time you were working handling cargo, you were doing your real job, gaining our confidence. Then you betrayed us, also part of your job. Do you understand that if we had found out about you early enough, our job would have been to kill you?"

"Those are the rules," Donnie said.

"And I trust you to follow all of them, my friend. We have our own code of honor. Men are nothing without that." The hand, empty, came out from beneath the coat.

"Before you begin talking," Donnie said, "I've got to warn you the information has to be worthwhile for there to be any sort of deal."

"I think you'll find it worthwhile. It's about the anthrax containers."

"That's a start toward worthwhile."

"When they left the club they went to Dr. Aquasian because it took someone with medical expertise to combine the anthrax with the charges."

"Charges?"

"In the fireworks. Fortunately for us, they were already shipped from the Pyromagic warehouse when you raided it last night."

"Shipped to where?"

"Not long ago you had a president who uttered some very wise words: 'Trust, but verify.' "

"Meaning?"

"You have my trust, but this is also business. I guarantee that if I don't have secure immunity in a very short time, there will be a great catastrophe in this city. I'm not lying to you. Those are the rules." He motioned with his head. "There is the phone, Donnie Brasco."

"How much time?" Donnie asked.

"Ah, you know what's important. As I do. Time the thief." Barkov glanced at his watch. "You have less than an hour."

"Is that enough time to prevent it from happening?"

"If you hurry, there's a chance."

Donnie believed him. He went to the phone, called Jules Donavon and explained. He found himself vouching for Barkov, who smiled and nodded to him from across the room.

"Any news on Daisy?" Donnie asked.

"Not yet," Jules said. "I'll pass on Barkov's offer and call you back."

And he did call back, a long fifteen minutes later.

There was still no word on Daisy.

But word on Barkov had come down from on high. Very high. If he was telling the truth and it brought results, he had his immunity. Jules told Donnie to call him back as soon as he had the information.

When Donnie told Barkov, the Russian seemed to relax even further in relief. Donnie figured that meant he had the goods to seal the agreement. And he was ready to talk.

"The very important leader of a South American drug cartel was shot and killed last year," Barkov began, "and the CIA is blamed. The cartel cannot allow this to go unanswered. It obtained the anthrax spores from an Iraqi source, then in a roundabout way shipped them to us. In exchange for the Russian Mafia releasing anthrax bacteria effectively in the U.S., the Russians will be given the franchise to sell most of the narcotics smuggled into the country. So the drug cartel will have its revenge, Iraq will strike a blow against an enemy, and we will obtain a rich drug franchise. Everybody gains."

"Except the people who die," Donnie said.

"It's always that way, my friend. In this country it's said that time is money, but there is an old Russian saying: Time is lives. Originally the anthrax was to be used against Israel, with intermediate range missiles as the delivery system. Our operation will be done on a smaller scale. The anthrax bacteria will be made airborne through pyrotechnic skyrockets tonight, where it will drift down on a large, unknowing crowd, infecting almost all of them."

"What crowd?"

Barkov tilted his head toward the newspaper on the

floor. The sports section. "Tonight's opening night, first baseball game of the season for the Yankees. The stadium is sold out. The ball club has a contract with Pyromagic. Each time the Yankees hit a home run, there will be a colorful fireworks display. Skyrockets. Clouds of what the admiring crowd assumes to be only residual smoke will be more than smoke. The anthrax bacteria, odorless, colorless, will settle throughout the stadium. It's extremely infectious. Within five or six days those infected will assume they are catching a simple cold, but within a few days after the symptoms appear, difficulty breathing, then shock and death will occur."

Donnie felt a dark dread seep into him like cold water. He numbly repeated what he'd been told, trying to comprehend it. "Each fireworks display after a home run will be releasing airborne anthrax above the stadium crowd."

"Only after Yankee home runs," Barkov pointed out. "The rules."

"What if the Yankees don't hit any home runs?"

"Then there will be a grand fireworks display immediately after the game. Not only over the stadium, but over the parking lots and surrounding neighborhood."

"So even more people will be infected."

"It could work out that way. There is almost always a breeze."

"What about the people setting off the fireworks? Won't they be exposed? Or is this a suicide mission?"

"They will be wearing Yankee caps and souvenir

rubber Babe Ruth masks that are actually aspirators—gas masks."

Donnie found himself trying not to believe this. "Thousands of people will die."

"Surely tens of thousands." Barkov glanced again at his watch. "The first pitch will be thrown in less than forty-five minutes. Are you going to play ball?"

Donnie called Jules Donavon.

Time was lives.

Nobody realized it more than Donnie.

47

"I don't understand why he bunted this early in the game."

The play-by-play announcer on the car radio was puzzled.

Jules was driving the Bureau unmarked. Donnie was in the passenger seat. Two agents from the New York field office were in back, a thin blond man named Nilson who dildn't look strong enough to pull his hat off, and Kaster, a hulking African American who looked as if he could play lineman for the Dallas Cowboys.

"The Yankees are cooperating," Jules said. "Word's been passed down to the field so the manager's making sure nobody hits a home run and causes a fireworks display."

"He better be damned careful," said Kaster from the back seat. "If word gets to the terrorists, they won't wait for home runs or the end of the game. They'll set off everything at once."

Donnie noticed that the Russian mobsters had become "terrorists." That's probably what the news media would call them when the story got out. Donnie knew they were thugs whose only cause was money and power.

"That's why we cautioned the ball club not to try to deal with these people or to use stadium security," Donavon said. "We have to catch them cold and nail them before they can get suspicious and make a move."

There were almost a hundred law enforcement personnel closing in on the Bronx and Yankee Stadium in dozens of vehicles. Most of them were in plainclothes. They had orders to drive the speed limit, not to draw any attention to themselves.

"Why would he lay down a sacrifice bunt when the Yankees are up in the bottom of the first, with a man on first base and only one out?" The Yankees announcer still couldn't get over it.

"I can't give you an answer," his radio sidekick said. "But he did move the runner over to second."

"How close are we?" Donnie asked nervously.

"Ten minutes away," said Nilson. "Middle of the lineup coming up. Yanks might hit a home run by accident."

And invisible, odorless death will begin to settle over the crowd.

It was difficult for Donnie to sit still. He could imagine the fireworks exploding high above the stadium in bursts of color, the crowd, plenty of kids mixed in, staring up with their mouths open, *oooohing* and *ahhhing* at the noise and kaleidoscope brilliance against the night sky. Over 55,000 people gathered in a bowl, unknowing subjects in a simple laboratory procedure on a grand scale. There was hardly any breeze, but even if one kicked up, whoever was detonating the fireworks would know how to compensate for it.

A van eased through a yellow light and blocked the intersection, cutting off the Bureau car. Windows were cranked down. All four men in the car yelled. Donavon leaned hard on the horn.

The terrified van driver maneuvered his vehicle so one wheel was up on the sidewalk, and the unmarked FBI car roared past.

"This hitter's gotta strike out on purpose," Kaster said in back.

"If anything suspicious happens down on the field, it might start an unscheduled fireworks display," Donnie reminded him. "If the hitter's an unconvincing actor and the Russians understand baseball, they might detonate all the fireworks at once. It'd be the biggest strikeout in history."

"Then we're sunk," Kaster said. "It'll take us a little while to get operational even after we get in the ballpark, and that's still a mile away in this traffic."

The first two pitches were called strikes.

Donnie breathed easier. The agents in the car looked at each other, feeling better.

"There's a long fly ball!" the announcer suddenly shouted. "Waaay back! If it stays fair it's outta here! It's . . . *foul* by about three feet! Oh, brother, that woulda been two runs!"

"Hold on!" his sidekick said. "We got us an argument here. The Yankees are claiming the ball was fair and a home run!"

"Are they crazy?" Nilson blurted.

"Calm down," Kaster said. "Yanks got something else in mind. Umpires don't change those kinda calls."

But Donnie knew that sometimes they did. Not often, but they did.

"The ump's scratching his head. He can't figure out why there's any question about that one. Now the Red Sox pitcher's going over to see what this is all about. He's all upset, jumping up and down. The third base coach is trying to calm him down. Now the Sox manager's running over there. Whoa! Both benches are emptying onto the field! Oh, brother! We've got us a major brouhaha here!"

Donnie turned around and smiled at the agents in back.

"Team's not in first place for nothing," Kaster said.

Theirs was among the first of the cars to arrive. About a dozen agents and some NYPD plainclothes cops were clustered in the stadium tunnel near a concession stand. There was still plenty of crowd noise. The bench-clearing brawl had ended and the umpires were trying to restore order and get the game going again. Judging by the boos from the crowd, somebody was still giving them trouble.

Donnie glanced over at the concession stand, where half a dozen people were lined up for hot dogs, beer, or soda. A kid had on one of the rubber Babe Ruth masks that vendors were selling. At least the masks didn't seem to be a popular item. The kid's was the only one Donnie saw.

A man in a gray silk suit approached. He had a brisk, bouncy walk and was trailed by a stooped, gray-haired guy in his sixties, trying to keep up. The one in the suit said he was Lawrence E. Elderhoff, the ranking Yankees executive in the stadium.

After checking Donavon's ID and a few others, Elderhoff introduced the gray-haired man as Johnny Edgy, a longtime Yankees employee. "Johnny knows every inch of this ballpark," Elderhoff said.

Donavon gave orders for the others to take up positions near the exits, then gathered Donnie, Nilson, Kaster, and three plainclothes New York SWAT team members.

"We've gotta pass for fans," Donavon told them.

"I thought you might," Elderhoff interrupted. He reached into a big paper sack he'd brought with him and handed out Yankees caps.

Jules thanked him.

Donnie stuck his cap on his head. As ordered, everyone was armed only with concealed handguns. Almost everyone. One of the SWAT team had a disassembled sniper's rifle in a leather case that Donavon had told him to bring along. The guy looked a little irked at having to take orders from the Bureau, but he didn't object. They all might be breathing in anthrax toxin if they didn't act fast. It might happen anyway. That was enough to squelch the territorial instinct.

Donavon looked at Johnny Edgy, who appeared to be nearer to seventy than sixty up close. "What's the best way to get to where the fireworks will be set off?"

"It's outside the stadium, beyond the left field foul pole," Edgy said. "We best follow the tunnel six sections over, then we'll go up some steps to street level."

"Lead the way," Donavon said.

Edgy set off without looking back. Donavon fell in behind him. Donnie, who knew how to blend, thought they all looked a little conspicuous in their brand-new Yankees caps. He removed his and tossed it aside.

After taking the steps, Edgy unlocked and opened a door and led them alongside the stadium and through a parking lot. They were looking at a small stretch of grass outside the ballpark. A van was parked there, and there were some portable outdoor lights. The fireworks, ready for launching, were arranged in a rough-hewn wooden framework that hugged the ground and supported dozens of tubes angled slightly toward the stadium like military mortars. There was a folding table and three collapsible aluminum lawn chairs, but three men in dark blue coveralls were all standing. Two of them had on Yankees caps and rubber Babe Ruth masks. The other had on only a cap and would slip his mask-aspirator on just before the skyrockets were launched. They were all staring at a small television monitor on the table. *"Oh, brother!"* Donnie heard the Yankees announcer yell from the tiny speaker.

"They know you?" Jules asked Johnny Edgy.

"They seen me."

"When I tell you, lead us over there like you're showing us around, tell us this is where they set off the fireworks, then tell us to hold on a minute and you walk back here, not fast, and get out of sight and out of danger. Can you do that and stay cool?"

"Hell, yes," Edgy said. "Ever hear of a place called Korea?"

Seventy-five at least, Donnie thought, looking again at Edgy's seamed face.

"I heard," Jules told him. "Let's do it."

Walking loose-jointed, putting on the casual act, all six men ambled across the field toward the fireworks, Edgy leading the way.

"This here's where we set off the fireworks on special occasions like opening night," Edgy was saying loudly. "How ya doin', fellas?" He waved to the men in the blue coveralls.

"Hi ya," said one of them from beneath his mask.

"I'm givin' these folks the tour," Edgy said.

The one whose face was visible casually slipped on his Babe Ruth mask. Donnie caught a glimpse of clear plastic tube dangling from the bottom of the mask.

Inside the stadium the crowd roared. Donnie looked at the TV monitor on the table. The batter was down on the ground, dusted back or maybe struck by a pitch.

"Hold on a minute," Edgy was saying to the group.

Donnie saw that he was pressing a cell phone to his ear.

Edgy flipped the phone closed and returned it to his pocket. "Gotta check on something. I'll be right back."

He turned and walked stooped over, very slowly, toward the rows of parked cars.

Good enough, Donnie thought. Smooth.

"Nice old guy," Kaster remarked.

The three men in Babe Ruth masks were silent, staring after the retreating Edgy. The masks weren't meant to be very lifelike, more caricatures. Donnie didn't like the way Babe Ruth was grinning.

When it happened it was fast. One of the men made a move toward the open side door of the van. Another toward the armed fireworks structure.

"FBI!" Donavon yelled. "Don't move!"

The agents dashed toward the three men, drawing their weapons as they ran.

The Russian near the van had made it to the open door and was spinning back around, already laying down a field of fire with an automatic weapon.

Donnie dropped to the ground, hearing a grunt as one of the NYPD plainclothes took a bullet and staggered a few steps before collapsing. Single shots then, almost as one shot. The man by the van dropped his weapon and hugged his midsection, curling to the ground. Babe Ruth smiled through the pain.

Lying on his stomach, Donnie drew a bead on the one bending over the fireworks display. He saw the man pick up something small with a wire trailing from it, probably a remote control to launch the skyrockets. There was more shooting, more screaming. No point in ordering the man to drop the control. No time.

Donnie aimed carefully and shot at the arm holding the control. The man dropped it, but the bullet must have missed the arm or simply plucked at his sleeve. Seemingly unhurt, he produced a handgun from a pocket of his coveralls at the same time he stooped to retrieve the control.

Maybe because the grass was slippery, or he was in

a hurry, the man lost his balance and fell backward, then scrambled to his feet. Donnie squeezed the trigger again but was out of ammunition. Very calmly, the Russian stood holding the gun with both hands, aiming at Donnie.

Donnie tried to roll to the left but the bad arm, out of the sling and aching, stopped him with a stab of pain.

Good thing it did. The bullet struck the ground a couple of feet to his left, kicking up dirt.

The man had given up any idea of trying to pick up the control and was running now, sprinting like an Olympian for the darkness beyond the field.

Then he stopped. There were winking pinpoints of light, muzzle flashes, in front of him. More of the Bureau and NYPD had arrived and were approaching from the opposite direction. The fleeing man got off a single shot before dropping lifeless and disappearing among the shadows on the grass.

Donnie struggled to his feet and looked around. Nilson from the backseat was on the ground, as was the NYPD cop. And there was the body by the van.

"Where's the other one?" Donnie asked.

Jules was still holding his 9mm, looking hopped-up from the action and glancing all around. A desk jockey high on adrenaline. "He got away."

"Not that way," somebody said. "He musta gone back in the stadium."

"Nail this site down," Donavon ordered Kaster. "C'mon, Donnie!"

When they reached the door to reenter the stadium, Donnie stepped on Johnny Edgy's hand. Edgy was lying with his head on level ground, his legs spread wide on the concrete steps. There was blood all over his white shirt, an ugly exit wound in the side of his neck.

As they were taking the steps, Donavon was on his two-way, telling everyone their position. Donnie was trying to reload, fumbling to jam a fresh clip into the gun with his bad hand.

He gave up and had to put the clip out of sight along with the gun when they were back among fans in the stadium tunnel. A hundred feet into it, they linked with two more agents from the New York office. Then more reinforcements came up from the rear. A bigger crowd than up in the stadium, Donnie thought.

"Check the restrooms," Donavon told them. "Our man'll try shedding those coveralls and the gas mask."

"Babe Ruth!" one of the agents said. "The bastards oughta be ashamed."

Letting the others move ahead of him, Donnie got near a wall and turned his back, then drew the clip and gun out from beneath his shirt. It was easy enough to slide the clip home, now that he wasn't bouncing on the stairs. He worked the mechanism to jack a round into the chamber.

When he turned back and prepared to catch up with the others, something caught his eye. A man in brown suitpants, pale blue shirt and navy tie, red suspenders, walking toward an exit. He was wearing a rubber Babe Ruth mask.

If he was the escaping Russian and had had time to get out of the blue coveralls, why was he still wearing the mask? It would only serve to help identify him. The man must simply be a fan, leaving the ball park.

But why would he leave in the first inning of the opening game, one of New York's hot tickets? Donnie knew there were possibilities. Maybe the man was a doctor who'd been called away on an emergency.

A doctor who'd forgotten his suit coat and was walking with deliberate slowness.

A doctor in a Babe Ruth mask.

Donnie decided to follow the man.

As he trailed him, moving closer, Donnie realized there was something familiar about his walk, but he couldn't quite pin it down.

Babe Ruth grinned at Donnie. In a parking lot the man had realized someone was behind him and glanced back.

He walked faster, faster, then peeled off the mask and began to run.

And Donnie knew why he'd been wearing the mask—so he wouldn't be recognized. He was the organizer of the Russian operation. The thief-in-law. Zelensky. Though he only infrequently visited the U.S. and had no doubt delegated the details of the plan to someone else—most likely Barkov—Zelensky deemed the operation important enough to observe first hand.

Donnie began running after him, the bad arm aching with every stride and throwing him off balance. But Zelensky was older and stockier, not a runner. Donnie almost smiled back at the discarded Babe

Ruth mask lying on the blacktop. He knew he could catch Zelensky.

And he did.

Halfway up one of the endless rows of vehicles, Zelensky was leaning against the fender of a pickup truck with both hands, his back to Donnie. He was winded, loudly sucking in air, his head bowed.

Donnie slowed down, held his 9mm at the ready, and approached Zelensky. "You have a gun within reach," he said. "You're going to try to turn and fire it before I have a chance to react. It'll be suicide."

He stopped five feet from Zelensky, aiming the gun with both hands at the center of the broad back, between the crescents of perspiration on the pale blue shirt, exactly midpoint between the red suspenders.

"You would like me to be alive so you can deal with me," Zelensky said, out of breath but in control. "You think I could be a good source of information."

A *great* source, Donnie thought. "I would also like to shoot you."

"*Distvitilna?* You could bring yourself to do that?"

"I could. I'd consider it a home run.'

"It would be a mistake. My knowledge extends to operations all over the world."

"Right now your world is just me, this gun, and a bullet."

The back heaved as Zelensky drew a deep breath.

"I am not suicidal," he said.

He slowly raised his empty hands, then turned around.

Leaving his pistol lying on the fender.

Donnie knew there must be an old Russian saying that covered the situation, but he couldn't think of it.

He read Zelensky his rights, then asked if he'd understood them.

"I have only one question," Zelensky said. "Who is Babe Ruth?"

48

They were still at the ballpark, or just outside it, when Jules Donavon got the call on his cell phone. He approached Donnie and led him over to where the car they'd driven to the stadium was parked.

"She's alive," he said.

Donnie felt his legs turn to dead wood and almost bend and break beneath him. Jules opened the car door for him, and he sat down on the edge of the seat, his feet still on the ground. "Lily called?" he heard his voice ask.

Jules said that she had. "But it didn't work exactly like you said. Daisy wasn't buried. Roma was only playing with your mind when he told you that, increasing the pressure. She was being held in an abandoned farmhouse. The lumber and tool purchase was to board up the windows. But the car was parked far enough away they didn't hear the phone ringing, what with the car windows up and the boarded up windows in the house. When Lily arrived at the signal's emanation, she saw Charlie Farrato and another man come out of the farmhouse with Daisy. Then she and the St. Louis agent she'd brought with her moved in to make the arrests. Neither of them saw the third man come out of the house. He shot the St. Louis agent. Another bullet hit Lily and wounded her in the side."

Donnie looked up. "I thought you said—"

"Wait. She said what happened next was automatic weapon fire, quick and precise. It killed two of the men and left the other shot up and unable to move. Then the shooter came out of the nearby woods, and at first she thought he was a woman or a young boy."

"Marishov. He must have followed her there thinking she might lead him to me."

"Right, Donnie. He shot the wounded man through the head, then he took care of Daisy."

"You mean—"

"No. He put her in Lily's car with a blanket and called on the cell phone for help. Then he disappeared back into the woods."

"*Marishov* saved her? Saved Daisy?"

"Lily said he's cold and dangerous and he won't give up on you, that you need to know that about him. She thinks he only left her alive so she could make sure Daisy was cared for until help came, and to give you his message."

"What message?"

"That he had honor and didn't condone the killing of children, but that it changed nothing between you."

Donnie sat staring at the ground, trying to sort his thoughts, his emotions. Daisy was safe, her life saved by a man with a genius for killing. A professional with honor, and with ethics that Donnie understood and feared.

Jules handed him the cell phone so he could call Elana, then left him there.

As Jules had done for him, Donnie gave her the news immediately to end her agony. "She's okay, Elana. Daisy's alive."

"Are you sure?"

"Count on it." He heard her begin to cry. "Elana, get the next flight to St. Louis. Go to her."

"I'm already packed, don't you think I'm packed? Oh, God . . ."

"Tell her I love her."

The sound of sniffling, Elana regaining her poise. "You mean you're not going?"

"I can't."

"Why *not*? She's your daughter!"

He decided not to tell her the real reason, that Marishov would be waiting for him there, hoping he'd be drawn by the bait, that he'd show the fatal weakness of emotion. Was that why Marishov had saved Daisy, so he could use her to lure Donnie and kill him? "It's impossible for me to go to her. You have to believe me."

He heard her exhale like a smoker after a deep drag. "Sure. Your job."

"Not entirely that."

"I won't ask you anything more. You'll call her?"

"Of course I'll call her." He was angry, not only because of her question but because he knew that now that the thing that had drawn the two of them together and held them, the mutual terror and concern for their daughter, was gone, they were already pulling apart from each other as inexorably as planets in opposing orbits, moving away again.

She hung up, and he knew it was over.

Again.

Donnie held tight to what he had. Daisy was alive. The smuggling operation at La Guardia would be closed down in both directions, and the Russians and what was left of the Italians would talk. With Zelensky and Barkov as sources, the Bureau and Interpol would mine information more valuable than diamonds. Donnie had done his job. The infiltration of Russian crime into the U.S. would be severely hampered.

For a while.

Donnie would be put under wraps and closely guarded. He would give depositions and eventually testify in person during the legal action that followed this kind of operation. Then he had no idea what would happen, what his identity would be, where he would go, or why.

The only comfort in it was that Marishov also wouldn't know.

For a while.